INTERZONE

The 1st Anthology

New science fiction and fantasy writing

Edited by John Clute,
Colin Greenland and David Pringle

J. M. Dent & Sons Ltd
London   Melbourne

This selection first published by J. M. Dent & Sons Ltd 1985
Selection copyright © J. M. Dent & Sons Ltd 1985
Introduction copyright © John Clute 1985
'O Happy Day!' copyright © Geoff Ryman 1985

The copyright information on the Acknowledgements page constitutes
an extension to this copyright notice

Phototypeset in 10/11½ Linotron Sabon by
Inforum Ltd, Portsmouth
Printed in Great Britain by
Guernsey Press Co. Ltd, Guernsey, C.I. for
J. M. Dent & Sons Ltd
Aldine House, 33 Welbeck Street, London W1M 8LX

British Library Cataloguing in Publication Data

Interzone: the first anthology. — (Everyman fiction)
    I. Science fiction, English
    I. Clute, John   II. Greenland, Colin   III. Pringle, David
    823'.0876'08[FS]   PR1309.53

ISBN 0 460 02294 6

CONTENTS

INTRODUCTION
John Clute

Here are thirteen stories about the way things are going. It has been a long century for the world, and there is much to talk about. In 1985, we have already been told a good deal. We have been told that the fabric of life, having gone rotten in 1914, has been replaced by synthetic fibres, which itch terribly. We have been told that the novel, through which earlier generations learned how to make some sense of life, has died, because the stable organic culture it described has given way. No longer, we have been told, can fiction cope with the harrowing speed and inde-terminacy and scale of the catastrophes presently shaking apart this small planet.

For most modern fiction the world which we inherit has become a quicksand out of Limbo, bereft of landscape, without a sure sense of the passage of historical time; and most modern fiction of any worth focuses darkly inwards upon human con-sciousness floating in the dream of words. Fiction is no longer reliable. It has abandoned Time's arrow and the measurable world. It seems to have abandoned the task of envisioning this century, whose end, all the same, most of us hope to witness and to comprehend.

We come to science fiction, which may have begun with Mary Shelley's *Frankenstein* (1818), or Jules Verne, or H. G. Wells, but which became an identifiable and self-conscious genre, with a name of its own, in America in the 1920s. Only then was properly established the long-lived science fiction claim to confront and to explain our world, generally through stories set in a future extra-polated from some version of the present as defined, however crudely, by the sciences. Given a brief of this positivist crudity, it is not surprising that many of the novels which staked the science fiction claim were philistine, absurdly hopeful about the efficacy of rational decision-making and heroic action in the task of shaping the world for the future, unwittingly comical. In humanity's march of progress, what could not be measured did not exist, what could not be tinkered with was junk. It was a literature for children.

But it grew up. (So did some of the children.) The proto-Fascist space operas of 1930 became the doubting satires of 1950; and the deft apocalypses of 1960 turned into the complex novels of today, when the outcome of speculation about the course of the world no longer seems distant or unlikely. We live in the Dreadful Warnings of earlier generations. As a consequence, the old science fiction confidence in the marvels of the coming world has gradually darkened, just as the world itself has grown problematical. All the same, something has remained of the bright origins of science fiction, and it continues to inspire the writers of today. For them, the history of the genre provides not answers but a certain perspective, an angle of vision. Science fiction offers a sense that the world itself is a legitimate subject-matter.

The contributors to *Interzone: The First Anthology* are modern writers; most of them are also heirs to that science fiction tradition which claims that the world is addressable. The stories in this anthology reflect the double inheritance. In Michael Blumlein's 'Tissue Ablation and Variant Regeneration', what seems an exercise in the blackest of black humour gradually reveals itself as a savage political statement. By rewriting history so that America becomes a saner, simpler, kinder imperium, Neil Ferguson's 'The Monroe Doctrine' pays homage to an earlier, more naive time; but before we have finished reading, we find that the pathos of this almost pastoral vision bites very deep indeed, in the charnel-house of Czechoslovakia. Geoff Ryman's 'Oh Happy Day!' delivers a near-future America to the dark embrace of a discourse between the sexes which we may have dreamed of, but never thought to envision so clearly.

Blumlein, Ferguson and Ryman have all published their first significant work in *Interzone* magazine which, since its inception in 1982, has been able to introduce several substantial talents. Other new writers represented here are Scott Bradfield, Malcolm Edwards and Kim Newman. At the same time, by including stories by Angela Carter, Keith Roberts, Rachel Pollack, David

Redd, John Shirley, J. G. Ballard and Cherry Wilder, we are presenting work of established writers from a broad literary spectrum. That Ballard was shortlisted for the Booker Prize in 1984 — but that *Empire of the Sun* did not gain the award — is less a comment on Ballard, and the tradition of speculative writing for which he stands, than it is on the literary establishment.

None of the contents of *Interzone: The First Anthology* has appeared in the UK in book form. Geoff Ryman's long story appears here for the first time anywhere; all other stories are from the first nine issues of *Interzone*. We are proud of them.

GEOFF RYMAN
O HAPPY DAY!

They're fooled by history. They think they won't be killed until they get into camps. So when we load them onto a different train, they go willingly. They see an old country railroad station with a big red hill behind it, and they think it's just a stop along the way.

They slip down from the cars and can't keep their feet on the sharp-edged rubble of the track. They're all on testosterone specifics, a really massive dose. They're passive and confused, and their skin has a yellow taint to it, and their eyes stare out of patches of darkness, and they need a shave. They smell. They look like a trainload of derelicts. It must be easier to kill people who look like that, easier to call them Stiffs, as if they were already dead.

We're probably on specifics, too, but a very mild dose. We have to work, after all.

We load the Stiffs into cars, the Cars with the special features, and the second train goes off, and ten minutes later it comes back, and we unload them, dead, and that is life under what we call the Grils.

We are the Boys. We get up each morning and we shave. We're male, so we shave. Some of us do our make-up then, a bit of lipstick and slap, and an earring maybe. Big Lou always wore an earring and a tight short-sleeved T-shirt that showed off his arms. It was very strange, all those muscles with his pudding basin haircut and hatchet face, all pressed and prim around the lips.

Big Lou thought what was happening was good. I remember him explaining it to me my first day, the day he recruited me. 'Men are violent,' he said. 'All through history, you look at violence, and it's male. That was OK in the jungle, but not now, with the gangs and the bombs and everything else. What is happening here is simple evolutionary necessity. It's the most liberating event in human history. And we're part of it.' Then he kissed me. It was a political kiss, wet and cold. Then he introduced me to the work.

After we unload the trains, we strip the corpses. There are still shortages, so we tie up the clothes in bundles and save everything else of value — money, watches, cigarette lighters — and send them back on the train. It would be a terrible job for anyone, but it's worse for a faggot. Most of the bodies are young. You feel tender toward them. You want them to wake up again and move, and you think, surely there must be something better to do with this young brown body than kill it? We work very quickly, like ants on a hill.

I don't think we're mad. I think the work has become normal for us, and so we're normal within it. We have overwhelming reasons for doing it. As long as we do this work, as long as there is this work to do, we stay alive. Most of the Boys volunteered, but not for this. At first, it was just going to be internal deportation, work camps for the revolution. They were just going to be guards. Me, I was put on that train to die, and I don't know why. They dope whole areas, and collect the people they want. Lou saw me on the platform, and pulled me in. Recruited me, he called it. I slept with him, out of gratitude and fear. I still remember sleeping with him.

I was the one who recruited Royce. He saw me first. He walked up to me on the gravel between the trains, nothing out of the ordinary, just a tall black man in rumpled khaki. He was jingling the keys in his pockets, housekeys, as if he was going to need them again. He was shaking, and he kept blinking, and swaying where he stood, and he asked in a sick and panicky voice, 'It's cold. It's cold. Isn't there any food?'

The information that he was good-looking got through slowly. The reaction was neutral, like you'd get from looking at a model on a billboard. Then I thought: in ten minutes' time, he's going to be dead.

You always promise yourself 'just once'. Just once, you'll tell the boss off; just once, you'll phone in sick and go out to the lakes. Just once. So here, I thought, is my just once: I'm going to save one of them.

'Are you gay?' I asked him. I did it without moving my lips. The cameras were always on us.

'What?' Incomprehension.

2

Oh God, I thought, he's going to be difficult, this is dumb. I got scared.

'What did you ask me?'

'Nothing. Go on.' I nodded toward the second train.

'Am I gay?' He said it quickly, glancing around him. I just nodded.

The last of the other Stiffs were being loaded on, the old ones, who had to be lifted up. I saw Big Lou look at us and start walking towards us, sauntering, amiable, with a diamanté earring.

'Yes,' said Royce. 'Why?'

'Make like you know me. My name's Richard.'

'Royce,' he said, but I couldn't catch it.

Then Lou was standing next to us. 'A little tête-à-tête?' he asked.

'Hi Lou,' I said. I leaned back on my heels, away from him. 'We got ourselves a new recruit.'

'Don't need one, Rich,' he said, still smiling.

'Lou, look. We were lovers. We lived together for two years. We did a lot of work for the movement together. He's OK, really.'

Lou was looking at Royce, at Royce's face. Being black was in Royce's favour, ideologically. All the other Boys were white. No one wanted the Station to be accused of racism.

'I don't believe a word of it,' said Lou. 'But OK.'

Lou walked toward one of the cameras. 'Hey!' he shouted up to it. The camera was armed. It turned toward him, slowly. 'We've got a new recruit.'

'What was that?' asked the camera, or rather the voice of the Gril behind it. The sound was flat and mechanical, the tone off-hand and bored.

'A new recruit. A new Boy. He's with us, so don't burn him, OK?'

'OK, OK,' said the camera. Lou turned back, and patted Royce's bare, goose-pimpled arm. Royce lurched after him, and I grabbed hold of his shirt to stop him. I was frightened he was going to get back onto the train. I waited until it was pulling out, creaking and crashing, so that the noise would cover what I said.

'It's terrible here,' I told Royce. 'But it's better than dying. Watch what you say. The cameras don't always hear, but usually they can. It's all right to look disgusted. They don't mind if you

3

look a bit sick. They like us to do the job with distaste. Just don't ever say you think it's wrong.'

'What's wrong?' he asked, and I thought: Oh God, he doesn't know. He doesn't know what's going on here. And I thought: now what do I do with him?

I showed him around the Station. It's a small, old-fashioned building made of yellow and black brick, with no sign on it to tell us where we are. One hundred years ago women in long dresses with children would have waited on its platform for the train to take them shopping in the city. There would have been a ticket-seller behind the counter who knew all the women by their last name, and who kept a girlie calendar pinned on the wall. His booth still has ornate iron bars across it, the word 'Tickets' in art nouveau scrolling, still slightly gilded. The waiting-room is full of temporary metal beds. The walls are painted a musty pistachio, and the varnish on the wooden floor has gone black. There are games machines in the corner, and behind the ticket counter is an electric cooker. We eat sitting on our beds. There are cold showers, outside by the wall, and there are flower-boxes in the windows. James the Tape Head — he's one of the Boys — keeps them full of petunias and geraniums. All around it and the hill behind, are concentric rows of wire mesh, thirty feet high and thirty feet deep, to keep the Stiffs controlled, and us in. It isn't a Station, it's a mass graveyard, for them and probably for us.

I tried to get Royce to go to bed, but he wouldn't. He was frightened to be left alone. He followed me out onto the platform where we were unloading the Stiffs, rolling them out. Sometimes the bodies sigh when they hit the concrete.

Royce's eyes went as wide as a rabbit's that's been run over by a car.

'What are you doing? What are you doing?' he yelped, over and over.

'What the fuck does it look like?' I said.

We strip them on the platform, and load them into trolleys. We shake them out of their trousers, and go through the pockets. Getting them out of their shirts is worse; their arms flop, and their heads loll. We're allowed to leave them in their underwear.

'They're doing it. Oh God, oh Jesus, they're killing them! Nobody knows that! Nobody believes that!'

4

'Help me carry them,' I said. I said it for his sake. He shook his head, and stepped back, and stumbled over arms and legs and fell into a tangle of them.

Only the worst, we're told, only the most violent of men. That means the poor bastards who had to pick up a gun, or join a gang, or sign up for the police or the army. In other words, most of the people we kill are either black or Latino. I tried to tell them, I tried to tell the women that would happen.

Royce was suddenly sick. It was partly the drugs wearing off. Charlie and I hoisted him up and dragged him, as limp as a Stiff, into the showers. We got him cleaned up and into bed — my bed, there wasn't any other — and after that he was very quiet. Everybody was interested in him. New dog in the pound. Harry offered him one of his peppermints. Harry came up smiling, but then Harry is always smiling like the Man who Laughed, yellow teeth in a red beard. He'd got the peppermints off a Stiff. Royce didn't know how precious they were. He just shook his head, and lay there staring under the blanket, as one by one we all came back from the platform. Lou was last, thumping in and sighing, like he was satisfied with something. He slumped down on my bed next to Royce's knees, and I thought: uh-oh, Lou likes him too.

'Bad day, huh,' Lou said. 'Listen, I know, the first day is poison. But you got to ask yourself why it's happening.'

'Why is it?' asked Royce, his face and mouth muffled in the crook of his elbow. He sounded like he was going to be sick again.

'Why?' Lou sounded shocked. 'Royce, you remember how bad things got. The assassinations, the military build-up, the bombs?'

Only in America: the gangs got hold of tactical nuclear weapons. They punched out their rivals' turf: parts of Detroit, Miami, Houston, Chicago and then the big DC.

'I know,' said Royce. 'I used to live in Los Angeles.'

Los Angeles came later. I sometimes wonder now if Los Angeles wasn't a special case. Ever hear of the Reichstag fire? Lou went respectful and silent, and he sat back, head bowed. 'I am really sick at heart to hear that. I am so sorry. It must be like your whole past life has been blown away. What can I say? You probably know what I'm talking about better than anyone else here. It just had to be stopped, didn't it?'

'It did stop,' said Royce.

'Yeah, I know, and that was because of the testosterone specifics. The women gave us that. Do you remember how great that felt, Royce? How calm you felt. That's because you'd been released from your masculinity, the specifics set men free from themselves. It was a beautiful thing to do.'

Lou rocked back on the bed, and recited the old doggerel slogan. 'TSI, in the water supply, a year-round high. I remember the first day I could leave my gun at home, man. I got on the subway, and there was this big Kahuna, all beads and tattoos, and he just smiled at me and passed me a joint. I really thought the specifics were the answer. But they hurt women, not many, but that's enough. So the specifics were withdrawn, and look what happened. Six months later, Los Angeles went up. The violence had to stop. And that's what we're going for here, Royce. Not men per se, but violence: the military, the police, criminals, gangsters, pornographers. Once they go, this whole thing here stops. It's like a surgical operation.'

'Could you let me sleep?' Royce asked.

'Yeah sure,' said Lou gently, and leaned forward and kissed him. 'Don't worry, Royce, we take care of our own here. These guys are a really great bunch of people. Welcome home.'

The Boys went back to playing computer games in the waiting room. Bleep bleep bleep. One of the guys started yelling because a jack was missing from his deck of cards. James the Tape Head sat on his bed, Mozart hissing at him through his headphones. I looked at Royce, and I thought of him: you are a good person.

That's when I began to have the fantasy. We all have the fantasy, of someone good and kind and strong, who sees who we really are when we're not messed up. Without knowing I was doing it, I began to make Royce my fantasy, my beautiful, kind, good man. The strange thing was that in a way the fantasy was true. So was it a fantasy at all?

The next day — it was the very next day — Royce began his campaign.

I volunteered us both to get the food. The food comes down the tracks very early in a little automatic car. Someone has to unload it and take it into the kitchen. I wanted to get Royce and me away from the Boys to talk. He was unsure of me; he pulled on his socks and looked at me, solemnly, in the eye. Fair enough, I thought, he doesn't know me. Lou loaned him a big duffle coat, and Royce led us both out through the turnstiles and onto the platform.

We didn't have our talk. Like he was stepping out onto a stage, under the cameras, Royce started to play a part. I don't like to say this, but he started to play the part of a black man. It was an act, designed to disarm. He grinned and did a Joe Cool kind of movement. 'Hey! How are you?' he said to one particular camera.

The camera stayed still, and silent.

'You can't fool me, I know there's someone there. What's your name?' he asked it. Silence, of course.

'Aw, come on, you can tell me that, can't you? Listen I have got a terrible name. It's Royce. How would you like to be called after a car? Your name can't be as bad as that. What is it? Grizelda? Hortensia? My favourite aunt's called Hortensia. How about Gertrude? Ever read Hamlet? What about . . . Lurleen?'

There was a hollow sound, like in a transatlantic phone call, when you talk over someone and it cuts out what they're saying for a couple of seconds afterwards. The camera did that. It had turned off its voice. And I thought, I didn't know it could do that; and I thought, why did it do it?

'Look. I have to call you something. My sister is called Alice. You don't mind if I call you Alice? Like in Wonderland?' Royce stepped forward. The camera did not have to bristle; its warm-up light went on.

'You see, Alice. I — uh — have a personal question.'

The camera spoke. 'What is it?' The voice was sharp and wary. I had the feeling that he had actually found her real name.

'Alice — uh — I don't want to embarrass anyone, but, um, you see I got this little emergency, and everywhere I look there are cameras, so, um, where can I *go*?'

A pause from the camera. 'I'm sorry,' it said. 'There are toilet facilities, but I'm afraid we have to keep you under observation.'

'Really, I don't do anything that much different from anyone else.'

'I'm sure you don't.'

'I mean sometimes I try it standing on the seat or in a yoga position.'

'Fine, but I'm afraid you'll still have to put up with the cameras.'

'Well I hope you're recording it for posterity, 'cause if you get rid of all the men, it'll have real historical interest.'

There was a click from the camera again. I stepped out of the line of fire. Royce presented himself at the turnstiles, and they buzzed to let him through. He made his way toward the john singing 'That's Entertainment'.

All the cameras turned to watch him.

Just before he went into the shed, he pulled out his pecker and waggled it at them. 'Wave bye-bye,' he said.

He'll get us all killed, I thought. The john was a trench with a plywood shed around it, open all along one side. I went to the wire mesh behind it, to listen.

'Alice?' I heard him ask through the plywood.

'I'm not Alice,' said another voice from another camera. She meant in more ways than one, she was not Alice.

'Uh — Hortensia? Uh. There's no toilet paper, Hortensia.'

'I know.'

'Gee, I wish you'd told me first.'

'There are some old clothes on the floor. Use some of them and throw them over the side.'

Dead men's shirts. I heard a kind of rustle and saw a line of shadow under the boards, waddling forward, crouched.

'I must look like a duck, huh?'

'A roast one in a minute.'

Royce was quiet for a while after that. Finally he said, grumbling, 'Trust me to pick tweed.'

He kept it up, all morning long, talking to the Grils. During breakfast, he talked about home cooking and how to make tostadas and enchiladas. He talked about a summer job he'd had in Los Angeles, working in a diner that specialized in Kosher Mexican Food. Except for Royce, everyone who worked there including the owners was Japanese. That, said Royce, shaking his head, was LA. He and his mother had to move back east, to get away from the gang wars.

As the bodies were being unloaded, Royce talked about his grandmother. He'd lived with her when he was a child, and his father was dying. His grandmother made ice cream in the bathtub. She filled it full of ice and spun tubs of cream in it. Then she put one of the tubs in a basket with an umbrella over it on the

8

front of her bicycle. She cycled through the neighbourhood, selling ice cream and singing 'Rock of Ages'. She kept chickens, which was against the zoning regulations, and threw them at people who annoyed her, especially policemen. Royce had a cat, and it and a chicken fell in love. They would mew and cluck for each other, and sit for contented hours at a time, the chicken's neck snugly and safely inside the cat's mouth.

It was embarrassing, hearing someone talk. Usually we worked in silence. And the talk was confusing; we didn't think about things like summer jobs or household pets anymore. Royce's face as he talked, as the bodies were dumped and stripped, was hard and shiny with sweat, like polished wood.

That afternoon, we had our talk. Since we'd gotten the food, it was our turn to cook lunch. So I got him away from the Boys.

We took our soup and crackers up to the top of the mound. The mound is dug out of a small hill behind the Station. James makes it in his bulldozer, listening to Mozart. He pulls the trolleys up a long dirt ramp, and empties them, and smooths the sandstone soil over each day's addition of Stiffs. I get the feeling he thinks he works like Mozart. The mound rises up in terraces, each terrace perfectly level, its slope at the same angle as the one below it. The dirt is brick red and there are seven levels. It looks like Babylon.

There are cameras on top, but you can see over the fence. You can see the New England forest. It looks tired and small, maybe even dusty, as if it needed someone to clean the leaves. There's another small hill. You can hear birds. Royce and I climbed up to the top, and I gathered up my nerve and said, 'I really like you.'

'Uh-huh,' he said, balancing his soup, and I knew it wasn't going to work.

Leave it, I thought, don't push, it's hard for him, he doesn't know you.

'You come here a lot,' he said. It was a statement.

'I come here to get away.'

Royce blew out through his nostrils: a kind of a laugh. 'Get away? You know what's under your feet?'

'Yes,' I said, looking at the forest. Neither one of us wanted to sit on that red soil, even to eat the soup. I passed him his crackers, from my coat pocket.

'So why did you pick me? Out of all the other Stiffs?'

'I guess I just liked what I saw.'

'Why?'

I smiled with embarrassment at being forced to say it; it was as if there were no words for it that were not slightly wrong. 'Because I guess you're kind of good-looking and I . . . just thought I would like you a lot.'

'Because I'm black?'

'You are black, yes.'

'Are most of your boyfriends black?'

Bullseye. That was scary. 'I, uh, did go through a phase where I guess I was kind of fixated on black people. But I stopped that, I mean, I realized that what I was actually doing was depersonalizing the people I was with, which wasn't very flattering to them. But that is all over. It really isn't important to me now.'

'So you went out and made yourself sleep with white people.'

He does not, I thought, even remotely like me.

'I found white people I liked. It didn't take much.'

'You toe the line all the way down the line, don't you?' he said.

I thought I didn't understand.

'Is that why you're here?' A blank from me. 'You toe the line, the right *line*, so you're here.'

'Yes,' I said. 'In a way. Big Lou saw me on the platform, and knew me from politics. I guess you don't take much interest in politics.' I was beginning to feel like hitting back.

'Depends on the politics,' he said, briskly.

'Well you're OK, I guess. You made it out.'

'Out of where?'

I just looked back at him. 'Los Angeles.'

He gave a long and very bitter sigh, mixed with a kind of chortle. 'Whenever I am in this . . . situation, there is the conversation. I always end up having the same conversation. I reckon you're going to tell me I'm not black enough.'

'You do kind of shriek I am middle class.'

'Uh-huh. You use that word class, so that means it's not racist, right?'

'I mean, you're being loyal to your class, to which most black people do not belong.'

'Hey, bro', you can't fool me, we're from the same neighbourhood. That sort of thing?' It was imitation ghetto. 'You want somebody with beads in his hair and a beret and a semi who hates white people, but likes you because you're so upfront movement? Is that your little dream? A big bad black man?'

I turned away from him completely.

He said, in a very cold still voice. 'Do you get off on corpses, too?'

'This was a mistake,' I said. 'Let's go back.'

'I thought you wanted to talk.'

'Why are you doing this?'

'Because,' he said, 'you are someone who takes off dead men's watches, and you look like you could have been a nice person.'

'I am,' I said, and nearly wept, 'a nice person.'

'That's what scares the shit out of me.'

'You think I want this? You think I don't hate this?' I think that's when I threw down the soup. I grabbed him by the shirt sleeves and held him. I remember being worried about the cameras, so I kept my voice low and rapid, like it was scuttling.

'Look, I was on the train, I was going to die, and Lou said, you can live. You can help here and live. So I did it. And I'm here. And so are you.'

'I know,' he said, softly.

'So OK, you don't like me, I can live with that, fine, no problem, you're under no obligation, so let's just go back.'

'You come up here because of the forest,' he said.

'Yes! Brilliant!'

'Even mass murderers need love too, right?'

'Yes! Brilliant!'

'And you want me to love you? When you bear the same relation to me, as Lou does to you?'

'I don't know. I don't care.' I was sitting down now, hugging myself. The bowl of soup was on the ground by my foot, tomato sludge creeping out of it. I kicked it. 'Sorry I hassled you.'

'You didn't hassle me.'

'All I want is one little part of my life to have a tiny corner of goodness in it. Just one little place. I probably won't, but I feel like if I don't find it soon, I will bust up into a million pieces. Not love. Not necessarily. Just someone nice to talk to, who I really like. Otherwise I think one day I will climb back into one of those trains.' When I said it, I realized it was true. I hadn't known I was that far gone. I thought I had been making a play for sympathy.

Royce was leaning in front of me, looking me in the face. 'Listen, I love you.'

'Bullshit.' What kind of mind-fuck now?

He grabbed my chin, and turned my head back round. 'No. True. Not maybe in the way you want, but true. You really do look, right now, like one of those people on the train. Like someone I just unloaded.'

I didn't know quite what he was saying, and I wasn't sure I trusted him, but I did know one thing. 'I don't want to go back to that bunkhouse, not this afternoon.'

'OK. We'll stay up here and talk.'

I felt like I was stepping out onto ice. 'But can we talk nicely? A little bit less heavy duty?'

'Nicely. Sounds sweet, doesn't mean anything. Like the birds?'

'Yes,' I said. 'Like the birds.'

I reckon that, altogether, we had two weeks. A Lullaby in Birdland. Hum along if you want to. You don't need to know the words.

Every afternoon after the work, Royce and I went up the mound and talked. I think he liked talking to me, I'll go as far as that. I remember one afternoon he showed me photographs from his wallet. He still had a wallet, full of people.

He showed me his mother. She was extremely thin, with dark limp flesh under her eyes. She was trying to smile. Her arms were folded across her stomach. She looked extremely kind, but tired.

There was a photograph of a large red brick house. It had white window sills and a huge white front door, and it sagged in the way that only very old houses do.

'Whose is that?' I asked.

'Ours. Well, my family's. Not my mother's. My uncle lives there now.'

'It's got a confederate flag over it!'

Royce grinned and folded up quietly; his laughter was almost always silent. 'Well, my great-grandfather didn't want to lose all his slaves, did he?'

One half of Royce's family were black, one half were white. There were terrible wedding receptions divided in half where no one spoke. 'The white people are all so embarrassed, particularly the ones who want to be friendly. There's only one way a black family gets a house like that: Grandfather messed around a whole bunch. He hated his white family, so he left the house to us. My uncle and aunt want to open it up as a Civil War museum and put their picture on the leaflet.' Royce folded up again. 'I mean, this is in Georgia. Can you imagine all those rednecks showing up and finding a nice black couple owning it, and all this history about black regiments?'

'Who's that?'

'My cousin. She came to live with us for a while.'

'She's from the white half.'

'Nope. She's black.' Royce was enjoying himself. The photograph showed a rather plump, very determined teenage girl with orange hair, slightly wavy, and freckles.

'Oh.' I was getting uncomfortable, all this talk of black and white.

'It's really terrible. Everything Cyndi likes, I mean *everything*, is black, but her father married a white woman, and she ended up like that. She wanted to be black so bad. Every time she met anyone, she'd start explaining how she was black, really. She'd go up to black kids and start explaining, and you could see them thinking "Who is this white girl and is she out of her mind?" We were both on this *programme*, so we ended up in a white high school and that was worse because no one knew they'd been integrated when she was around. The first day this white girl asked her if she'd seen any of the new black kids. Then her sister went and became a top black fashion model, you know, features in *Ebony*, and that was it. It got so bad, that whenever Cyndi meant white, she'd say "the half of me I hate".'

'What happened to her?'

'I think she gave up and became white. She wanted to be a lawyer. I don't know what happened to her. She got caught in LA.'

I flipped over the plastic. There was a photograph of a mother and a small child. 'Who's that?'

'My son,' said Royce. 'That's his mother. Now *she* thinks she's a witch.' An ordinary looking girl stared sullenly out at the camera. She had long frizzy hair and some sort of ethnic dress.

'She'll go up to waiters she doesn't like in restaurants and whisper spells at them in their ears.'

'How long ago was this?' I felt an ache, as if I'd lost him, as if I had ever had him.

'Oh ten years ago, before I knew anything. I mean, I wouldn't do it now. I'd like any kid of mine to have me around, but his mother and I don't get on. She told my aunt that she'd turned me gay by magic to get revenge.'

'Were they in LA too?'

Royce went very still, and nodded yes.

'I'm sorry,' I said.

He passed me back the wallet. 'Here. That's all of them. Last time we got together.'

There was a tiny photograph, full of people. The black half. On the far right was a very tall, gangling fifteen-year-old, looking bristly and unformed, shy and sweet. Three of the four people around him were looking at him, bursting with suppressed smiles. I wish I'd known him then, as well. I wanted to know him all his life.

'I got a crazy, crazy family,' he said, shaking his head with affection. 'I hope they're all still OK.' It was best not to think about what was happening outside. Or inside, here.

It was autumn, and the sun would come slanting through the leaves of the woods. It would make a kind of corona around them, especially if the Boys were burning garbage and there was smoke in the air. The light would come in shafts, like God was hiding behind the leaves. The leaves were dropping one by one.

There was nothing in the Station that was anything to do with Royce. Everything that made him Royce, that made him interesting, is separate. It is the small real things that get obliterated in a holocaust, forgotten. The horrors are distinct and do not connect with the people, but it is the horrors that get remembered in history.

When it got dark, we could go back down, and I hated it because each day it was getting dark earlier and earlier. We'd get back and find that there had been — oh — a macaroni fight over lunch, great handprints of it over the windows and on the beds, that had been left to dry. Once we got back to the waiting room, and there had been a fight, a real one. Lou had given one of the

Boys a bloody nose, to stop it. There was blood on the floor. Lou lectured us all about male violence, saying anyone who used violence in the Station would get violence back.

He took away all of Tom's clothes. Tom was beautiful, and very quiet, but sometimes he got mad. Lou kicked him out of the building in punishment. It was going to be a cold night. Long after the Grils had turned out the lights, we could hear Tom whimpering, just outside the door. 'Please, Lou. It's cold. Lou, I'm sorry. Lou? I just got carried away. Please?'

I felt Royce jump up and throw the blanket aside. Oh God, I thought, don't get Lou mad at us. Royce padded across the dark room, and I heard the door open, and I heard him say, 'OK, come in.'

'Sorry, Lou,' Royce said. 'But we all need to get to sleep.'

Lou only grunted. 'OK,' he said, in a voice that was biding its time.

And Royce came back to my bed.

I would hold him, and he would hold me, but only, I think, to stop falling out of the bed. It was so narrow and cold. Royce's body was always taut, like each individual strand of muscle had been pulled back, tightly, from the shoulder. It was as tense through the night as if it were carrying something, and nothing I could do would soothe it. What I am trying to say, and I have to say it, is that Royce was impotent, at least with me, at least in the Station. 'As long as I can't do it,' he told me once on the mound, 'I know I haven't forgotten where I am.' Maybe that was just an excuse. The Boys knew about it, of course. They listened in the dark and knew what was and was not happening.

And the day would begin at dawn. The little automatic car, the porridge and the bread, the icy showers, and the wait for the first train. James the Tape Head, Harry with his constant grin, Gary who was tall and ropey, and who kept tugging at his pigtail. He'd been a trader in books, and he talked books and politics and thought he was Lou's lieutenant. Lou wasn't saying. And Bill the Brylcreem, and Charlie with his still, and Tom. The Boys. Hating each other, with no one else to talk to, waiting for the day when the Grils would burn us, or the food in the cart would have an added secret ingredient. When they were done with us.

Royce talked, learning who the cameras were.

There were only four Grils, dividing the day into two shifts. Royce gave them names. There was Alice and Hortensia, and Miss Scarlett who turned out to be from Atlanta. Only one of the Grils took a while to find a name, and she got it the first day one of the cameras laughed.

She'd been called Greta, I think because she had such a low, deep voice. Sometimes Royce called her Sir. Then one morning, Lou was late, and as he came, Royce said. 'Uh-oh. Here comes the Rear Admiral.'

Lou was very sanctimonious about always taking what he assumed was the female role in sex. The cameras knew that; they watched all the time. The camera laughed. It was a terrible laugh; a thin, high, wailing, helpless shriek.

'Hey, Sir, that's really Butch,' said Royce, and the name Butch stuck.

So did Rear Admiral. God bless all who sail in him.

'Hiya, Admiral,' gasped the camera, and even some of the Boys laughed too.

Lou looked confused, a stiff and awkward smile on his face. 'It's better than being some macho prick,' he said.

That night, he took me to one side, by the showers.

'Look,' he said. 'I think maybe you should get your friend to ease up a bit.'

'Oh Lou, come on, it's just jokes.'

'You think all of this is a joke!' yelped Lou.

'No.'

'Don't think I don't understand what's going on.' The light caught in his eyes, pinprick bright.

'What do you think is going on, Lou?'

I saw him appraising me. I saw him give me the benefit of the doubt. 'What you've done, Rich, and maybe it isn't your fault, is to import an ideological wild card into this station.'

'Oh Lou,' I groaned. I groaned for him, for his mind.

'He's not with us. I don't know what these games are that he's playing with the women, but he's putting us all in danger. Yeah, sure, they're laughing now, but sooner or later he'll say the wrong thing, and some of us will get burned. Cooked. And another thing. These little heart to heart talks you have with each other. Very nice. But that's just the sort of thing the Station cannot tolerate.

We are a team, we are a family, we've broken with all of that nuclear family shit, and you guys have re-imported it. You're breaking us up, into little compartments. You, Royce, James, even Harry, you're all going off into little corners away from the rest of us. We have got to work together. Now I want to see you guys with the rest of us. No more withdrawing.'

'Lou,' I said, helpless to reply. 'Lou. Fuck off.'

His eyes had the light again. 'Careful, Rich.'

'Lou. We are with you guys 22 hours a day. Can you really not do without us for the other two? What is wrong with a little privacy, Lou?'

'There is no privacy here,' he said. 'The cameras pick up just about every word. Now look. I took on a responsibility. I took on the responsibility of getting all of us through this together, show that there is a place in the revolution for good gay men. I have to know what is going on in the Station. I don't know what you guys are saying to each other up there, I don't know what the cameras are hearing. Now you lied to me, Rich. You didn't know Royce before he came here, did you. We don't know who he is, what he is. Rich, is Royce even gay?'

'Yes! Of course!'

'Then how does he fuck?'

'That's none of your business.'

'Everything here is my business. You don't fuck him, he doesn't fuck you, so what goes on?'

I was too horrified to speak.

'Look,' said Lou, relenting. 'I can understand it. You love the guy. You think I don't feel that pull, too, that pull to save them? We wouldn't be gay if we didn't. So you see him on the platform, and he is very nice, and you think, Dear God, why does he have to die?'

'Yes.'

'I feel it! I feel it too!' Lou made a good show of doing so. 'It's not the people themselves, but what they are that we have to hold onto. Remember, Rich, this is just a programme of containment. What we get here are the worst, Rich, the very worst — the sex criminals, the transsexuals, the media freaks. So what you have to ask yourself, Rich, is this: what was Royce doing on that train?'

'Same thing I was. He got pulled in by mistake.'

17

Lou looked at me with a kind of blank pity. Then he looked down at the ground. 'There are no mistakes, Rich. They've got the police files.'

'Then what was I doing on the train?'

Lou looked back up at me and sighed. 'I think you probably got some of the women very angry with you. There's a lot of in-fighting, particularly where gay men fit in. I don't like it. It's why I got you out. It may be something similar with Royce.'

'On the train because I disagreed with them?' Everything felt weak, my knees, my stomach.

'It's possible, only possible. This is a revolution, Rich. Things are pretty fluid.'

'Oh God, Lou, what's happening?'

'You see why we have to be careful? People have been burned in this station, Rich. Not lately, because I've been in charge. And I intend to stay in charge. Look.'

Lou took me in his arms. 'This must be really terrible for you, I know. All of us were really happy for you, when you and Royce started. But we have to protect ourselves. Now let's just go back in, and ask Royce who and what he is.'

'What do you mean?'

'Just ask him. In front of the others. What he was. And not take no for an answer.' He was stroking my hair.

'He'll hate me if I do that!' I tried to push him away. He grabbed hold of my hair, and pulled it, smiling, almost as if he were still being sexy and affectionate.

'Then he'll just have to get over that kind of mentality. What has he got to hide if he needs privacy? Come on, Rich. Let's just get it over with.' He pulled me back, into the waiting-room.

Royce took one look at us together as we came in, and his face went still, as if to say, 'Uh-huh. This is coming now, is it?' His eyes looked hard into mine, and said, 'Are you going to put up with it?' I was ashamed. I was powerless.

'Rich has a confession to make,' said Lou, a friendly hand still on the back of my neck. 'Don't you, Rich?'

They all seemed to sit up and close in, an inquisition, and I stood there thinking, Dear God, what do I do? What do I do?

'Rich,' Lou reminded me. 'We have to go through this. We need to talk this through.'

Royce sat there, on our bed, reclining, waiting.

Well, I *had* lied. 'I don't really know who Royce is. We weren't lovers before. We are lovers now.'

'But you don't know what he was doing, or who he was, do you, Rich?'

I just shook my head.

'Don't you want to know that, Rich? Don't you want to know who your lover was? Doesn't it seem strange to you that he's never told you?'

'No,' I replied. 'We all did what we had to do before the revolution. What we did back then is not who we are.' See, I wanted to say to Royce, I'm fighting, see I'm fighting.

'But there are different ways of knuckling under, aren't there, Rich? You taught history. You showed people where the old system had gone wrong. You were a good, gay man.'

Royce stood up, abruptly, and said, 'I was a prison guard.'

The room went cold and Lou's eyes gleamed.

'And there are different ways of being a prison guard. It was a detention centre for juveniles, young guys who might have had a chance. Not surprisingly, most of them were black. I don't suppose you know what happens to black juvenile prisoners, do you? I'd like to know.'

'Their records are looked at,' said Lou. 'So. You were a gay prison guard in charge of young men.'

'Is that so impossible?'

'So, you were a closet case for a start.'

'No. I told my immediate superior.'

'*Immediate superior*. You went along with the hierarchy. Patriarchy, I should say. Did you have a good time with the boys?'

'This camp is a hierarchy, in case you hadn't noticed. And no, I kept my hands off the boys. I was there to help them, not make things worse.'

'Helping them to be gay would be worse?' Every word was a trap door that could fall open. The latch was hatred. 'Did you ever beat one of the boys up? Did you deal dope on the side?'

Royce was still for a moment, his eyes narrow. Then he spoke.

'About four years ago, me and the kids put on a show. We put on a show for the girls' centre. The girls came in a bus, and they'd all put their hair in ringlets, and they walked into the gym with too much make-up on, holding each other's hands, clutching each other's forearms, like this, because they were so nervous. And the kids, the boys, they'd been rehearsing, oh, for weeks. They'd built and painted a set. It was a street, with lights in the windows, and a big yellow moon. There was this one kid, Jonesy. Jonesy kept sticking his head through the curtain before we started. "Hey everybody! I'm a star!" '

Royce said it again, softly. 'Hey everybody, I'm a star. And I had to yell at him, Jonesy, get your ass off that stage. The girls sat on one side of the gymn, and the boys on the other, and they smiled and waved and threw things at each other, like gum wrappers. It was all they had.'

Royce started to cry. He glared at Lou and let the tears slide down his face. 'They didn't have anything else to give each other. The show started and one of the kids did his announcing routine. He'd made a bow tie out of a white paper napkin, and it looked so sharp. And then the music came up and one of the girls just shouted. "Oh, they're going to *dance*!" And those girls screamed. They just screamed. The boys did their dance on the stage, no mistaking what those moves meant. The record was "It's a Shame".'

His face contorted suddenly, perhaps with anger. 'And I had to keep this god-damned aisle between them, the whole time.'

'So?' said Lou, unmoved.

'So,' said Royce, and gathered himself in. He wiped the moisture from his face. 'So I know a lot about prisons. So, some of those kids are dead now. The boys and the girls wanted each other. That must be an ideological quandary for you, Lou. Here's a big bad guard stopping people doing what they want, but what they want to do is het-ero-sex-u-ality.' He turned it into a mock dirty word, his eyes round.

'No problem,' said Lou. 'All women are really lesbians.'

Royce stared at him for a moment. Then he began to laugh.

'I wouldn't expect you to understand. But the first experience of physical tenderness that any woman has is with her mother.'

'Gee, I'm sure glad my old aunt Hortensia didn't know that. She would be surprised. Hey, Alice. Are you a dyke?'

Lou went pale, and lines of shadow encircled his mouth.

'Yes,' said Alice, the camera.

'Well, I'm a faggot, but it doesn't mean everyone else is.'

Lou launched himself from the bed, in a fury. He was on his feet, and shouting, flecks of spit propelled from his mouth. 'You do not use demeaning language here!' His voice cracked.

Alice had been working nine hours, and now she was alone, on the night shift. She had been watching, silently, for nine hours. Now, she wanted to talk.

'I had a girlfriend once who was straight,' she said. 'No matter how hard she tried, women just didn't bring her off. Mind you, that's better than those lust lesbians. They just want your body. Me, I'm totally dedicated to women, but it's a political commitment. It's something I decided. I don't let my body make my decisions for me.'

'Yah, I know what you mean,' said Royce. 'It's these lust faggots, I can't stand.' He cast his eyes about him at the Boys, and they chuckled.

'We do not use the word "dyke" in this station,' said Lou.

Royce looked rather sad and affectionate, and shook his head. 'Lou. You are such a prig. Not only are you a prig. You are a dumb prig.'

The floor seemed to open up under my feet with admiration. Only Royce could have said that to Lou. I loved him, even though I did not love myself. The Boys chuckled again, because it was funny, and because it was true, and because it was a little bit of a shock.

'Alice,' said Lou. 'He has just insulted women.'

'Funny,' said Alice. 'I thought he'd just insulted you.'

Lou looked like he was in the middle of a nightmare; you could see it in his face. 'Alice is being very tolerant, Royce. But from now on, you talk to and about the women with respect. If you want to live here with us, there are a few ground rules.'

'Like what?'

'No more jokes.'

Royce was leaning against the bar at the foot of our bed, and he was calm, and his ankles were crossed. He closed his eyes, and smiled. 'No more jokes?' he asked, amused.

'You mess around with the women, you put us all in danger. You keep putting us in danger, you got to go.'

'Lou,' said Alice. 'Can I remind you of something? You don't decide who goes on the trains. We do.'

'I understand that, Alice.' He slumped from the shoulders and his breath seeped out of him. He seemed to shrink.

'Lou,' said Royce. 'I think you and I are on the same side?' It was a question.

'We'd better be,' said Lou.

'Then you do know why I talk to the women.'

'Yeah,' said Lou. 'You want to show off. You want to be the centre of attention. You don't want to take responsibility for anything.'

He didn't understand. Lou was dangerous because he was stupid.

'I've been a prison guard,' said Royce, carefully. 'I know what it's like. You're trapped, even worse than the prisoners.'

'So?' He was going to make Royce say it, in front of a camera. He was going to make him say that he was talking to the Grils so that they would find it hard to kill us when the time came.

'I'm talking to the women, so that they'll get to know us,' said Royce, 'and see that there is a place for gay men within the revolution. They can't know that unless we talk to them. Can they?'

Bullseye again. That was the only formulation Lou was ever likely to accept.

'I mean, can they, Lou? I think we're working with the women on this thing together. There's no need for silence between us, not if we're on the same side. OK, so maybe I do it wrong. I don't want to be the only one who does all the talking. We all should talk to them, Lou, you, me, all of us. And the women should feel that they can talk with us as well.'

'Oh yeah, I am so bored keeping schtum,' said Alice.

Lou went still, and he drew in a deep breath. 'OK,' he said. 'We can proceed on that basis. We all communicate, with each other and with the cameras. But Royce. That means no more withdrawing. No more going off in a corner. No more little heart to hearts on the mound.'

'I didn't know that was a problem, Lou. There will be no more of those.'

'OK, then,' said Lou, murmurous in defeat. Royce strode towards him, both hands outstretched, and took Lou's hand in both of his.

'This is really good, Lou. I'm really glad we talked.'

Lou looked back at him, looking worn and heavy, but he was touched. Big Lou was moved, as well, and he gave a slightly forlorn flicker of a smile.

So Royce became head of the Station.

He gave me a friendly little nod, and moved his things away from our bed. He slept in Tom's; Tom never did. It didn't matter, because I still had my little corner of goodness, even if we didn't talk. Royce was still there, telling jokes. I was happy with that because I knew that I had deserted him before he had deserted me; and I understood that I was to be the visible victory he gave to Lou. None of that mattered. Royce had survived. I didn't cry the first night alone; I stopped myself. I didn't want the Boys to hear.

Things started to change. The cameras stopped looking at us on the john. We could see them turn and look away. Then one morning, they were just hanging, dead.

'Hey, Rich!' Harry called me. It was me and Harry, unloading the food cart, as winter finally came. Harry was hopping up and down in front of the camera. He leapt up and tapped it, and the warm up light did not even go on.

'They've turned it off, Rich! The camera's off. It's dead!'

He grabbed my arms, and spun me around, and started doing a little dance, and I started to hoot with laughter along with him. It was like someone had handed you back part of your pride. It was like we were human enough to be accorded that again.

'Hey Royce, the camera in the john's off!' shouted Harry, as we burst through the canteen doors with the trolley.

'Maybe they're just broken,' said Gary, who was still loyal to Lou.

'Naw, man, they'd be telling us to fix it by now. They've turned it off!'

'That so, Alice?' Royce asked the camera in the canteen.

'Oh. Yeah,' said Alice. Odd how a mechanical voice could sound so much more personal than a real one, closer somehow, as if in the middle of your ear.

'Thanks, Alice.'

' 'S OK,' said Alice, embarrassed. 'We explained it to the Wigs. We told them it was like pornography, you know, demeaning to us. They bought it. Believe me, you guys are not a lovely sight first thing in the morning.'

I could see Royce go all alert at that word 'Wig', like an animal raising its ears. He didn't mention the Wigs again until later that afternoon.

'Alice, is our talking ever a problem for you?'

'How d'you mean?'

'Well, if one of the Wigs walked in . . .'

Alice kind of laughed. 'Huh. They don't get down this far. What do you know about them, anyhow?'

'Nothing. Who are they?'

'Mind your own business. The people who run things.'

'Well if someone does show up and you want us to shut up, just sneeze, and we'll stop talking.'

'Sneeze?'

'Well, you could always come right out and say cool it guys, there's someone here.'

'Hey Scarlett,' said Alice. 'Can you sneeze?'

'Ach-ooo,' said Miss Scarlett, delicately.

'Just testing, guys,' said Alice.

Big Lou hung around, trying to smile, trying to look like somehow all this w   going on under his auspices. Nobody was paying attention.

The next d . , the train didn't show.

It was very cold, and we stood on the platform, thumping our feet, as the day grew more sparkling, and the shadows shorter.

'Hey, Butch, what's up?' Royce asked.

'I'll check, OK?' said the camera. There was a long silence.

'The train's broken down. It's in a siding. It'll be a while yet. You might as well go back in, have the day off.'

That's how it would begin, of course. No train today, fellas, sorry. No need for you, fellas, not today, not ever, and with what you know, can you blame us? What are ten more bodies to us?

Trains did break down, of course. It had happened before. We'd had a holiday then, too, and the long drunken afternoon became a long drunken day.

'Well let's have some fun for a change,' said Lou. 'Charlie, you got any stuff ready? Let's have a blow-out man.'

'Lou,' said Royce, 'I was kind of thinking we could get to work on the hot water tank.'

'Hot water tank?' said Lou. 'Are we going to need it, Royce?' There was a horrified silence. 'So much for talking. Go on, Charlie, get your booze.'

Then Lou came for me. 'How about a little sex and romance, Rich?' Hand on neck again.

'No thanks, Lou.'

'You won't get it from him, you know.'

'That's my problem. Lou, lay off.'

'At least I can do it.' Grin.

'Surprise, surprise,' I said. His face and body were right up against mine, and I turned away. 'You can't get at him through me, you know, Lou. You just can't do it.'

Lou relented. He pulled back, but he was still smiling. 'You're right,' he said. 'For that, he'd have to like you. Sucker.' He flicked the tip of my nose with his fingers, and walked away.

I went and sat down beside Royce. I needed him to make everything seem normal and ordinary. He was leaning on his elbows, plucking at the grass. 'Hi,' I said. It was the first time we'd spoken since the inquisition.

'Hi,' he said, affectionate and distant.

'Royce, what do you think's going to happen?'

'The train will come in tomorrow,' he said.

'I hate it when it comes in,' I said, my breath rattling out of me in a kind of chuckle, 'and I hate it when it doesn't. I just hate it. Royce, do you think we could go to work on the tank?'

He considered the implications. 'OK,' he said. 'Charlie? Want to come work with us on the tank?'

Charlie was plump with a grey beard, and had a degree in engineering, a coffee tin and a copper coil. He was a sort of Santa Claus of the booze. 'Not today,' he said, cheerily. 'I made all of this, I might as well get to drink some of it myself.' It was clear and greasy-looking and came in white plastic screw-top bottles.

Charlie had sacrificed one of the showers to plumb in a hot water tank. We'd hammered the tank together out of an old train door. It was more like a basin, really, balanced in the loft of the Station. There were cameras there, too.

Royce sat looking helplessly at an electric hot plate purloined from the kitchen stove. We'd pushed wiring through from the floor below. 'Charlie should be here,' he said.

'I really love you, Royce.'

He went very still for a moment. 'I know,' he said. 'Rich, don't be scared. You're afraid all the time.'

'I know,' I said, and felt my hand tremble as I ran it across my forehead.

'You gotta stop it. One day, you'll die of fear.'

'It's this place,' I said, and broke down, and sat in a heap. 'I want to get out!'

He held me, gently. 'Someday we'll get out,' he said, and the hopelessness of it made me worse. 'Someday it'll be all right.'

'No, it won't.'

'Hi, guys,' said Alice. 'They're really acting like pigs down there.'

'They're scared,' said Royce. 'We're all scared, Alice. Is that train going to come in tomorrow?'

'Yup,' she said brightly.

'Good. You know anything about electricity?'

'Plenty. I used to work for Bell Telephone.'

Royce disengaged himself from me. 'OK. Do I put the plate inside the tank or underneath it?'

'Inside? Good Lord no!'

So Royce went back to work again, and said to me. 'You better go back down, Rich.'

'The agreement?' I asked, and he nodded yes. The agreement between him and Lou.

When I got down, the Boys looked like discarded rags. There was piss everywhere, and blood on Lou's penis.

I went up to the top of the mound. All the leaves were gone now. For about the first time in my life, I prayed. Dear God, get me out of here. Dear God, please, please, make it end. But there wasn't any answer. There never is. There was just an avalanche inside my head.

I could shut it out for a while. I could forget that every day I saw piles of corpses bulldozed and mangled, and that I had to chase the birds away from them, and that I peeled off their clothes and looked with inevitable curiosity at the little pouch of genitals in their brightly coloured underwear. And the leaking and the sudden haemorrhaging and the supple warmth of the dead, with their marble eyes full of seeming questions. How many had we killed? Was anybody keeping count? Did anyone know their names? Even their names had been taken from them, along with their wallets and watches.

Harry had found his policeman father among them, and had never stopped smiling afterwards, saying 'Hi!' like a cartoon chipmunk without a tail.

I listened to the roaring in my head as long as I could and then I went back down to the Boys. 'Is there any booze left, Charlie?' I asked, and he passed me up a full plastic bottle, and I drank myself into a stupor.

It got dark and cold, and I woke up alone, and I pulled myself up, and walked back into the waiting-room, and it was poison inside. It was as poison as the stuff going sour in our stomachs and brains and breath. We sat in twitchy silence, listening to the wind and our own farts. Nobody could be bothered to cook. Royce was not there, and my stomach twisted around itself like a bag full of snakes. Where was he? What would happen when he got back?

'You look sick,' said Lou in disgust. 'Go outside if you have to throw up.'

'I'm fine, Lou,' I said, but I could feel a thin slime of sweat on my forehead.

'You make me sick just looking at you,' he said.

'Funny. I was just thinking the same about you.' Our eyes locked, and there was no disguising it. We hated each other.

It was then that Royce came back in, rubbing his head with a towel. 'Well, there are now hot showers,' he announced. 'Well, tepid showers. You guys can go clean up.'

The Boys looked up to him, smiling. The grins were bleary, but they were glad to see him.

'Phew-wee!' he said, and waved his hand in front of his face. 'That's some stuff you come up with, Charlie, what do you make it out of, burnt tyres?'

Charlie beamed. 'Orange peel and grass,' he said proudly. I thought it was going to be all right.

Then Lou stood up out of his bed, and flopped naked toward Royce. 'You missed all the fun,' he said.

'Yeah, I know, I can smell it.'

'Now who's being a prig?' said Lou. 'Come on, man, I got something nice to show you.' He grabbed hold of Royce's forearm, and pulled him towards his own bed. Tom was in it, lying face down, like a ruin, and Lou pulled back the blanket. 'Go on, man.'

Tom was bleeding. Royce's face and voice went very hard, and he pulled the blanket back up. 'He's got an anal fissure, Lou. He needs to be left alone. It could get badly infected.'

Lou barked, like a dog, a kind of laugh. 'He's going to die anyway!'

Royce moved away from his bed. With Tom in it, he had no place to sit down. Lou followed him. 'Come on, Royce. Come on. No more pussyfooting.' He tried to put his hand down the front of Royce's shirt. Royce shrugged it away, with sudden annoyance. 'Not tonight.'

'Not ever?' asked Lou, amused.

'Come on, Royce, give it up man,' said Harry. He grabbed Royce playfully, about the waist. 'You can't hold out on us forever.' He started fumbling with the belt buckle. 'Hell, I haven't eaten all day.'

'Oh yes you have,' said Lou, and chuckled.

'Harry, please let go,' said Royce, wearily.

The belt was undone, and Lou started pulling out his shirt. 'Let go,' warned Royce. 'I said let go,' and he moved very suddenly. His elbow hit Harry in the mouth, and he yelped.

'Hey, you fucker!'

'You turkey,' said Lou.

And all the poison rose up like a wave. Oh, this was going to be fun, pulling off all of Royce's clothes. Gary, and Charlie, they all came, smiling. There was a sound of cloth tearing and suddenly Royce was fighting, fighting very hard, and suddenly the Boys were fighting too, grimly. They pulled him down, and he tried to hit them, and they held his arms, and they launched themselves on him like it was a game of tackle football. I thought, there is a word for this. The word is rape.

'Alice!' I shouted up to the camera. 'Alice, stop them! Alice? Burn one of them, stop it!'

Then something slammed into the back of my head, and I fell, the floor scraping the skin of my wrists and slapping me across the cheeks. Then I was pulled over, and Lou was on top of me, forearm across my throat.

'Booby booby booby booby,' he said all blubbery lips, and then he kissed me. Well, he bit my upper lip. He bit it to hold me there; he nearly bit through it with his canine teeth, and my mouth was full of the taste of something metallic: blood.

The sounds the Boys made were conversational, with the odd laugh. Royce squealed like a pig. It always hurts beyond everything the first time. It finally came to me that Royce wasn't gay, at least not in any sense that we would understand. I looked up at the camera, at its blank, glossy eye, and I could feel it thinking: these are men; this is what men do; we are right. We are right to do this to them. For just that moment, I almost agreed.

Lou got up, and Charlie nestled in next to me, fat and naked, white hairs on his chest and ass, and he was still beaming like a baby, and I thought: don't you know what you've done? I tried to sit up, and he went no, no, no and waggled a finger at me. It was Lou's turn to go through him. 'Rear Admiral, am I?' asked Lou.

When he was through, Charlie helped me to my feet. 'You might as well have a piece,' he said, with a friendly chuckle. Lou laughed very loudly, pulling on his T-shirt. The others were shuffling back to their beds in a kind of embarrassment. Royce lay on the floor.

I knelt next to him. My blood splashed onto the floor. 'Can you get up, Royce?' I asked him. He didn't answer. 'Royce, let's go outside, get you cleaned up.' He didn't move. 'Royce, are you hurt? Are you hurt badly?' Then I called them all bastards.

'It was just fun, man,' said Harry.

'Fun!'

'It started out that way. He shouldn't have hit people.'

'He didn't want to do it. Royce, please. Do you want anything? Is anything especially painful?'

'Just his ass,' said Lou, and laughed.

'He'll be OK,' said Charlie, a shadow of confusion on his face.

'Like fuck he will. That was some way to say thanks for all he's done. Well? Are any of you going to give me a hand?'

Harry did. He helped me to get Royce up. Royce hung between us like a sack.

'It's that fucking poison you make, man,' said Harry, to Charlie.

'Don't blame me. You were the first, remember.'

'I was just playing.'

They began to realize what they'd done. He was all angles, like a doll that didn't work anymore.

'What the fuck did you do?' I shouted at them. He didn't seem to be bruised anywhere. 'Jesus Christ!' I began to cry because I thought he was dead. 'You fucking killed him!'

'Uh-uh, no,' said Gary. 'We didn't.'

'Pisshead!'

Charlie came to help too, and we got him outside, and into the showers, and he slumped down in the dark. I couldn't find a rag, so we just let the lukewarm water trickle down over him. All we did was get him wet on an evening in November.

'It's cold out here, we got to get him back in,' said Harry.

Royce rolled himself up onto his knees, and looked at me. 'You were there.'

'I wasn't part of it. I tried to stop it.'

'You were there. You didn't help.'

'I couldn't!'

He grunted and stood up. We tried to help him, but he knocked our hands away. He sagged a bit at the knees, but kept on walking, unsteadily. He walked back into the waiting-room. Silently, people were tidying up, straightening beds. Royce scooped up his clothes with almost his usual deftness. He went back to his bed, and dropped down onto it, next to Tom, and began to inspect his shirt and trousers for damage.

'The least you could have done!' I said. I don't know what I meant.

Lou was leaning back on his bed. He looked pleased, elbows sticking out from the side of his head. 'Look at it this way,' he said. 'It might do him some good. He shouldn't be so worried about his little problem. He just needs to relax a bit more, try it on for size. The worst thing you can do with a problem like that is hide from it.'

If I'd had an axe, I would have killed him. He knew that. He smiled.

Then the lights went out, without warning as always, but two hours early.

There was snow on the ground in the morning, a light dusting

30

of it on the roof and on the ground. There was no patter. Royce did not talk to the cameras. He came out, wearing his jacket; there was a tear in his shirt, under the armpit. He ate his breakfast without looking at anyone, his face closed and still. Hardly anyone spoke. Big Lou walked around with a little half-grin. He was so pleased, he was stretched tight with it. He'd won; he was Boss again. No one used the showers.

Then we went out, and waited for the train.

We could see its brilliant headlight shining like a star on the track.

We could see the layers of wire-mesh gates pulling back for it, like curtains, and close behind it. We began to hear a noise coming from it.

It was a regular, steady drumming against metal, a bit like the sound of marching feet, a sound in unison.

'Yup,' said Charlie. 'The drugs have worn off.'

'It's going to be a bastard,' said Gary.

Lou walked calmly towards the cameras. 'Alice? What do we do?' No answer. 'We can't unload them, Alice. Do we just leave them on the train, or what?' Silence. 'Alice. We need to know what you want done.'

'Don't call me Alice,' said the camera.

'Could you let us back in, then?' asked Lou.

No answer.

The train came grinding into the platform, clattering and banging and smelling of piss. We all stood back from it, well back. Away from us, at the far end of the platform, James stood looking at the silver sky and the snow in the woods, his back to us, his headphones on. We could hear the thin whisper of Mozart from where we stood. Still looking at the woods, James sauntered towards the nearest carriage.

'James!' wailed Charlie. 'Don't open the door!'

'Jim! Jimmy! Stop!'

'James! Don't!'

He waved. All he heard was Mozart, and a banging from the train not much louder than usual. With a practised, muscular motion, he snapped up the bolt, and pulled it back, and began to swing open the door.

It burst free from his grasp, and was slammed back, and a torrent of people poured down out of the carriage, onto him. His headphones were only the first thing to be torn from him. The Stiffs were all green and mottled, like leaves. Oh Christ, oh Jesus. Uniforms. Army.

We turned and ran for the turnstile. 'Alice! God-damn it, let us in!' raged Lou. The turnstile buzzed, angrily, and we scrambled through it, caught up in its turning arms, crammed ourselves into its embrace four at a time, and we could hear feet running behind us. I squeezed through with Gary, and heard Charlie behind us cry out. Hands held him, clawed at his forehead. Gary and I pulled him out, and Lou leapt in after us, and pulled the emergency gate shut.

They prowled just the other side of a wire mesh fence, thick necked, as mad as bulls, with asses as broad as our shoulders. 'We'll get you fuckers,' one of them promised me, looking dead into my eyes. They trotted from door to door of the train, springing them. They began to rock the turnstile back and forth. 'Not electric!' one of them called. They began to pull at the wire mesh. We had no weapons.

'Hey! Hey, help!' we shouted. 'Alice, Scarlett. Help!'

No answer. As if in contempt, the warm-up lights went on.

'We're using gas,' said Alice, her voice hard. 'Get your masks.'

The masks were in the waiting-room. We turned and ran, but the cameras didn't give us time. Suddenly there was a gush of something like steam, in the icy morning, out from under the platform. I must have caught a whiff of it. It was like a blow on the head, and my feet crossed in front of each other instead of running. I managed to hold my breath, and Royce's face was suddenly in front of me, as still as a stone, and he pushed a mask at me, and pulled on his own, walking towards the gate. I fumbled with mine. Harry, or someone, all inhuman in green, helped me. I saw Royce walking like an angel into white, a blistering white that caught the winter sunlight in a blaze. He walked right up to the fence, and stood in the middle of the poison, and watched.

The gas billowed, and the people billowed too, in waves. They climbed up over each other, in shifting pyramids, to get away, piling up against the fence. Those on top balanced, waving their arms like surfers, and there were sudden flashes of red light through the mist, and bars of rumpled flesh appeared across their eyes. One of them had fine light hair that burst into flame about his head. He wore a crown of fire.

The faces of those on the bottom of the heap were pressed against the fence into diamond shapes, and they twitched and jittered. The whole wave began to twitch and jitter, and shake, against the fence.

It must have been the gas in my head. I was suddenly convinced that it was nerve gas, and that meant that the nerves of the dead people were still working, even though they were dead. Even though they were dead, they would shake and judder against the fence until it fell, and they they would walk towards us, and take us into their arms, and talk to us in whispers, and pull off the masks.

I spun around, and looked at the mound, because I thought the dead inside it would wake. It did seem to swim and move, and I thought that Babylon would crack, and what had been hidden would come marching out. The dead were angry, because they had been forgotten.

Then the mist began to clear, blown. I thought of dandelion seeds that I had blown like magic across the fields when I was a child.

'Hockey games,' I said. I thought there had been a game of hockey. The bodies were piled up, in uniforms. They were still. We waited. Harry practised throwing stones.

'What a mess,' said Gary.

There were still wafts of gas around the bottom of the platform. We didn't know how long we would have to wait before it was safe.

Suddenly Lou stepped forward. 'Come on, let's start,' he said, his voice muffled by the mask. He pulled back the emergency gate. 'We've got masks,' he said.

None of us moved. We just didn't have the heart.

'We can't leave them there!' Lou shouted. Still none of us moved.

Then Royce sat down on the grass, and pulled off his mask, and took two deep breaths. He looked at the faces in front of him, a few feet away, purple against the mesh.

'Alice,' he said. 'Why are we doing this?'

No answer.

33

'It's horrible. It's the worst thing in the world. Horrible for us, horrible for you. That's why what happened last night happened, Alice. Because this is so terrible. You cage people up, you make them do things like this, and something goes, something inside. Something will give with you, too, Alice. You can't keep this up either. Do you have dreams, Alice? Do you have dreams at night about this? While the Wigs are at their parties, making big decisions and debating ideology? I don't believe anyone could look at this and not feel sick.'

'You need to hear any more?' Lou asked the cameras, with a swagger.

'I mean. How did it happen?' Royce was crying. 'How did we get so far apart? There were problems, sure, but there was love, too. Men and women loved each other. People love each other, so why do we end up doing things like this? Can you give me a reason, Alice?'

'You do realize what he's saying, don't you?' asked Lou. He pulled off his mask, and folded his arms. 'Just listen to what is coming out of his closet.'

'I am not going to move those bodies, Alice,' said Royce. 'I can't. I literally cannot move another body. I don't think any of us can. You can kill us all if you want to. But then, you'd have to come and do it yourselves, wouldn't you?'

Lou waited. We all waited. Nothing happened.

'They'll — uh — start to stink if we don't move them,' said Gary, and coughed, and looked to Lou.

'If we don't move them,' said Harry, and for once he wasn't smiling, 'another train can't come in.'

'Alice?' said Lou. 'Alice?' Louder, outraged. 'You hear what is happening here?'

There was a click, and a rumbling sound, a sort of shunting. A gate at the far end of the platform rolled back. Then another, and another, all of them opening at once.

'Go on,' said Alice.

We all just stood there. We weren't sure what it meant, we didn't even know that all those gates could open at once.

'Go *on*. Get out. Hurry. Before one of the Wigs comes.'

'You mean it?' Harry asked. We were frightened. We were frightened to leave.

'We'll say you got killed in the riot, that you were gassed or something. They'll never know the difference. Now move!'

'Alice, god-damn it, what are you doing, are you crazy?' Lou was wild.

'No. She ain't crazy. You are.' That was Royce. He stood up. 'Well you heard her, haul some ass. Charlie, Harry, you go and get all the food there is left in the canteen. The rest of you, go get all the blankets and clothes, big coats that haven't been shipped back. And Harry, fill some jugs with water.'

Lou didn't say anything. He pulled out a kitchen knife and he ran toward Royce. Royce just stood there. I don't think he would have done anything. I think he was tired, tired of the whole thing. I mean he was tired of death. Lou came for him.

The Grils burned him. They burned Lou. He fell in a heap at Royce's feet, his long, strong arms all twisted. 'Aw hell,' said Royce, sad and angry. 'Aw hell.'

And a voice came cutting into my head, clear and blaring. I was crazy. The voice said, 'This is radio station KERB broadcasting live from the First Baptist Church of Christ the Redeemer with the Reverend Thomas Wallace Robertson and the Inglewood Youth Choir, singing *O Happy Day.*'

And I heard it. I heard the music. I just walked out onto the platform, reeling with the sound, the mass of voices inside my head, and I didn't need any blankets. O Happy Day! When Jesus wash! And Los Angeles might be gone, and Detroit and Miami, a lot of things might be gone, but that Sunday night music was still kicking shit, and if there wasn't a God, there was always other people, and they surprised you. Maybe I'd been fooled by history too. I said goodbye to the cameras as I passed them. Goodbye Alice. Goodbye Hortensia. See ya, Scarlett. Butch, I'm sorry about the name.

They were making funny noises. The cameras were weeping. I walked on toward the open gate.

For America

ANGELA CARTER
THE CABINET OF
EDGAR ALLAN POE

Imagine Poe in the Republic! when he possesses none of its virtues; no Spartan, he. Each time he tilts the jug to greet the austere morning, his sober friends reluctantly concur: 'No man is safe who drinks before breakfast.' Where is the black star of melancholy? Elsewhere; not here. Here it is always morning; stern, democratic light scrubs apparitions off the streets down which his dangerous feet must go.

Perhaps . . . perhaps the black star of melancholy was hiding in the dark at the bottom of the jug all the time . . . it might be the whole thing is a little secret between the jug and himself . . .

He turns back to go and look; and the pitiless light of common day hits him full in the face like a blow from the eye of God. Struck, he reels. Where can he hide, where there are no shadows? They split the Republic in two, they halved the apple of knowledge, white light strikes the top half and leaves the rest in shadow; up here, up north, in the levelling latitudes, a man must make his own penumbra if he wants concealment because the massive, heroic light of the Republic admits of no ambiguities. Either you are a saint; or a stranger. He is a stranger, here, a gentleman up from Virginia somewhat down on his luck, and, alas, he may not invoke the Prince of Darkness (always a perfect gentleman) in his cause since, of the absolute night which is the antithesis to these days of rectitude, there is no aristocracy.

Poe staggers under the weight of the Declaration of Independence. People think he is drunk.

He *is* drunk.

The prince in exile lurches through the new-found land.

So you say he overacts? Very well; he overacts. There is a past history of histrionics in his family. His mother was, as they say, born in a trunk, greasepaint in her bloodstream, and made her first appearance on any stage in her ninth summer in a hiss-the-villain melodrama entitled *Mysteries of the Castle*. It was the evening of the eighteenth century; twilight falls on the Age of Reason.

Poe's future mother skipped onto a stage in the fresh-hatched American republic to sing an old-world ballad clad in the pretty rags of a ballet gypsy. Her dancer's grace, piping treble, dark curls, rosy cheeks — cute kid! And eyes with something innocent, something appealing in them that struck directly to the heart so that the smoky auditorium broke out in raucous sentimental cheers for her and clapped its leather palms together with a will. A star was born that night in the rude firmament of fit-ups and candle-footlights, but she was to be a shooting star; she flickered briefly in the void, she continued the inevitable trajectory of the meteor, downward. She hit the boards and trod them.

But, well after puberty, she was still able, thanks to her low stature and slim build, to continue to personate children, clever little ducks and prattlers of both sexes. Yet she was versatility personified; she could do you Ophelia, too.

She had a low, melodious voice of singular sweetness, an excellent thing in a woman. When crazed Ophelia handed round the rosemary and rue and sang: 'He is dead and gone, lady,' not a dry eye in the house, I assure you. She also tried her hand at Juliet and Cordelia and, if necessary, could personate the merriest soubrette; even when racked by the nauseas of her pregnancies, still she would smile, would smile and oh! the dazzling candour of her teeth!

Out popped her firstborn, Henry; her second, Edgar, came jostling after to share her knee with her scripts and suckle at her bosom meanwhile she learned her lines, yet she was always word-perfect even when she played two parts in the one night, Ophelia or Juliet and then, say, Little Pickle, the cute kid in the afterpiece, for the audiences of those days refused to leave the theatre after a tragedy unless the players changed costumes and came back to give them a little something extra to cheer them up again.

Little Pickle was a trousers role. She ran back to the green room and undid the top buttons of her waistcoat to let out a sore, milky breast to pacify little Edgar who, wakened by the hoots and catcalls that had greeted her too voluptuous imitation of a boy, likewise howled and screamed.

A mug of porter or a bottle of whisky stood on the dressing table all the time. She dipped a plug of cotton in whisky and gave it to Edgar to suck when he would not stop crying.

The father of her children was a bad actor and only ever carried a spear in the many companies in which she worked. He often stayed behind in the green room to look after the little ones. David Poe tipped a tumbler of neat gin to Edgar's lips to keep him quiet. The red-eyed Angel of Intemperance hopped out of the bottle of ardent spirits and snuggled down in little Edgar's longclothes. Meanwhile, on stage, her final child, in utero, stitched its flesh and bones together as best it could under the corset that preserved the theatrical illusion of Mrs Elizabeth Poe's eighteen inch waist until the eleventh hour, the tenth month.

Applause rocked round the wooden O. Loving mother that she was — for we have no reason to believe that she was not — Mrs Poe exited the painted scene to cram her jewels on her knee while tired tears ran rivers through her rouge and splashed upon their peaky faces. The monotonous clamour of their parents' argument sent them at last to sleep but the unborn one in the womb pressed its transparent hands over its vestigial ears in terror.

(To be born at all might be the worst thing.)

However, born at last this last child was, one July afternoon in a cheap theatrical boarding house in New York City after many hours on a rented bed while flies buzzed at the windowpanes. Edgar and Henry, on a palette on the floor, held hands. The midwife had to use a pair of blunt iron tongs to scoop out the reluctant wee thing; the sheet was tented up over Mrs Poe's lower half for modesty so the toddlers saw nothing except the midwife brandishing her dreadful instrument and then they heard the shrill cry of the new-born describing a jagged arc in the exhausted silence like the sound of the blade of a skate on ice and something was twitching between the midwife's pincers, bloody as a fresh-pulled tooth.

David Poe spent his wife's confinement in a nearby tavern, wetting the baby's head. When he came back and saw the mess he vomited.

Then, before his sons' bewildered eyes, their father began to grow insubstantial. He unbecame. All at once he lost his outlines and began to waver on the air. It was twilit evening. Mama slept on the bed with a fresh mauve bud of flesh in a basket on the chair beside her. The air shuddered with the beginning of absence.

He said not one word to his boys but went on evaporating until he melted clean away, leaving behind him in the room as proof he had been there only a puddle of puke on the splintered wooden floor.

As soon as the deserted wife got out of bed, she posted down to Virginia with her howling brats because she was booked for a tour of the South and she had no money put away so all the babies got to eat was her sweat. She dragged them with her in a trunk to Charleston; to Norfolk; then back to Richmond.

Down there, it is the foetid height of summer.

Stripped to her chemise in the airless dressing-room, she milks her sore breasts into a glass; this latest baby must be weaned before its mother dies.

She coughed. She slapped more, yet more rouge on her now haggard cheekbones. 'My children! what will become of my children?' Her eyes glittered and soon acquired a febrile brilliance that was not of *this* world. Soon she needed no rouge at all; red spots brighter than rouge appeared of their own accord on her cheeks while veins as blue as those in Stilton cheese but muscular, palpitating, prominent, lithe, stood out on her forehead. In Little Pickle's vest and breeches it was not now possible for her to create the least suspension of disbelief and something desperate, something fatal in her distracted playing both fascinated and appalled the witnesses, who could have thought they saw the living features of death itself upon her face. Her mirror, the actress's friend, the magic mirror in which she sees whom she has become, no longer acknowledged any but a death's head.

The moist, sullen, Southern winter signed her quietus. She put on Ophelia's madwoman's nightgown for her farewell.

When she summoned him, the spectral horseman came. Edgar looked out of the window and saw him. The soundless hooves of black-plumed horses struck sparks from the stones in the road outside. 'Father!' said Edgar; he thought their father must have reconstituted himself at this last extremity in order to transport them all to a better place but, when he looked more closely, by the light of the gibbous moon, he saw the sockets of the coachman's eyes were full of worms.

They told her children that now she could come back to take no curtain-calls no matter how fiercely all applauded the manner of her going. Lovers of the theatre plied her hearse with bouquets: 'And from her pure and uncorrupted flesh May violets spring.' (Not a dry eye in the house.) The three orphaned infants were dispersed into the bosoms of charitable protectors. Each gave the clay-cold cheek a final kiss; then they too kissed and parted, Edgar from Henry, Henry from the tiny one who did not move or cry but lay still and kept her eyes tight shut. When shall these three meet again. The church bell tolled: never never never never never.

Kind Mr Allan of Virginia, Edgar's own particular benefactor, who would buy his bread henceforward, took his charge's little hand and led him from the funeral. Edgar parted his name in the middle to make room for Mr Allan inside it. Edgar was then three years old. Mr Allan ushered him into Southern affluence, down there; but do not think his mother left Edgar empty handed, although the dead actress was able to leave him only what could not be taken away from him, to whit, a few tattered memories.

Testament of Mrs Elizabeth Poe

Item: nourishment. A tit sucked in a green room, the dug snatched away from the toothless lips as soon as her cue came, so that, of nourishment, he would retain only the memory of hunger and thirst endlessly unsatisfied.

Item: transformation. This is a more ambivalent relic. Something like this . . . Edgar would lie in prop-baskets on heaps of artificial finery and watch her while she painted her face. The candles made a profane altar of the mirror in which her vague face swam like a magic fish. If you caught hold of it, it would make your dreams come true but Mama slithered through all the nets desire set out to catch her.

She stuck glass jewels in her ears, pinned back her nut brown hair and tied a muslin bandage round her head, looking like a corpse for a minute. Then on went the yellow wig. Now you see her, now you don't; brunette turns blonde in the wink of an eye.

Mama turns round to show how she has changed into the lovely lady he glimpsed in the mirror.

'Don't touch me, you'll mess me.'

And vanishes in a susurration of taffeta.

Item: that women possess within them a cry, a thing that needs to be extracted . . . but this is only the dimmest of memories and will reassert itself in vague shapes of unmentionable dread only at the prospect of carnal connection.

Item: the awareness of mortality. For, as soon as her last child was born, if not before, she started to rehearse in private the long part of dying; once she began to cough she had no option.

Item: a face, the perfect face of a tragic actor, his face, white skin stretched tight over fine, white bones in a final state of wonderfully lucid emaciation.

Ignited by the tossed butt of a still-smouldering cigar that had lodged in the cracks of the uneven floorboards, the theatre at Richmond where Mrs Poe had made her last appearance burned to the ground three weeks after her death. Ashes. Although Mr Allan told Edgar that all of his mother that was mortal had been buried in her coffin, Edgar knew that the somebody elses she so frequently became lived in her dressing-table mirror and were not constrained by the physical laws that made her body rot. But now the mirror, too, was gone: and all the lovely and untouchable, volatile, unreal mothers went up together in a puff of smoke on a pyre of props and painted scenery.

The sparks from this conflagration rose high in the air, where they lodged in the sky to become a constellation of stars that only Edgar saw and then only on certain still nights of summer, those hot, rich, blue, mellow nights that the slaves have brought from Africa, weather that ferments the music of exile, weather of heartbreak and fever. (Oh, those voluptuous nights, like something forbidden!) High in the sky these invisible stars marked the points of a face folded in sorrow.

Nature of the theatrical illusion: everything you see is false.

Consider the theatrical illusion with special reference to this impressionable child, who was exposed to it at an age when there is no reason for anything to be real.

He must often have toddled onto the stage when the theatre was empty and the curtains down so all was like a parlour prepared for a séance, waiting for the moment when the eyes of the observers make the mystery.

Here he will find a painted backdrop of, say, an antique castle — a castle! such as they don't build here; a Gothic castle all complete with owls and ivy. The flies are painted with segments of trees, massy oaks or something like that, all in two dimensions. Artificial shadows fall in all the wrong places. Nothing is what it seems. You knock against a gilded throne or horrid wrack that looks perfectly solid, thick and immovable, but when you kick it sideways, it turns out to be made of papier mâché, it is as light as air — a child, you yourself, could pick it up and carry it off with you and sit in it and be a king or lie in it and be in pain.

A creaking, an ominous rattling scares the little wits out of you; when you jump round to see what is going on behind your back, why, the very castle is in mid-air! Heave-ho and up she rises, amid the inarticulate cries and muttered oaths of the stagehands, and down comes Juliet's tomb or Ophelia's sepulchre, and a super scuttles in, clutching Yorick's skull.

The foul-mouthed whores who dandle you on their pillowy laps and tip mugs of sour porter against your lips now congregate in the wings, where they have turned into nuns or something. On the invisible side of the plush curtain that cuts you off from the beery, importunate, tobacco-stained multitude that has paid its pennies on the nail to watch these transcendent rituals now come the thumps, bangs and clatter that make the presence of their expectations felt. A stage hand swoops down to scoop you up and carry you off, protesting, to where Henry, like a good boy, is already deep in his picture book and there is a poke of candy for you and the corner of a handkerchief dipped in moonshine and Mama in crown and train presses her rouged lips softly on your forehead before she goes down before the mob.

On his brow her rouged lips left the mark of Cain.

Having, at an impressionable age, seen with his own eyes the nature of the mystery of the castle — that all its horrors are so much painted cardboard and yet they terrify you — he saw another mystery and made less sense of it.

Now and then, as a great treat, if he kept quiet as a mouse, because he begged and pleaded so, he was allowed to stay in the wings and watch; the round-eyed baby saw that Ophelia could, if necessary, die twice nightly. All her burials were premature.

A couple of brawny supers carried Mama on stage in Act Four, wrapped in a shroud, tipped her into the cellarage amidst displays of grief from all concerned but up she would pop at curtain call having shaken the dust off her graveclothes and touched up her eye make-up, to curtsey with the rest of the resurrected immortals, all of whom, even Prince Hamlet himself, turned out, in the end, to be just as un-dead as she.

How could he, then, truly believe she would not come again, although, in the black suit that Mr Allan provided for him out of charity, he toddled behind her coffin to the cemetery? Surely, one fine day, the spectral coachman would return again, climb down from his box, throw open the carriage door and out she would step wearing the white nightdress in which he had last seen her, although he hoped this garment had been laundered in the interim since he last saw it all bloody from a haemorrhage.

Then a transparent constellation in the night sky would blink out; the scattered atoms would reassemble themselves to the entire and perfect Mama and he would run directly to her arms.

It is mid-morning of the nineteenth century. He grows up under the black stars of the slave states. He flinches from that part of women the sheet hid. He becomes a man.

As soon as he becomes a man, affluence departs from Edgar. The heart and pocketbook that Mr Allan opened to the child now pull themselves together to expel. Edgar shakes the dust of the sweet South off his heels. He hies north, up here, to seek his fortune in the places where the light does not permit that chiaroscuro he loves; nevertheless, now Edgar Poe must live by his disordered wits.

The dug was snatched from the milky mouth and tucked away inside the bodice; the mirror no longer reflected Mama but, instead, a perfect stranger. He offered her his hand; smiling a tranced smile, she stepped out of the frame.

'My darling, my sister, my life and my bride!'

He was not put out by the tender years of this young girl whom he soon married; was she not just Juliet's age, just thirteen summers?

The magnificent tresses forming great shadowed eaves above her high forehead were the raven tint of nevermore, black as his suits the seams of which his devoted mother-in-law painted with ink so that they would not advertise to the world the signs of wear and, nowadays, he always wore a suit of sables, dressed in readiness for the next funeral in a black coat buttoned up to the stock and he never betrayed his absolute mourning by so much as one flash of white shirtfront. Sometimes, when his wife's mother was not there to wash and starch his linen, he economised on laundry bills and wore no shirt at all.

His long hair brushes the collar of his coat, from which poverty has worn off the nap. How sad his eyes are; there is too much sorrow in his infrequent smile to make you happy when he smiles at you and so much of bitter gall, also, that you might mistake his smile for a grimace or a grue except when he smiles at his young wife with her forehead like a tombstone. Then he will smile and smile with as much posthumous tenderness as if he saw already: *Dearly Beloved Wife Of* . . . carved above her eyebrows.

For her skin was white as marble and she was called — would you believe! — 'Virginia', a name that suited his expatriate's nostalgia and also her condition, for the child-bride would remain a virgin until the day she died.

Imagine the sinless children lying in bed together! The pity of it!

For did she not come to him stiffly armoured in taboos — taboos against the violation of children; taboos against the violation of the dead — for, not to put too fine a point on it, didn't she always look like a walking corpse? But such a pretty, pretty corpse!

And, besides, isn't an undemanding, economic, decorative corpse the perfect wife for a gentleman in reduced circumstances, upon whom the four walls of paranoia are always about to converge?

Virginia Clemm. In the dialect of Northern England, to be 'clemmed' is to be very cold. 'I'm fair clemmed.' Virginia Clemm.

She brought with her a hardy, durable, industrious mother of her own, to clean and cook and keep accounts for them and to outlive them, and to outlive them both.

Virginia was a perfect child and never ceased to be so. The slow years passed and she stayed as she had been at thirteen, a simple little thing whose sweet disposition was his only comfort and who never ceased to lisp, even when she started to rehearse the long part of dying.

She was light on her feet as a revenant. You would have thought she never bent a stem of grass as she passed across their little garden. When she spoke, when she sang, how sweet her voice was; she kept her harp in their cottage parlour, which her mother swept and polished until all was like a new pin. A few guests gathered there to partake of the Poes' modest hospitality. There was his brilliant conversation though his women saw to it that only tea was served, since all knew his dreadful weakness for liquor, but Virginia poured out with so much simple grace that everyone was charmed.

They begged her to take her seat at her harp and accompany herself in an Old World ballad or two. Eddy nodded gladly: 'Yes,' and she lightly struck the strings with white hands of which the long, thin fingers were so fine and waxen that you would have thought you could have set light to the tips to make of her hand the flaming Hand of Glory that casts all the inhabitants of the house, except the magician himself, into a profound and death-like sleep.

She sings:

> Cold blows the wind, tonight, my lore,
> And a few drops of rain.

With a taper made from a ms. folded into a flute, he slyly takes a light from the fire.

> I never had but one true love
> In cold earth she was lain.

He sets light to her fingers, one after the other.

> A twelve month and a day being gone
> The dead began to speak.

Eyes close. Her pupils contain in each a flame.

> Who is that sitting on my grave
> Who will not let me sleep?

All sleep. Her eyes go out. She sleeps.

He rearranges the macabre candelabrum so that the light from her glorious hand will fall between her legs and then he busily turns back her petticoats; the mortal candles shine. Do not think it is not love that moves him; only love moves him.

He feels no fear.

An expression of low cunning crosses his face. Taking from his back pocket a pair of enormous pliers, he now, one by one, one by one by one, extracts the sharp teeth just as the midwife did.

All silent, all still.

Yet, even as he held aloft the last fierce canine in triumph above her prostrate and insensible form in the conviction he had at last exorcised the demons from desire, his face turned ashen and sere and he was overcome with the most desolating anguish to hear the rumbling of the wheels outside. Unbidden, the coachman came; the grisly emissary of her high-born kinsman shouted imperiously: 'Overture and beginners, please!' She popped the plug of spiritous linen between his lips; she swept off with a hiss of silk.

The sleepers woke and told him he was drunk; but his Virginia breathed no more!

After a breakfast of red-eye, as he was making his toilet before the mirror, he suddenly thought he would shave off his moustache in order to become a different man so that the ghosts who had persistently plagued him since his wife's death would no longer recognise him and leave him alone. But, when he was clean-shaven, a black star rose in the mirror and he saw that his long hair and face folded in sorrow had taken on such a marked resemblance to that of his loved and lost one that he was struck like a stock or stone, with the cut-throat razor in his hand.

And, as he continued, fascinated, appalled, to stare in the reflective glass at those features that were his own and yet not his own, the bony casket of his skull began to agitate itself as if he had succumbed to a tremendous attack of the shakes.

Goodnight, sweet prince.

He was shaking like a back-cloth about to be whisked off into oblivion.

Lights! he called out.

Now he wavered; horrors! *He was starting to dissolve!*

Lights! more lights! he cried, like the hero of a Jacobean tragedy

when the murdering begins, for the black star was engulfing him.
  On cue, the laser light of the Republic blasts him.
  His dust blows away on the wind.

SCOTT BRADFIELD
THE FLASH! *KID*

Rudy McDermott's siege of the termite nest was inspired by the funny word 'attrition', introduced to him by his birthday book, *We Were There at the Hundred Years War*. He shovelled a moat circumscribing the infested oak-log and filled it generously with Pennzoil looted from Father's outboard. The termites, busy inside their mouldering apartments, exhibited no immediate concern, and Rudy dashed home for lunch. He returned a half-hour later to find the insects constructing a bridge across the moat with accumulating drowned corpses. They swarmed headlong into the muck in a sort of conscientious frenzy. Rudy struck a match and ignited the moat. The ring of fire flashed and heat rushed his face. The fried insects smelled like burnt popcorn. Greasy black smoke lifted into the bright mountain sky, flames dwindled into the scorched earth. Rudy replenished the moat and lay back against a warm flinty hill, watching the discombobulated insects struggle and squirm in the ashy sludge. He flicked small stones at them as they carted their sizzling brethren into deep, buzzing tombs. Rudy reignited the moat and ran home for an ice-cream and a brief chat with Father.

Father was out back on the raised sun-deck with Mom. *Bushwah!* Father roared, and flung the newspaper over the railing. A few white sheets skimmed down the surface of the hill like mantarays. What's *this* I read? My tax-deductible religious contributions provide flak jackets for Sister Maria Theresa's guerilla force in Uruguay! And who's Sister Maria fighting for? Subversives, that's who! And who do subversives hate most of all? Successful men like me, that's who!

For godsake, Mom groaned, prone on her lawn-chair and bikinied, brown and glistening with oil like a very old salad. If there's one thing you sound stupid about it's politics.

Father grumbled, his face flush. A black vein pulsed ominously in his forehead. He poured himself another icy Margarita, sprinkled it with salt.

Termites, huh? Father said later, solaced by now with his fishing rod. He reeled in line from a spool that twitched and tumbled on the deck. Rudy watched raptly over his dribbling ice-cream. My old pal Bob Probosky and I knew all about termites. Or at least I did, yessir. When I was your age I busted open a termite nest, that's what I did. Bob was chicken, scared he'd get stung. Not me, though. I reached in and yanked out that mamatermite with my bare hands, diced her for bait. She caught trout like a goddamn gattling gun — yessir, she did! But did I let that fag Probosky use any? Nosir, I didn't! Sure I got stung. But I knew what I had to do and I did it — and *I* reaped the reward. The world's a jungle, boy, and only the fittest survive. You have to act fast if you want to make your mark on the world. That's how you become a successful man like your Father —

For godsake, Mom said, and reached for her sunglasses. If there's one thing you sound stupider about than politics it's your crummy childhood.

With a sledge-hammer Rudy returned and demolished the nest, pried back sheaves of rotted wood. The mamatermite was enormous, Rudy startled. Gravid and glistening, as long and thick as Father's forearm, the queen's convoluted envelope fitted snugly inside the log like the meat of some gigantic walnut. Reach in and yank it out? He would need a bucket. Rudy improvised, swung the sledge-hammer again. Pus and slime spattered his arms and face. The stench was terrible; he wiped the sour taste from his lips. He ran away crying and crashed through bushes and a small stream. The crowd of trees stood around making shadows, birds chirped in the leaves. Rudy stopped shivering, obligated by Father's nostalgic courage. He walked back solemnly to the ruined nest. Termites swarmed around the exploded queen, dragging away slivers of flesh. Rudy unscrewed the lid from a jellyjar, crouched, shut his eyes. He scooped blindly at the nest and the jar made a thwucking sound. He screwed back the lid and flung the jar against the flinty hill where it thudded soundly. Rudy's hands were sticky, he wiped them against the ground. The ground was dry and crusty and broke apart in shards. Rudy threw the flinty dirt across the ruined nest, cut more dirt loose with his bowie knife. Something metallic clanged and the knife bucked against his hand. He scraped the dirt curiously. Metal screeched. Gradually Rudy cleared a patch of gunmetal black. The black was remarkably smooth, like the surface of an eyeball. A sense of heaviness surfaced in his mind when he touched the buried object. Like déjà vu, abstract but firm. Patiently he uncovered the statue's entire surface. Two feet long, tubular, black and smooth and unblemished, without any markings or delineations whatever, seamless as the skin of an egg. He struck it sharply with his knife and the knife-point cracked. His fingers were drawn again and again across the smooth surface, as if here was condensed the enigmatic stuff of the universe. He clenched his teeth. Overhead the moon hooked vague clouds, and Rudy wondered, Who to tell? Who, indeed?

Sure, we'll take a look at it, Father agreed. Some day, some day soon. But not today, not right this minute. Right this minute there was fishing to do, imported beer to drink, Mom to bicker with inanely. Mom drove to Tahoe and returned by dinner, her freshly dyed hair piled high atop her dry red face, accompanied by a strange noisy couple. The man was in the stock market, the woman in the Book-of-the-Month Club. The woman hugged Rudy viciously. The man said ha ha ha, what's that, young buck? A termite *how* big? I saw that movie. Jon Agar saves the world, doesn't he?

The image of the submerged, neglected statue infiltrated Rudy's dreams. They were deep black dreams without faces, a quicksand effluvium which filled his mind like molten ore, as if his identity and the identity of the statue were being inverted. The dreams encased Rudy in darkness; he was warm, secure; his body was a vessel hard and unimpressionable, like something fired in a kiln, like the heart of a planet, like the fine black powder he discovered inside the abandoned jelly-jar the next morning. The fine kinetic powder jingled sibilantly as he swirled it around the inside of the glass, keening, eerie, celestial, like purported music of the spheres.

The first person Rudy lured to the statue took it away from him. A young surveyor had been prowling the woods for several days, unshaven, muttering, scratching himself, toting a small intricate telescope and clipboard. Rudy's approach was determinedly casual. He was learning that a child's enthusiasm is inversely proportional to the scale of adult priorities. Hey, Mister. Want to see something weird? Hey, Mister. It's right over here. Maybe somebody lost it. Hey, Mister.

Okay, okay, the young man conceded finally. Show me something weird. But then promise you'll go home, all right? Could you do that for me? Promise?

Mmmmmmmmmm. Interesting . . . The surveyor touched the statue briefly, as if testing a hot iron. Cautiously he laid his palm flat against the frictionless surface, whistled slowly through his teeth. So heavy, he said, and clenched his jaws.

As the surveyor stared, Rudy's sanctioned enthusiasm ran free. He babbled hectically of his discovery: the doomed termites, the Pennzoil, Father's nostalgic fishbait, Mom's new hairstyle, the gravid queen, the immanent dreams and the fine black powder.

The surveyor grumbled, scratched his oily hair, scrawled something on his clipboard, and proceeded to the fishing lodge.

Hey, Mister, can I come? Rudy asked, was not refused.

Rudy pressed his face against the glass-panelled telephone booth, breathing mist against the glass and pretending he was an enormous fish in a bowl.

Andy? the surveyor said. This is Steve. Yeah, the connection's bad. I'm up at Caple's Lake . . . What? Dunnigan, Steve Dunnigan. No, I don't have a sister. We were in Dr Tennyson's seminar together, remember? Okay, okay — just forget it. I've found something you'll want to take a look at —

Here, Dunnigan said, shutting the glass booth behind him. Buy yourself some baseball cards.

Rudy accepted the quarter cordially, slipped it in his pocket, went to the lodge and bought a pound bag of beef jerky with one of the twenties from his genuine cowhide wallet. He sat on the front steps and chewed as he watched Dunnigan hurry bags and equipment from his cabin into a battered red Toyota. When Dunnigan drove off, the Toyota's flimsy clutch rattled like a marble in a soup can.

Rudy went home for dinner, rapidly consumed two steaks, a potato, no broccoli, three hot slices of cherry pie, and a frozen Snicker's bar. Upstairs in his loft he was only mildly queasy, and watched the portable television underneath his bedcovers. He fell asleep and resumed the dreams again, awoke in a cold sweat, his stomach protuberant and growling. He slipped downstairs and managed a pair of ice-cream sandwiches, returned to bed and the dreams again. It was as if his mind was being fed on a very short loop. Eggs for breakfast, four or five scrambled. Mom was pleased, offered encouragement. Another sandwich? Cookies? More milk, Rudy? Eat, *eat*! Marie and the girls are always talking about your skinny arms . . . Father said, Good for you, boy! Build those muscles. You can't be a skinny little wimp all your life. You have to be tough, you have to take care of yourself in this world, boy. You think I'm not tough? Go on, then; try me. Hit me in the stomach. Go ahead, *hit* me. Harder. *Harder*, now! Show some muscle, boy! I've swatted gnats harder than that!

Dunnigan returned in the afternoon with a goateed, circumspect man. They conferred beside the sunken statue, consulted pocket-sized devices, and departed in a jeep. Dunnigan returned again the following morning with more men, equipment, jeeps. Rudy visited the site daily, saw crowbars snap like popsicle sticks, pneumatic hammers grind to a halt, strong men with ringed underarms herniate in chorus, puny forklifts roar as cables snapped everywhere. Helicopters beat overhead above the secluded lakefront property, CB radios spluttered and squawked in the crisp mountain air. Still, the object did not budge. It would not budge. It was stubborn, heroic and invulnerable, Rudy thought. Just like Superman.

Father and Mom budged quite readily, however, packed Rudy up with the belongings and relocated to the relative sanctity of their San Francisco mansion, where Rudy explored the daily paper with casual regularity. The initial notice appeared in the back pages of the *Chronicle*, amidst advertisements for lingerie and quick-weight-loss clinics. Rudy's name was included in the blurb, Dunnigan's, date and location of find, difficulties encountered. A mere journalistic kernel, yet fecund, persevering, it rooted and advanced to page two as *Life Buried in Strange Object?* and blossomed ultimately in frontpage headlines:

LIFE BURIED IN STRANGE OBJECT!
Child Unearths Cosmic Treasure

Father and Mom began introducing Rudy to their friends as 'the little archaeologist in the family' before posting him off to bed when another reporter infiltrated the party. The phone rang ceaselessly, and Mom had the number changed. Reporters and cameramen populated the front porch, lunatics verged on the perimeters. The streets resounded with cymbals and tambourines, bullhorns proclaimed the sovereignty of Jesuschristallmighty. *The Flying Saucer Gazette* accused Rudy of conspiring with sentient vegetable protein from Betelgeuse, Satanists dropped by evenings for coffee and, rebuked, splattered sheep's blood on the lawn, driveway, and deluxe Mercedes convertible. A flurry of Dianetic brochures arrived daily with the harried postman. Red journalism complemented topical hysteria. *Cosmic Statue Predicts Earthquakes!!! Jeanne Dixon Communicates With Telepathic Statue in Esperanto!!! Cosmic Boon for Acne Sufferers???* Rudy chatted happily with the interchangeable lunatics and newsmen until his family's tolerance was 'overextended', Father's press release declared. All he can tell you, Mom shouted one day, yanking Rudy inside, is that he found the thing, gave it away, and then came right home! Crestfallen, Rudy was denied permission to pose for the covers of *Jack and Jill Monthly* and *Isaac Asimov's Science Fiction Magazine*. For the rest of the summer Rudy was relegated to the video entertainment console of his isolate bedroom.

Dunnigan, along with the 'cosmic treasure', was appropriated by UC Regents Berkeley. An Associate Professorship in Archaeology compensated the former while the elaborate wing of the Physical Research Center secluded the latter. Dunnigan appeared frequently on network news programs and *The Tonight Show, Starring Johnny Carson*. Frankly, Johnny, we're baffled, he conceded. We can't penetrate the object's shell, but ultrasound has detected embedded proteins, minerals, rudimentary enzymes — materials implicit in the genesis of life. As I told you over dinner, the statue's shell is so dense that the molecules are virtually impacted together. Conceivably billions of years old, it's perhaps the byproduct — or so contend the latest theories — of some titanic implosion, the devastating force of which would be unconscionable even in our nuclear-conscious age. Dunnigan gave the unconscionable audience an ingratiating, winsome smile, like a Nobel Laureate confronted by some giddy coed, and Johnny said they *must* play tennis again real soon.

Rudy switched off the television. It was late. He couldn't sleep. The resumption of grammar school foreclosed upon the vanished summer like some formidable mortgage. Rudy awoke the next morning in an empty house. Dad in Rio, Mom in bed. The lunch, prepared by the maid, was folded inside a double bag on the kitchen counter. Rudy scanned the *Chronicle*'s comics page and devoured an eight-ounce box of Rice Puffies. Public concern over the statue had receded in the wake of renewed Mideast skirmishes. Rudy went to the bathroom, vomited anxiously, brushed his teeth, removed a frozen Snicker's bar from the freezer, and chewed as he departed for the bus stop. Father had won the debate years ago concerning Rudy's education. He's going to public, not be a sissy, just like me.

On the streetcorner Kent Crapps and Marty Femester were passing an untidy cigarette back and forth, inexpertly rolled from Bugle tobacco and parting at the seam. Rudy sat on the curb and handled his lunchbag to tatters.

Hey. If it ain't the rich kid. Hey, Crapps. Ain't that the poor little rich kid?

Sure is, Crapps said. It looks like *two* rich kids, if you ask me. Hey, fat boy. You better stop eating so much. You're liable to *explode!*

Rudy sat forlornly as he heard them approach. The wrecked cigarette bounced off his knee and he brushed at sparks.

Hey, maybe the fat boy's hungry. You think so, Crapps? You think he might like a marshmallow? There's a marshmallow, there in the gutter. It's a little muddy, but maybe the fat boy's *real* hungry.

Rudy hunkered submissively, anticipating customary ridicule.

Hey, fat boy. Look what we fixed you to eat —

As the imperative mud-filled hand clamped Rudy's mouth, something unfamiliar activated abruptly in his mind. Something alert, canny, uncompromising.

Help help help quit it no no help help *blech*! Marty struggled weakly, like a small damaged sparrow. There, Rudy thought, his arm not strong so much as intent. *You* eat the mud this time. At a discreet distance Kent Crapps bounded up and down and shrieked for the police. Rudy wasn't even angry. He just wanted them to know he could take care of himself now. He had new responsibilities, through his discovery of the statue a sort of implied integrity. The weight of the buried statue filled the deep part of his mind. Nothing can hurt you, the deep voice confirmed, resounding in the immensity of remembered dreams that whirled, unalterable and patient, impervious and eternal.

Young men have responsibilities. I don't care who started it you can't carry on like hoodlums what if everybody behaved like that I'm doing this for your own good, the principal pronounced, and down came their pants. The secretary pulled shut the office door. Rudy neither whined nor protested at his turn. He was supremely confident, and listened to the deep dreamy monotone of the buried voice. Returning to class he met wary eyes and whispers. He ate a magnanimous lunch alone in the cafeteria and cached burps to be released later, in class, in improvisatory bleats.

Grade school was a breeze.

Ha ha ha, everybody laughed, orbiting him in the schoolyard. Occasionally Rudy grabbed the scrawniest of them — a homely, wheezing asthmatic — and twisted his limbs one at a time. He commanded the asthmatic to confess explicit sex crimes with his mother, his father, his dog. Everybody laughed and even the asthmatic grinned plaintively. You're a riot, Rudy. You are — you're the funniest guy I know. You oughta be a comedian. Rudy never suspected himself of bullying. He was merely amusing his friends. He viewed popularity as a social obligation, like the ballot. When the bell rang the timid orbiting boys dispersed readily to their classes and Rudy, in his own time, lumbered along behind, thirteen years old and one hundred and ninety-seven pounds, and nobody threatened him anymore. Not even his parents.

Rudy! Rudy, stop that! You *heard* me, young man! Let go of your mother — I mean *right this minute!* Father bellowed punily.

Damn, Rudy thought, releasing Mom's red perfumed arm. Damn if anybody sends *me* to military school, and flung the academy brochure in the trash. I'm not a failure. I will succeed. I am tough, too, and I will make my mark on the world. Just watch.

Father and Mom departed for the Riviera, and left Rudy under the aegis of a reluctant maid. Just fine with me, Rudy thought. I don't need anybody. I'm happy to be me, just like they recommend on television talk shows. He deposited himself at the kitchen table and trooped through a stack of grilled cheese sandwiches as if through so many Saltines.

Rudy dropped out of school at sixteen. Father leased him a two-bedroom apartment in the Financial District and promptly departed with Mom to Rio where, it was rumoured, they developed a successful liaison with two blonde, liquid women Mom had met in Toronto the year before. Rudy, meanwhile, ate. Mountains of toast, vistas of jelly and syrup, acres of Rice Puffies and Sugar Dongs and Candy Cakes and Twinky Pies. Crushed plastic cereal toys littered the floors of his apartment. A mobile landmark, Rudy strolled immensely through the neighborhood, easily visible from office buildings, helicopters, incoming passenger planes. He visited Taco Heaven, Mrs Mary's Candy House, Happy Jack's Ice Cream Palace, and returned home munching candy apples, barbecued sides of beef, Big Macs. He squeezed blithely through crowds of slim, fashionable secretaries, and never glanced twice at their slit skirts, high heels, polished nails. Desire never pestered Rudy, his pubic hair remained downy, innocent. The family doctor proposed hormonal 'supplementation'. Adamant, Rudy refused. He was not sick. He was inconceivably healthy. His life was purposeful, coherent and determined: he ate, he slept, he waited.

Steve Dunningan appeared at Rudy's door one summer afternoon. Rudy was uncertain of the year. The seasons had flitted past like moths. Rudy shifted his weight away from the door and Dunnigan sidled into the cluttered apartment. Dunnigan wore a faded Grateful Dead T-shirt, stained Levis, tattered Keds. My, how you've grown, Dunnigan said. Rudy slumped into a beanbag chair and the straining plastic envelope burst with a pop, spewing brown varnished beans everywhere. Rudy sagged unconcernedly as the chair depleted, listening to the vague familiar man through his stuffy brain.

I came to warn you, Dunnigan said.

Rudy yawned. Dunnigan scratched his head, and white dandruff spilled onto the floor.

Have you ever heard of IRM, Rudy?

No, Rudy croaked, and massaged his adam's apple circumspectly.

Innate Releaser Mechanism. Genetic knowledge, knowledge coded into the DNA. Instinct, really. But an instinct, a mechanism, which must be triggered by a behavioural cue, understand? Mother bird does a little dance, perhaps, and activates the fledgeling's migratory program. Then the fledgeling departs for Tehachapi, Capistrano, Guam.

Rudy reached for a crushed Ritz Cracker box, rattled crumbs into his mouth.

The cue was tactile, Rudy.

Rudy tore open the box, licked more yellow crumbs from waxed paper.

A few years ago, undergraduates in the UC Research Programme came into contact with the statue. Today these students are withdrawn, anti-social, disrespectful of authority, obese, and under heavy sedation at UC Medical. The doctors and scientists have agreed on a tentative diagnosis. The prognosis is catastrophe . . . Rudy, are you listening?

Rudy picked up the telephone and dialled Chicken Delite. Three buckets of centre breast, he thought, and a gallon of coleslaw. The line was busy.

The statues are containers, Rudy, distributing life's essential ingredients throughout the universe. But the molecules of the container must be fused, the container launched. Think of a simple atomic reaction. A solitary atom is split, and the devastation is well publicized. Your body is composed of how many trillions of atoms, Rudy?

Rudy put down the phone, his head lolled against the wall. A few last beans dribbled from the exhausted plastic envelope.

Cosmic evolution — just think of it, Rudy. Life is forged from calamity, catastrophe, annihilation. The ultimate purpose of life

— mere perserverence. And the law of evolution? Survival of the fittest —

Father, Rudy said. Hypnagogic, he stared at the ceiling.

Rudy, wake up!

Rudy started upright. Chicken Delite? he asked.

Would you like to see the statue again, Rudy? Would you like that?

Yes, Rudy thought. Yes yes. He raised himself courageously to his feet. The varnished beans seethed on the floor.

There's food in my car. Hungry, Rudy? Come on, Rudy, come on . . . Dunnigan led Rudy out the door, rolled open the side of his van.

Rudy clambered inside, smelling pizza. Three cardboard containers streaked with oil. He opened the top box. The pizza was still warm, the cheese stiff and congealed. He divided the slices and transferred them, slice by slice, into his mouth. The door of the van slammed shut, bolts were thrown. Rudy chewed pepperoni, mozzarella, briny anchovies.

The van's engine erupted, along with a nervous spasm in Rudy's gut.

The van moved. An air vent communicated with the driver's seat.

Everything will be fine, Rudy. They dig out a tiny chunk of your brain — no bigger than a sausage. You'll be happy, then. People will like you; you'll like people. We'll start you on an exercise regimen, a diet. Hell, with your money, you can just take your pick of the ladies. You won't be lonely anymore. You'll be just like everybody else.

But I'm *not* like everybody else, Rudy reassured himself, and placed his palm against his stomach. Something percolated deep inside, his bowels contracted. He tried to hold it in. Father would get very mad. Father hated when Rudy smelled up the car, and rolled down the electric windows.

Just you wait and see, Rudy. We can command top dollar from the university, once I inform them of your condition. Let me handle it. Did I tell you they fired me? I used to know Johnny Carson and his wife personally. Now what's my doctorate worth? A job delivering all-night pizza to junkies, high school parties, perverts. But I've learned. This time they'll deal on *my* conditions. This time I'll demand *tenure* —

The pressure mounted in Rudy's stomach. He cried out.

What's that? Watch your temper, Rudy. I don't want you ending up like the others at UC Med. Armstraps and thorazine — very uncomfortable. And more than anything, Rudy, I want you to be comfortable. The fridge at our Motel is packed with Candy Cakes, Twinky Pies, Rice Puffies, and plenty of that white soul food — mayonnaise and Wonderbread.

Rudy returned the final slice of pizza to the container, closed the lid. He had lost his appetite.

— Did I mention the colour TV?

Rudy lay flat on his back, gripping his stomach with both hands. Just when the pain grew intolerable, the deep voice interposed. Life is light. Life is calamity, catastrophe, annihilation. You are life, Rudy. Annihilate. Annihilate colour TV, Rice Puffies, UC Medical, Innate Releaser Mechanisms, the Financial District, military school, the homely asthmatic, the monotone principal, marshmallows, Johnny Carson, icy Margaritas, Sister Maria Theresa, Uruguay, Father and Mom. Will they see me in Rio? Rudy asked. Just before they feel the impact of your cosmic prestige, the voice answered. Rudy chuckled contentedly. His colon fluttered.

Will they be proud? What will they think when they see me?

What the termites thought when the hammer came down. Life is light.

Every muscle in Rudy's body contracted abruptly. And then, just before the flash, Rudy realized he would finally make his mark on the world.

MALCOLM EDWARDS
AFTER-IMAGES

After the events of the previous day Norton slept only fitfully, his dreams filled with grotesque images of Richard Carver, and he was grateful when his bedside clock showed him that it was nominally morning again. He always experienced difficulty sleeping in anything less than total darkness, so the unvarying sunlight, cutting through chinks in the curtains and striking across the floor, marking it with lines that might have been drawn by an incandescent knife, added to his restlessness. He had tried to draw the curtains as closely as possible, but they were cheap and of skimpy manufacture — a legacy from the previous owner of the flat, who for obvious reasons could not be bothered to take them with her when she moved — and even when, after much manoeuvring, they could be persuaded to meet along much of their length, narrow gaps would always appear at the top, near the pleating.

Norton felt gripped by a lassitude born of futility, but as on the eight other mornings of this unexpected coda to his existence, fought off the feeling and slid wearily out of bed. After dressing quickly and without much thought, he pulled back the curtains to admit the brightness of the early-afternoon summer sun.

The sun was exactly where it had been for the last eight days, poised a few degrees above the peaked roof of the terraced house across the road. It had been a stormy day, and a few minutes before everything had stopped a heavy shower had been sweeping across London; but the squall had passed and the sun had appeared — momentarily, one would have supposed — through a break in the cloud. The visible sky was still largely occupied by lowering, soot-coloured clouds, which enfolded the light and gave it the peculiar penetrating luminosity which presages a storm; but the sun sat in its patch of blue sky like an unblinking eye in the face of the heavens, and Norton and the others spent their last days and nights in a malign parody of the mythical, eternally sunlit English summer.

Outside the heat was stale and oppressive and seemed to settle heavily in his temples. Drifts of rubbish, untended now for several weeks, gave off a ripe odour of decay and attracted buzzing platoons of flies. Marlborough Street, where Norton lived, was one of a patchwork of late-Victorian and Edwardian terraces filling an unfashionable lacuna in the map of west London. At one end of the road was a slightly wider avenue which called itself a High Road on account of a bus route and a scattering of down-at-heel shops. Norton walked towards it, past houses which gave evidence of their owners' hasty departure, doors and windows left open. The house across the road, which for three days had been the scene of an increasingly wild party held by most of the few teenagers remaining in the area, was now silent again. They had probably collapsed from exhaustion, or drugs, or both, Norton thought.

At the corner Norton paused. To the north — his left — the street curved away sharply, lined on both sides by shabby three-storey houses with mock-Georgian facades. To the south it was straight, but about a hundred yards away was blocked off by the great baleful flickering wall of the interface, rising into the sky and curving back on itself like a surreal bubble. As always he was drawn to look at it, though his eyes resisted as if under autonomous control and tried to focus themselves elsewhere.

It was impossible to say precisely what it looked like, for its surface seemed to be an absence of colour. When he closed his eyes it left swimming variegated after-images; protoplasmic shapes which crossed and intermingled and blended. When Norton forced himself to stare at it, his optic nerves attempted to deny its presence, warping together the flanking images of shop-fronts so that the road seemed to narrow to a point.

Norton suffered occasional migraine headaches and often experienced an analogous phenomenon as the prelude to an attack: he would find that parts of his field of vision had been excised, but that the edges of the blanks were somehow pulled together, so it was difficult to be sure something *was* missing. Just as then it was necessary sometimes to turn sideways and look obliquely to see an object sitting directly in front of him, so now, as he turned away, he could see the interface as a curving wall the colour of a bruise from which pinpricks of intense light occasionally escaped as if through faults in its fabric. Then, too, he could glimpse more clearly the three human images printed, as though by some sophisticated holographic process, upon the interface. In the centre of the road were the backs of Carver and himself as they disappeared beyond the interface, the images already starting to become fuzzy as the wavefront slowly advanced; to one side, slightly sharper, was the record of his lone re-emergence, his expression clearly pale and strained despite the heavy polarised goggles which covered half his face.

Norton had been sitting the previous morning at a table outside the Café Hellenika, slowly drinking a tiny cup of Greek coffee. He had little enthusiasm for the sweet, muddy drink, but was unwilling as yet to move on to beer or wine.

The café's Greek Cypriot proprietor had reacted to the changed conditions in a manner which under other circumstances would have seemed quite enterprising. He had shifted all his tables and chairs out on to the pavement, leaving the cooler interior free for the perennial pool players and creating outside a passable imitation of a street café remembered from happier days in Athens or Nicosia. Many of the remaining local residents were of Greek origin, and the men gathered here, playing cards and chess, drinking cheap Demestica, and talking in sharp bursts which sounded dramatic however banal and ordinary the conversation. There was a timelessness to the scene which Norton found oddly apposite.

He was staring into his coffee, thinking studiously about nothing, when a shadow fell across him and he simultaneously heard the chair next to his being scraped across the pavement. He looked up to see Carver easing himself into the seat. He was dressed bizarrely in a thickly padded white suit which looked as though it should belong to an astronaut or a polar explorer. He was carrying a pair of thick goggles which he placed on the formica surface of the table. He signalled the café owner to bring him a coffee.

Norton didn't want company, but he was intrigued despite himself. 'What on Earth is that outfit?' he asked.

'Explorer's gear . . . bloody hot, too,' said Carver, dragging the sleeve cumbersomely across his perspiring forehead.

'What's to explore, for God's sake?'

'The . . . whatever you call it. The bubble. The interface. I've been into it.'

Norton felt irritated. Carver seemed incapable of taking their situation seriously. He had attached himself to Norton four days ago as he sat getting drunk and had sought him out every day since, full of jokes of dubious merit and colourful stories of his life in some unspecified, but probably menial, branch of the diplomatic service. He was the sort of person Norton hated finding himself next to in a bar. Now he was obviously fantasizing.

'Don't be ridiculous. You'd be dead.'

'Do I look dead?' Carver gestured at himself. His face, tanned and plump with eyes of a disconcertingly pure aquamarine, looked as healthy as ever.

'It's impossible,' Norton repeated.

'Don't you want to know what I found?'

Losing patience, Norton shouted: 'I *know* what you'd have found. You'd have found a fucking nuclear explosion. Don't tell me you went for a stroll through *that!*'

The café owner came up and slapped a cup on to the table in front of Carver, slopping the coffee into the saucer. Carver took a long slow sip of the dark liquid, looking at Norton expressionlessly over the rim of the cup as he did so. Norton subsided, feeling foolish.

'But I did, Norton,' Carver finally said calmly. 'I did.'

Norton remained silent, stubbornly refusing to play his part in the choreography of the conversation, knowing that Carver would carry on without further prompting.

'I didn't just walk in,' Carver said, after a few seconds. 'I'm not suicidal. I tried probing first, with a stick. I waggled it about a bit, pulled it out. It wasn't damaged. That set me thinking. So I tried with a pet mouse of mine. No damage — except that its eyes were burned out, poor little sod. So I thought, all right, it's very bright, but nothing more. What does that suggest?'

Norton shrugged.

'It suggested to me that the whole process is slowed down in there, that there's a whole series of wavefronts — the light flash, the fireball, the blastwave — all expanding slowly, but all separate.'

'It seems incredible.'

'Well, the whole situation isn't precisely normal, you know —'

They were interrupted by a commotion at another table. There seemed to be some disagreement between two men over a hand of cards. One of them, a heavy-set middle-aged man wearing a greying string vest through which his bodily hair sprouted abundantly, was standing and waving a handful of cards. The other, an older man, remained seated, banging his fist repeatedly on the table. Their voices rose in a fast, threatening gabble. Then the man in the vest threw the cards across the table with a furious jerk of his arm and stamped into the café. The other continued to talk loudly and aggrievedly to the onlookers, his words augmented by a complex mime of gesture.

Norton was glad of the distraction. He couldn't understand what Carver was getting at, and wasn't sure he wanted to. 'It's amazing the way they carry on,' he said. 'It's as though nothing had happened, as though everything *was* normal.'

'Very sensible of them. At least they're consistent.'

'Are you serious?'

'Of course I am. The whole thing has been inevitable for years. We all knew that, but we tried to pretend otherwise even while we carried on preparing for it. We said that it wouldn't happen, because so far it hadn't happened — some logic! We buried our heads like ostriches and pretended as hard as we could. Now it's here — it's just down the road and we can see it coming and we know there's no escape. But we knew that all along. If you tie yourself to a railway line you don't have to wait until you can see the train coming before you start to think you're in danger. So why not just carry on as usual?'

'I didn't know you felt like that.'

'Of course you didn't. As far as you're concerned I'm just the old fool in the saloon bar. End of story.'

Carver had a point, Norton supposed. If anyone had asked him whether there was going to be a nuclear war in his lifetime he would probably have said yes. If anyone had asked what he was doing about it he would have shrugged and said, well, what could you do? He had friends active in the various protest movements, but couldn't help viewing their efforts as futile. Some of them would virtually admit as much sometimes, if pressed. The difference was that they couldn't bear to sit still while some hope — however remote — remained, whereas he couldn't be bothered with gestures which seemed extremely unlikely to produce results. He would rather watch TV or spend the evening in the pub.

The other difficulty was that he couldn't really picture it in his mind's eye, couldn't visualize London consumed by blast and fire, couldn't imagine the millions of deaths, the survivors of the blast explosion dying in fallout shelters, the ensuing chaos and anarchy. And because he found it unimaginable, on some level he told himself it could never happen, not here, not to him.

Being apathetic about politics — especially Middle-Eastern politics — he hadn't even been properly aware of the crisis developing until it reached flashpoint, with Russian and American troops clashing outside Riyadh. Then there had been government announcements, states of emergency, panic. Despite advice to stay at home the great mass of the population had headed out of the cities; unconfirmed rumours filtered back of clashes with troops on roads commandeered for military use. A few had stayed behind: some dutifully obeying government instructions, some doubtless oblivious to the whole thing, some, like Norton, unable to imagine an aftermath they would want to live in.

And then the sirens had sounded and he had sat waiting for the end; and they had stopped, and there was a silence which went on and on and on until Norton, like others, had gone into the streets and found himself in the middle of a situation far stranger than anything he could have imagined. The small urban island in which they stood — an irregular triangle no more than half a mile on a side — was bracketed by three virtually simultaneous ground-burst explosions which had caused . . . what? A local fracture in space-time? That was as good an explanation as any. Whatever the cause, the effect was to slow down subjective time in the locality by a factor of millions, reducing the spread of the detonations to a matter of a few yards every day, hemming them into their strange and fragile-seeming shells.

At first people hoped that the miracle — for so it seemed — allowed some possibility of rescue, but they soon learned better. Between two of the wave-fronts was a narrow corridor which coincided with a side road and led apparently to safety. One family, who had miscalculated their evacuation plans, piled into a car and drove off down the corridor, but halfway their car seemed suddenly to halt, as if frozen. Norton still looked at it occasionally. Through the rear window could be seen two young children, faces caught in smiles, hands arrested in mid-wave. It was clear that the phenomenon was only local, and crossing some invisible threshold they had emerged into the real-time world. At least, he thought, they would never have time to realize that their escape attempt had failed; it was left to those still trapped to experience anguish on their behalf.

Norton wondered what one of the many spy satellites which he supposed crossed overhead would make of the scene, if any of their equipment was sensitive enough to register anything. Perhaps some future historian, analysing the destruction of London, would slow down the film and wonder at an apparent burst of high-speed motion in the area on which the explosions converged. The historian would probably rub his or her eyes in puzzlement and dismiss it as an optical trick, like the after-images which played behind one's eyelids after staring into a bright light.

'So will you come?' Carver was saying.

Norton dragged his attention back to the conversation, aware that Carver had been talking and that he had not been taking in what he was saying.

'Come? Where?'

'Through the interface. I want somebody else to see it. It's amazing, Norton. The experience of a lifetime. The *last* experience of a lifetime. Why miss it?'

Norton's first instinct was to protest that he wasn't interested, that there seemed little point in seeking out new experiences when extinction was, at best, days away, but then he realized that in fact some purposeful action — even a pretence at purposeful action *would* be welcome. Terminal patients given the bad news by their doctors didn't just lie down and wait to die, if they had any spirit: they got up and got on with their lives for as long as they could. In the last analysis that was all anyone could do, and here everybody — the Greek card players, the partygoers, Carver — seemed to be doing it except him.

'Sure,' he said. 'But what about protective clothing? You've got all that . . .' He gestured at Carver's bulky and absurd-looking outfit.

'It's unnecessary. In fact it's hotter out here than it is there. I don't know what I was thinking about — if I had run into the heat a thousand of these would have been no protection. All you need is goggles, and I've got a spare pair at home.'

Carver got up, tossed a £5 note on the table and walked away, gesturing Norton to follow. He lived just off the High Road, in a large, double-fronted redbrick Victorian house, most of whose neighbours had been turned into bedsits. His house was still intact, though the front garden was a tangle of hollyhocks choking amid brambles, and the wood in the window sashes was visibly rotten. Little attention was evidently paid to its upkeep.

Inside was a dim hallway floored with cracked brown linoleum and cluttered with coatstands and hatracks. There was a heavy odour of dust, old leather, and indefinable decay.

Carver went through into one of the rear rooms. Norton followed, then paused in the open doorway. It was a large room, with French windows opening on to the garden. It was impossible to tell what the decorations might have once been like, because the whole room was choked with a profusion of different objects. All the walls were lined from floor to ceiling with books, old and expensive bindings jammed alongside garish paperbacks seemingly at random. More books were heaped on the floor, in chairs and on tables. The rest of the room was a wild assortment of clocks, globes, stuffed animals, model ships and engines, old scientific and medical equipment, porcelain, musical instruments and countless other items. Carver made his way — almost wading through the detritus — to a desk, where some of the clutter had been pushed aside and a second pair of goggles lay amid knives, glues and offcuts of polarized plastic.

'Don't mind the mess,' he said jovially, seeing Norton still hovering uncertainly by the door. 'The whole house is like this, I'm afraid. Never could stop accumulating stuff. Never could throw anything out. My wife used to say I'd been a jackdaw in my previous lives. That's why I didn't leave, you know. I couldn't start off again somewhere else without all this. Sometimes I think there's more of me here —' his gesture took in the room, and the other rooms beyond it — 'than *here*.' He tapped the side of his skull.

Norton suddenly warmed to the man, seeing him properly for the first time as another human being, not just an irritating presence. Carver seemed to sense this and turned to fiddle with the goggles for long seconds while embarrassment dispersed from the atmosphere. 'I made these up myself,' he said. 'Ordinary dark glasses are no good. You need extra thicknesses, lots of them. Trouble is, if you put the things on anywhere else you can't see a damn thing.'

Carver insisted on showing Norton the place where he had gone exploring earlier, though he was equally adamant that this time they would cross over somewhere else. He had stripped off the cumbersome protective suit and now cut an unlikely figure as a pioneer in a Hawaiian-style shirt and corduroy slacks. He had uprooted two stout wooden poles, giving one to Norton and keeping the other himself. They walked away from the High Road, took the second turning on the left, and came face to face with another wall of shimmering, eye-wrenching colourlessness. On its surface, as if holographic images had been pasted to it, were images of Carver's back as he crossed the interface and his front view as he returned.

'You see,' Carver said, 'light can't escape, so the image is trapped there like a fly in amber until the thing moves forward far enough for it to break up. It's already starting to happen.'

Looking closely Norton could see that indeed the images were taking on a slightly unfocused aspect, as though viewed through a wavering heat haze.

They walked back to the High Road, passed the café — where a group of men were standing round a table watching five more play out an obviously tense card game; side bets were apparently being exchanged — and approached the interface which blocked the street.

'Right,' Carver said. 'Keep close by me. If in doubt wave the stick in front of you. If not in doubt *still* wave the stick in front of you.' He laughed, and Norton smiled in return. They pulled on their goggles and then, like blind men, tapping their way with their sticks, they walked through the interface, leaving their departing images stuck to its surface so that to anyone casually watching from the café it would have looked as if they had both suddenly and improbably halted in mid-stride.

Norton found himself enveloped in a soundless blizzard of brilliant light. Even through the thick laminations of polarized plastic the luminosity was almost painful; it was like looking too near to the sun, except that there was nowhere to turn away. The light seemed to bounce and swirl around him, to cascade on his head and fountain up from the ground. There was a singing in his ears, and he felt as though he was walking into a wind, a zephyr of pure incandescence, its photon pressure sufficient to resist his progress.

He felt exhilarated, almost ecstatic, as if he was coming face to face with God. The light was cleansing, purifying. He found that he was moving with an involuntary swimming motion of his arms, propelling himself into the cool heart of this artificial sun with a clumsy breaststroke.

'Norton! Be careful!' Carver's voice came as if from under water, far away; it splashed faintly against his ears but was washed away in the radiant tide.

Carver was at his side, tugging at his shirt. He turned and looked at the other man. Carver seemed to glow, to fluoresce. The intense effulgence overpowered ordinary colour, making him a surreal sculpture in degrees of brilliant white. His skin seemed luminous and translucent, and when Norton lifted his own hand he found it was the same; he fancied he could see dim outlines of bone through the flesh. When Carver moved he cut swathes through the light; a sudden motion of his stick sent splintered refractions in all directions.

'Carver —' Norton said, and his words seemed to be snatched away as if he was talking into a silent hurricane. 'This is extraordinary . . . incredible . . .' The sentence trailed away; he had no words to describe the experience.

Carver laughed. 'Who'd have thought that this lay in the heart of a nuclear explosion, eh? I don't know, though — those slow-motion films always *were* beautiful if you could forget what they were.'

'How far can we go?' Norton shouted, turning away and moving towards the heart of the radiance, using his cane like a mine-detector.

'Only a few yards. You'll see.'

Norton moved on a dozen paces, then the tip of his stick

abruptly exploded into brilliant fire, like a sparkler on Guy Fawkes' Night. He withdrew it, stamped on the burning end. Several inches had vanished from its tip in an instant.

Peering forwards he fancied he could see the further interface, the fireball advancing at its own slow, inexorable pace behind the light flash. Even through the radiance he thought he could detect flickering patterns of orange flame dancing across its surface. Norton was suddenly reminded of what lay beyond there . . . but for now it was enough to be drifting, clad in a nimbus of cool white fire.

Carver, a pale haloed ghost of a figure, was at his side. He swished his stick playfully through the fireball's surface, coming away each time with a couple of inches less on the tip. He was like a lion-tamer, holding inconceivable energy at bay with just the stick and the force of his personality.

'Don't get too close,' Norton warned, as the other man edged forward. Carver took no notice, so Norton tapped him on the shoulder with his own stick. Carver began to turn, but as he did so his foot caught on the kerbstone. He teetered, began to fall backwards, mouth widening in surprise: fell faster than Norton could lunge forwards, into the fireball.

Everything seemed to be happening in slow motion, as though Carver had fallen into still another time anomaly. He appeared to hang suspended as his hair burst into flame and his skin began to char. Puffs of steam rose from his body. His shirt was consumed so quickly that it simply seemed to vanish. His lips drew back as if he was about to say something, but they were only shrivelling with the heat. Behind them the guns burned away, exposing bone that blackened swiftly, though the teeth remained anomalously white until the enamel cracked and burst. The goggles melted, exposing steaming sockets in a face that was turning into a skull even as he fell. His body cooked, as if Norton was watching an accelerated film of meat being roasted. The skin crisped, then peeled away; the flesh followed, crumbling and flaking away from bones that snapped and popped from their sockets and themselves began to burn. By the time Carver hit the ground all that was left of him was a charred heap of smouldering detritus which blew away in clouds of ash even as it settled. It had taken only seconds; the only sound which reached Norton was a soft, almost plaintive sigh.

Norton watched, transfixed with horror. Then as nausea rose in him he stumbled away, dropping his stick. He burst out of the interface into total darkness — then ripped off the goggles and squatted by the pavement, retching until all he could wring from his stomach was a thin trickle of sour yellow bile.

Now, as Norton looked sidelong at the images recording the beginning and end of yesterday's tragic adventure, he saw that the interface was undergoing a change. Patterns played more vigorously across its surface; fans of light sprayed outwards briefly; it seemed to vibrate, as if to a deep bass tone. *It's breaking down*, he thought. *It won't be long now.*

To his surprise his major feeling was not fear but relief. He understood now why condemned prisoners sometimes sacked their lawyers and actively sought their execution rather than trying to delay it.

He felt he would prefer to be at home when it happened, so he turned back into Marlborough Street. As he passed number 6 a voice called out his name. It was Mr McDonald, a friendly and gregarious pensioner who lived there with his equally good-natured wife. Norton had always got on well with them on a pleasant superficial level. Lacking transport, the McDonalds had been unable to evacuate even if they had wanted to.

Mr McDonald was busily giving the sitting room windows a second coat of whitewash. 'Just putting the final touches,' he said cheerily. The McDonalds had spent the last eight days as they had spent the week before, turning part of their house into a fallout shelter, following an official instruction leaflet. To them the last week seemed to be a God-given opportunity to finish the job properly. Their house did not have a cellar, so they had fitted out the large cupboard under the stairs, protecting it with countless black dustbin bags filled with earth. Inside were carefully arranged supplies of food, water and medicine; bedding and primitive cooking equipment; and even a portable chemical toilet. Before retirement made such recreations impossible to afford the McDonalds had been keen campers, and regarded their expertise and lovingly-stored equipment as particular good fortune. A few days ago Mr McDonald had insisted on showing off their impressively well-organized shelter to Norton; had even offered to squeeze up and make room for three if he hadn't the materials to build his own defences. What was more, although the offer was made only out of politeness, Norton was sure the McDonalds would have gone through with it if he had pressed them. But he had declined politely, assuring them of the adequacy of his own preparations.

Now, with the image of Carver vivid in his mind, he felt like shouting at Mr McDonald, shocking him into a realization of how futile his efforts were in the face of the kind of forces held delicately in check all around him. But it would only hurt and confuse the old man, who was simply following the instructions which he had been told would keep him safe.

Norton waved goodbye to Mr McDonald and started to walk away. But even as his foot lifted, the air seemed to shudder and split around him, and before his senses were able properly to register the phenomenon the world was filled with an instantaneous, consuming brilliance, a white fire that was neither cool nor pure.

KEITH ROBERTS
KITEMASTER

The ground crew had all but finished their litany. They stood in line, heads bowed, silhouetted against the last dull flaring from the west; below me the launch vehicle seethed gently to itself, water sizzling round a rusted boiler rivet. A gust of warmth blew up toward the gantry, bringing scents of steam and oil to mingle with the ever-present smell of dope. At my side the Kitecaptain snorted, it seemed impatiently; shuffled his feet, sank his bull head even further between his shoulders.

I glanced round the darkening hangar, taking in the remembered scene; the spools of cable, head-high on their trolleys, bright blades of the anchor rigs, fathom on fathom of the complex lifting train. In the centre of the place above the wickerwork Observer's basket, the mellow light of oil lamps grew to stealthy prominence; it showed the spidery crisscrossings of girders, the faces of the windspeed telltales, each hanging from its jumble of struts. The black needles vibrated, edging erratically up and down the scales; beyond, scarcely visible in the gloom, was the complex bulk of the manlifter itself, its dark, spread wings jutting to either side.

The young priest turned a page of his book, half glanced toward the gantry. He wore the full purple of a Base Chaplain; but his worried face looked very young. I guessed him to be not long from his novitiate; the presence of a Kitemaster was a heavy weight to bear. His voice reached up to me, a thread of sound mixed with the blustering of the wind outside. '*Therefore we beseech Thee, Lord, to add Thy vigilance to ours throughout the coming night; that the Land may be preserved, according to Thy covenant . . .*' The final response was muttered; and he stepped back, closing the breviary with evident relief.

I descended the metal-latticed steps to the hangar floor, paced unhurriedly to the wicker basket. As yet there was no sign of Canwen, the Observer; but that was to be expected. A flier of his seniority knows, as the Church herself knows, the value of the proper form of things. He would present himself upon his cue; but not before. I sprinkled oil and earth as the ritual dictates, murmured my blessing, clamped the Great Seal of the Church Variant to the basket rim and stepped away. I said, 'Let the Watching begin.'

At once the hangar became a scene of ordered confusion. Tungsten arcs came to buzzing life, casting their harsher and less sympathetic glare; orders were shouted, and Cadets ran to the high end doors, began to roll them back. The wind roared in at once, causing the canvas sides of the structure to boom and crack; the arc globes swung, sending shadows leaping on the curving walls. The valve gear of the truck set up its fussing; I climbed back to the gantry as the heavy vehicle nosed into the open air. I restored the sacred vessels to their valise, clicked the lock and straightened.

The Kitecaptain glanced at me sidelong, and back to the telltales. 'Windspeed's too high, by eight or ten knots,' he growled. 'And mark that gusting. It's no night for flying.'

I inclined my head. 'The Observer will decide,' I said.

He snorted. 'Canwen will fly,' he said. 'Canwen will always fly . . .' He turned on his heel. 'Come into the office,' he said. 'You'll observe as well from there. In any case, there's little to see as yet.' I took a last glance through the line of rain-spattered windows, and followed him.

The room in which I found myself was small, and as spartan as the rest of the establishment. An oil lamp burned in a niche; a shelf held manuals and dog-eared textbooks, another was piled with bulky box files. A wall radiator provided the semblance at least of comfort; there was a square steel strongbox, beside it a battered metal desk. On it stood a silver-mounted photograph; a line of youths stood stiffly before a massive, old-pattern launch vehicle.

The Captain glanced at it and laughed, without particular humour. 'Graduation day,' he said. 'I don't know why I keep it. All the rest have been dead and gone for years. I'm the last; but I was the lucky one of course.' He limped to a corner cabinet, opened it and took down glasses and a bottle. He poured, looked over his shoulder. He said, 'It's been a long time, Helman.'

I considered. Kitecaptains, by tradition, are a strangely tempered breed of men. Spending the best part of their lives on the frontier as they do, they come to have scant regard for the social niceties most of us would take for granted; yet the safety of the Realm depends on their vigilance, and that they know full well. It gives them, if not a real, at least a moral superiority; and he seemed determined to use, or abuse, his position to the hilt. However if he chose to ignore our relative status, there was little I could do. In public, I might rebuke him; in private, I would merely risk a further loss of face. I accordingly remained impassive, and took the glass he proffered. 'Yes,' I agreed calmly. 'It has, as you say, been a very long time.'

He was still watching me narrowly. 'Well at least,' he said, 'one of us did all right for himself. I've little enough to show for twenty years' service; save one leg two inches shorter than the other.' He nodded at my robes. 'They reckon,' he said, 'you'll be in line for the Grand Mastership one day. Oh yes, we hear the chat; even stuck out in a rotting hole like this.'

'All things,' I said, 'are within the will of God.' I sipped cautiously. Outback liquor has never been renowned for subtlety, and this was no exception; raw spirit as near as I could judge, probably brewed in one of the tumbledown villages through which I had lately passed.

He gave his short, barking laugh once more. 'Plus a little help from Variant politics,' he said. 'But you always had a smooth tongue when it suited. And knew how to make the proper friends.'

'We are not all Called,' I said sharply. There are limits in all things; and he was pushing me perilously close to mine. It came to me that he was already more than a little drunk. I walked forward to the window, peered; but nothing was visible. The glass gave me back an image of a bright Cap of Maintenance, the great clasp at my throat, my own sombre and preoccupied face.

I sensed him shrug. 'We aren't all touched in the head,' he said bitterly. 'You won't believe it, I find it hard myself; but I once had a chance at the Scarlet as well. And I turned it down. Do you know, there was actually a time when I believed in all of this?' He paused. 'What I'd give, for my life back just once more,' he said. 'I wouldn't make the same mistakes again. A palace on the Middlemarch, that's what I'd have; servants around me, and decent wine to drink. Not the rotgut we get here . . .'

I frowned. Rough though his manner was, he had a way with him that tugged at memory; laughter and scents of other years, touches of hands. We all have our sacrifices to make; it's the Lord's way to demand them. There was a summer palace certainly, with flowering trees around it in the spring; but it was a palace that was empty.

I turned back. 'What do you mean?' I said. 'Believed in all of what?'

He waved a hand. 'The Corps,' he said. 'The sort of crap you teach. I thought the Kingdom really needed us. It seems crazy now. Even to me.' He drained the glass at a swallow, and refilled it. 'You're not drinking,' he said.

I set my cup aside. 'I think,' I said, 'I'd best watch from the outer gallery.'

'No need,' he said. 'No need, I'll shade the lamp.' He swung down before the light a species of hessian screen; then arcs flared on the apron down below, and all was once more clear as day. Anchors, I saw, had been run out in a half circle from the rear of the launch vehicle. 'We've never needed them yet,' said the Kite-captain at my elbow, 'but on a night like this, who can tell?'

A ball of bright fire sailed into the air, arced swiftly to the east. At the signal cadets surged forward, bearing the first of the kites shoulder-high. They flung it from them; and the line tightened and strummed. The thing hung trembling, a few feet above their heads; then insensibly began to rise. Steerable arc lamps followed it; within seconds it was lost in the scudding overcast. The shafts of light showed nothing but sparkling drifts of rain.

'The pilot,' said the Captain curtly; then glanced sidelong once more. 'But I needn't tell a Kitemaster a thing like that,' he said.

I clasped my hands behind me. I said, 'Refresh my memory.'

He considered for a while; then it seemed he came to a decision. 'Flying a Cody rig isn't an easy business,' he snapped. 'Those bloody fools back home think it's like an afternoon in Middle Park.' He rubbed his face, the iron-grey stubble of beard. 'The pilot takes up five hundred foot of line,' he said. 'Less, if we can find stable air. The lifter kites come next. Three on a good day, four; though at a need we can mount more. The lifters' job is to carry the main cable; the cables' job is to steady the lifters. It's all to do with balance. Everything's to do with balance.' He glanced sidelong once more; but if he expected a comment on his truism, he was disappointed.

Steam jetted from the launch vehicle, to be instantly whirled away. The Ground Controller squatted atop the big, hunched shape, one hand to the straining thread of cable, the other gesturing swiftly to the winchman; paying out, drawing in, as the pilot clawed for altitude. Others of the team stood ready to clamp the bronze cones to the main trace. The cone diameters decrease progressively, allowing the lifters to ride each to its proper station; and therein lies the skill. All must be judged beforehand; there is no room for error, no time for second thoughts.

An extra-heavy buffet shook the hangar's sides, set the Kitecaptain once more to scowling. Mixed with the hollow boom I thought I heard a growl of thunder. The main trace paid out steadily though, checked for the addition of the first of the vital cones. A second followed, and a third; and the Kitecaptain unconsciously gripped my arm. 'They're bringing the lifters,' he said, and pointed.

How they controlled the monstrous, flapping things at all was a mystery to me; but control them they did, hauling at the boxlike structures that seemed at any moment about to fling the men themselves into the air. The tail ring of the first was clipped about the line; orders echoed across the field, the kite sailed up smoothly into the murk. Its sisters followed it without a hitch; and the Captain visibly relaxed. 'Good,' he said. 'That was neatly done. You'll find no better team this side of the Salient.' He poured more spirit from the bottle, swallowed. 'Arms and legs enough have been broken at that game,' he said. 'Aye, and necks; in gentler blows than this.'

I restrained a smile. Despite his sourness, the quality of the man showed clear in the remark; the pride he still felt, justifiably, in a job well done. The rigs might look well enough in high summer, the lines of them floating lazy against the blue, as far as the eye could reach; or at the Air Fairs of the Middle Lands, flying, beribboned, for the delectation of the Master and his aides. It was here though, in the blustering dark, that the mettle of the Captains and their crews was truly tested.

All now depended on the Controller atop the launcher. I saw him turn, straining his eyes up into the night, stretch a gauntleted hand to the heavy trace. Five hundred feet or more above, the pilot flew invisible; below, the lifters spread out in their line, straining at their bridles of steel rope. The rig was aloft; but the slightest failure, the parting of a shackle, the slipping of an ill-secured clamp, could still spell disaster. All was well however; the Ground Controller pulled at the trace again, gauging the angle and tension of the cable, and the final signal was given. I craned forward, intrigued despite myself, brushed with a glove at the cloudy glass.

Quite suddenly, or so it seemed, the Observer was on the apron. A white-robed acolyte, his fair hair streaming, took from his shoulders his brilliant cloak of office. Beneath it he was dressed from head to foot in stout black leather; kneeboots, tunic and trews, close fitting helmet. He turned once to stare up at the hangar front. I made out the pale blur of his face, the hard, high cheekbones; his eyes though were invisible, protected by massive goggles. He saluted, formally yet it seemed with an indefinable air of derision, turned on his heel and strode toward the launch vehicle. I doubt though that he could have made out either the Kitecaptain or myself.

The ground crew scurried again. Moving with practised, almost military precision, they wheeled the basket forward; the Observer climbed aboard, and the rest was a matter of skilled, split-second timing. The manlifter, shielded at first by the hangar from the full force of the wind, swayed wildly, wrenching at its restraining ropes. Men ran back across the grass; the steam winch clattered and the whole equipage was rising into the night, the Observer already working at the tail-down tackle that would give him extra height. The winch settled to a steady, gentle clanking; and the Captain wiped his face. I turned to him. 'Congratulations,' I said. 'A splendid launch.'

Somewhere, distantly, a bell began to clang.

'They're all launched,' he said thickly. 'Right up to G6 in the northwest Salient; and south, down through the Marches. The whole Sector's flying; for what good it'll serve.' He glowered at me. 'You understand, of course, the principles involved?' he said sarcastically.

'Assuredly,' I replied. 'Air flows above the manlifter's surfaces faster than beneath them, thus becoming rarified. The good Lord abhors a vacuum; so any wing may be induced to rise.'

He seemed determined not to be mollified. 'Excellent,' he said. 'I see you've swallowed a textbook or two. There's a bit more to it than that though. If you'd ever flown yourself, you wouldn't be so glib.'

I lowered my eyes. I knew, well enough, the dip and surge of a Cody basket; but it was no part of my intention to engage him in a game of apologetics. Instead I said, 'Tell me about Canwen.'

He stared at me, then nodded to the valise. He said, 'You've got his file.'

'Files don't say everything,' I said. 'I asked you, Kitecaptain.'

He turned away, stood hands on hips and stared down at the launcher. 'He's a flier,' he said at length. 'The finest we've got left. What else is there to say?'

I persisted. 'You've known him long?'

'Since I first joined the Corps,' he said. 'We were cadets together.' He swung back, suddenly. 'Where's all this leading, Helman?'

'Who knows?' I said. 'Perhaps to understanding.'

He brought his palm down flat upon the desk. 'Understanding?' he shouted. 'Who in all the Hells needs understanding? It's explanations we're after, man . . .'

'Me too,' I said pointedly. 'That's why I'm here.'

He flung an arm out. 'Up in K7,' he said, 'an Observer slipped his own trace one fine night, floated off into the Badlands. I knew him too; and they don't come any better. Another sawed his wrists apart, up there on his own; and he'd been flying thirty years. Last week we lost three more; while you and all the rest sit trying to understand . . .'

A tapping sounded at the door. It opened to his shout; a nervous looking Cadet stood framed, his eyes on the floor. 'The Quartermaster sends his compliments,' he stammered, 'and begs to know if the Kitemaster — I mean My Lord — wishes some refreshment . . .'

I shook my head; but the Captain picked the bottle up, tossed it across the room. 'Yes,' he said, 'get me some more of this muck. Break it out of stores, if you have to; I'll sign the chitty later.' The lad scurried away on his errand; the other stood silent and brooding till he returned. Below, on the apron, the ratchet of the winch clattered suddenly; a pause, and the smooth upward flight was

79

continued. The Captain stared out moodily, screwed the cap from the fresh bottle and drank. 'You'll be telling me next,' he said, 'they've fallen foul of demons.'

I turned, sharply. For a moment I wondered if he had taken leave of his senses; he seemed however fully in command of himself. 'Yes,' he said, 'you heard me right first time.' He filled the glass again. 'How long has it really been,' he said, 'since the Corps was formed? Since the very first kite flew?'

'The Corps has always been,' I said, 'and always will be. It is the Way . . .'

He waved a hand dismissively. 'Save it for those who need it,' he said brutally. 'Don't start preaching your sermons in here.' He leaned on the desk. 'Tell me,' he said, 'what was the real idea? Who dreamed it up?'

I could I suppose have remained silent, or quit his company; but it seemed that beneath the bluster there lay something else. A questioning, almost a species of appeal. It was as if something in him yet needed confirmation of his heresy; the confirmation, perhaps, of argument. Certainly I understood his dilemma, in part at least; it was a predicament that in truth was by no means new to me. 'The Corps was formed,' I said, 'to guard the Western Realm, and keep its borders safe.'

'From demons,' he said bitterly. 'From demons and night walkers, all spirits that bring harm . . .' He quoted, savagely, from the Litany. '*Some plunge, invisible, from highest realms of air; some have the shapes of fishes, flying; some, and these be the hardest to descry, cling close upon the hills and very treetops . . .*' I raised a hand, but he rushed on regardless. '*These last be deadliest of all,*' he snarled. '*For to these the Evil One hath given semblance of a Will, to seek out and destroy their prey . . .* Crap!' He pounded the desk again. 'All crap,' he said, 'every last syllable. The Corps fell for it though, every man jack of us. You crook your little fingers, and we run; we float up there like fools, with a pistol in one hand and prayer-book in the other, waiting to shoot down bogles, while you live off the fat of the land . . .'

I turned away from the window and sat down. 'Enough,' I said tiredly. 'Enough, I pray you . . .'

'We're not the only ones of course,' he said. He struck an attitude. '*Some burst from the salt ocean,*' he mocked, '*clad overall in living flame* . . . So the Seaguard ride out there by night and day, with magic potions ready to stop the storms . . .' He choked, and steadied himself. 'Now I'll tell you, Helman,' he said, breathing hard. 'I'll tell you, and you'll listen. There are no demons; not in the sky, not on the land, not in the sea . . .'

I looked away. 'I envy,' I said slowly, 'the sureness of your knowledge.'

He walked up to me. 'Is that all you've got to say?' he shouted. 'You hypocritical bastard . . .' He leaned forward. 'Good men have died in plenty,' he said, 'to keep the folk in fear, and you in your proper state. Twenty years I flew, till I got this; and I'll say it again, as loud and clear as you like. *There are no demons* . . .' He swung away. 'There's something for your report,' he said. 'There's a titbit for you . . .'

I am not readily moved to anger. Enraged, we lose awareness; and awareness is our only gift from God. His last remark, though, irritated me beyond measure. He'd already said more than enough to be relieved of his command; enough, indeed, to warrant a court martial in Middlemarch itself. And a conviction, were I to place the information before the proper authorities. The sneer reduced me to the level of a Variant spy, peeping at keyholes, prying into ledgers. 'You fool,' I said slowly. 'You arrogant unreasoning fool . . .'

He stared, fists clenched. 'Arrogant?' he said. 'You call me arrogant. *You?*'

I stood up, paced back to the window. 'Aye, arrogant,' I said. 'Beyond all measure, and beyond all sense.' I swung back. 'Will you be chastised,' I said bitterly, 'like a first year Chaplain, stumbling in the Litany? If that's the height of your desire, it can readily be accomplished.'

He sat back at the desk, spread his hands on its dull-painted top. 'What do you want of me?' he said.

'The courtesy with which you're being used,' I said. 'For the sake of Heaven, man, act your age.'

He drained the glass slowly, and set it down. He stretched his hand toward the bottle, changed his mind. Finally he looked up, under lowering brows. 'You take a lot on yourself, Helman,' he said. 'If any other spoke to me like that, I'd kill him.'

'Another easy option,' I said shortly. 'You're fuller of them than a beggar's dog of fleas.' I shook my head. 'You alone, of all the Lord's creation,' I said. 'You alone, beg leave to doubt your Faith. And claim it as a novel sentiment . . .'

He frowned again. 'If you'd ever flown . . .'

'I've flown,' I said.

He looked up. 'You've seen the Badlands?' he asked sharply. I nodded. 'Yes,' I said. 'I have.'

He took the bottle anyway, poured another drink. 'It changes you,' he said. 'For all time.' He picked the glass up, toyed with it. 'Folk reckon nothing lives out there,' he said grimly. 'Only demons. I could wish they were right.' He paused. 'Sometimes on a clear day, flying low, you see . . . more than a man should see. But they're not demons. I think once, they were folk as well. Like us . . .'

I folded my arms. I too was seeing the Badlands, in my mind; the shining vista of them spread by night, as far as the eye could reach. The hills and valleys twinkling, like a bed of coals; but all a ghastly blue.

It seemed he read my thoughts. 'Yes,' he said, 'it's something to look at all right.' He drank, suddenly, as if to erase the memory. 'It's strange,' he said, 'but over the years, I wonder if a flier doesn't get to see with more than his normal eyes.' He rubbed his face. 'Sometimes,' he said, 'I'd see them stretching out farther and farther, all round the world; and nothing left at all, except the Kingdom. One little corner of a little land. That wasn't demons either, though. I think men did it, to each other.' He laughed. 'But I'm forgetting, aren't I?' he said bitterly. 'While the Watching goes on, it can never happen here . . .'

I touched my lip. I wasn't going to be drawn back into an area of barren cant. 'I sometimes wonder,' I said carefully, 'if it's not all merely a form of words. Does it matter, finally, how we describe an agent of Hell? Does it make it any more real? Or less?'

'Why, there you go,' he cried, with a return to something of his former manner. 'Can't beat a good Church training, that's what I always say. A little bit here, a little bit there, clawing back the ground you've lost; nothing ever alters for you, does it? Face you with reality though; that's when you start to wriggle.'

'And why not?' I said calmly. 'It's all that's left to do. Reality is the strangest thing any of us will ever encounter; the one thing, certainly, that we'll never understand. Wriggle though we may.'

He waved his glass. 'I tell you what I'll do,' he said. 'I'll propose a small experiment. You say the Watching keeps us from all harm . . .'

I shook my head. 'I say the Realm is healthy, and that its fields are green.'

He narrowed his eyes for a moment. 'Well then,' he said. 'For a month, we'll ground the Cody rigs. And call in all the Seaguard. That would prove it, wouldn't it? One way or the other.'

'Perhaps,' I said. 'You might pay dearly for the knowledge, though.'

He slammed the glass down. 'And what,' he said, 'if your precious fields stayed green? Would you concede the point?'

'I would concede,' I said gently, 'that Hell had been inactive for a span.'

He flung his head back and guffawed. The laughter was not altogether of a pleasant kind. 'Helman,' he said, 'you're bloody priceless.' He uncapped the bottle, poured. 'I'll tell you a little story,' he said. 'We were well off, when I was a youngster. Big place out in the Westmarch; you'd better believe it. Only we lost the lot. My father went off his head. Not in a nasty way, you understand; he never hurt a fly, right through his life. But every hour on the hour, for the last ten years, he waved a kerchief from the tower window, to scare off little green men. And you know what? We never saw a sign of one, not all the time he lived.' He sat back. 'What do you say to that?'

I smiled. 'I'd say, that he had rediscovered Innocence. And taught you all a lesson; though at the time, maybe you didn't see.'

He swore, with some violence. 'Lesson?' he cried. 'What lesson lies in that?'

'That logic may have circular propensities,' I said. 'Or approach the condition of a sphere; the ultimate, incompressible form.'

He pushed the bottle away, staring; and I burst out laughing at the expression on his face. 'Man,' I said, 'you can't put Faith into a test tube, prove it with a piece of litmus paper.'

A flash of brilliance burst in through the windows. It was followed by a long and velvet growl. A bell began to sound, closer than before. I glanced across to the Kitecaptain; but he shook his head. He said harshly, 'Observation altitude.'

I lifted the valise onto the desk edge, unlocked it once more. I assembled the receiver, set up the shallow repeater cone with its delicate central reed. The other stared, eyes widening. 'What're you doing?' he croaked.

'My function is to listen,' I said curtly. 'And as I told you, maybe to understand. I've heard you; now we'll see what Canwen has to say.' I advanced the probe to the crystal; the cone vibrated instantly, filling the room with the rushing of the wind, the high, musical thrumming of the Cody rig.

The Captain sprang away, face working. 'Necromancy,' he said hoarsely. 'I'll not have it; not on my Base.'

'Be quiet,' I snapped. 'You impress me not at all; you have more wit than that.' I touched a control; and the Observer roared with laughter. 'The tail-down rig of course,' he said. 'New since your day . . .'

The other stared at the receiver; then through the window at the launch vehicle, the thread of cable stretching into the dark. 'Who's he talking to?' he whispered.

I glanced up. 'His father was a flier, was he not?'

The Kitecaptain moistened his lips. 'His father died over the Salient,' he said. 'Twenty years ago.'

I nodded. 'Yes,' I said, 'I know.' Rain spattered sudden against the panes; I adjusted the control and the wind shrilled again, louder than before. Mixed as it was with the singing of the cables, there was an eerie quality to the sound; almost it was as if a voice called, thin and distant at first then circling closer. Canwen's answer was a great shout of joy. 'Quickly, Pater, help me,' he cried urgently. 'Don't let her go again . . .' Gasps sounded; the basketwork creaked in protest and there was a close thump, as if some person, or some thing, had indeed been hauled aboard. The Observer began to laugh. 'Melissa,' he said. 'Melissa, oh my love . . .'

'His wife,' I supplied. 'A most beautiful and gracious lady. Died of childbed fever, ten years ago in Middlemarch.'

'What?' cried Canwen. '*What?*' Then, 'Yes, I see it . . .' A snapping sounded, as he tore the Great Seal from the basket; and he began to laugh again. 'They honour us, beloved,' he cried. 'The Church employs thaumaturgy against us . . .'

The Kitecaptain gave a wild shout. 'No,' he cried, 'I'll hear no more of it.' I wrestled with him, but I was too late. He snatched the receiver, held it on high and dashed it to the floor. The delicate components shattered; and the room fell silent, but for the close sound of the wind.

The pause was of brief duration. Lightning flared again; then instantly the storm was all around us. Crash succeeded crash, shaking the very floor on which I stood; the purple flickering became continuous.

The Captain started convulsively; then it seemed he collected himself. 'Down Rig,' he shouted hoarsely. 'We must fetch him down.'

'No,' I cried. 'No.' I barred his way; for a moment my upflung arm, the sudden glitter of the Master's Staff, served to check him, then he had barged me aside. I tripped and fell, heavily. His feet clattered on the gantry steps; by the time I had regained my feet his thick voice was already echoing through the hangar. '*Down Rig . . . Down Rig*, for your lives . . .'

I followed a little dazedly, ran across the cluttered floor of the place. The great end doors had been closed; I groped for the wicket, and the wind snatched it from my hand. My robes flogged round me; I pressed my back to the high metal, offered up a brief and fervent prayer. Before me the main winch of the launcher already screamed, the great drum spun; smoke or steam arose from where the wildly driven cable snaked through its fairleads. Men ran to the threatened points with water buckets, white robed Medics scurried; Cadets, hair streaming, stood by with hatchets in their hands, to cut the lifter's rigging at a need. I stared up, shielding my face against the glaring arcs; and a cry of '*View-ho*' arose. Although I could not myself descry it, sharper eyes than mine had made out the descending basket. I started forward; next instant the field was lit by an immense white flash.

For a moment, it was as if Time itself was slowed. I saw a man, his arms flung out, hurled headlong from the launcher; fragments of superstructure, blown outward by the force of the concussion, arced into the air; the vehicle's cab, its wheels, the tautened anchor cables, each seemed lit with individual fire. The lightning bolt sped upward, haloing the main trace with its vivid glare; then it was as if the breath had been snatched from my lungs. I crashed to the ground again half stunned, saw through floating spots of colour how a young Cadet, blood on his face, ran forward to the winch gear. He flung his weight against the tallest of the levers, and the screaming stopped. The man-lifter, arrested within its last few feet of travel, crashed sideways, spilling the Observer unceremoniously onto the grass. A shackle parted somewhere, dimly heard through the ringing in my ears; the axes flashed, a cable end lashed viciously above my head. The lifter train whirled off into the dark, and was gone.

I got to my feet, staggered toward Canwen. By the time I reached him, the Medics were already busy. They raised him onto the stretcher they wheeled forward; his head lolled, but at sight of me he rallied. He raised an arm, eyes blazing, made as if to speak; then he collapsed, lying still as death, and was borne rapidly away.

The eastern sky was lightening as I packed the valise for the final time. I closed the lock hasp, clicked it shut; and the door was tapped. A fair-haired Cadet entered, bearing steaming mugs on a tray. I smiled at him. A fresh white bandage circled his brow, and he was a little pale; but he looked uncommon proud.

I turned to the Base Medic, a square-set, ruddy-faced man. I said, 'So you think Canwen will live?'

'Good God, yes,' he said cheerfully. 'Be up and about in a day or two at the latest. He's survived half a dozen calls like that already; I think this gives him the record.' The door closed behind him.

I sipped. The brew was dark and bitter; but at least it was hot. 'Well,' I said, 'I must be on my way. Thank you for your hospitality, Kitecaptain; and my compliments to all concerned for their handling of last night's emergency.'

He rubbed his face uncertainly. 'Will you not stay,' he said, 'and break your fast with us properly?'

I shook my head. 'Out of the question I'm afraid,' I said. 'I'm due at G15 by 0900 hours. But I thank you all the same.' I hefted the valise, and smiled again. 'Its Captain, I've no doubt, will have had too much to drink,' I said. 'I shall probably hear some very interesting heresy.'

He preceded me through the now-silent hangar. To one side a group of men was engaged in laying out long wire traces; but there were few other signs of activity. Outside, the air struck chill and sweet after the storm; by the main gate my transport waited, in charge of a smartly uniformed chauffeur/acolyte. I began to walk toward it; the Captain paced beside me, his chin sunk on his chest, still it seemed deep in thought. 'What's your conclusion?' he asked abruptly.

'About the recent loss rate?' I said. I shook my head. 'An all-round lessening of morale, leading to a certain slackness; all except here of course,' I added as his mouth began to open. It's a lonely and thankless life for all the Cody teams; nobody is more aware of it than I.'

He stopped, and turned toward me. 'What's to do about it then?' he said.

'Do?' I shrugged. 'Send Canwen to have a chat with them. He'll tell them he's seen the Face of God. If he doesn't, go yourself.'

He frowned. 'About the thaumaturgy. The things we heard . . .'

I began to walk again. 'I've heard them often enough before,' I said. 'I don't place all that much importance on them. It's a strange world, in the sky; we must all come to terms with it as best we may.' Which is true enough; sometimes, to preserve one's sanity, it's best to become just a little mad.

He frowned again. 'Then the report . . .'

'Has already been made,' I said. 'You gave it yourself, last night. I don't think I really have very much to add.' I glanced across to him. 'You'd have been best advised,' I said, 'to leave him flying, not draw him down through the eye of the storm. But you'd have seen that for yourself, had you not been under a certain strain at the time.'

'You mean if I hadn't been drunk,' he said bluntly. 'And all the time I thought . . .' He squared his shoulders. 'It won't happen again, Kitemaster; I'll guarantee you that.'

'No,' I said softly, 'I don't suppose it will.'

He shook his head. 'I thought for a moment,' he said, 'it was a judgement on me. I'd certainly been asking for it.'

This time I hid the smile behind my hand. That's the whole trouble, of course, with your amateur theologians. Always expecting God to peer down from the height. His fingers to His nose, for their especial benefit.

We had reached the vehicle. The acolyte saluted briskly, opened the rear door with its brightly blazoned crest. I stooped inside, and turned to button down the window. 'Goodbye, Kitecaptain,' I said.

He stuck his hand out. 'God go with you,' he said gruffly. He hesitated. 'Some day,' he said, 'I'll come and visit you. At that bloody summer palace.'

'Do,' I said. 'You'll be honourably received; as is your due. And Captain . . .'

He leaned close.

'Do something for me in the meantime,' I said. 'Keep the Codys flying; till something better comes along.'

He stepped back, saluting stiffly; then put his hands on his hips, stared after the vehicle. He was still staring when a bend of the green, rutted track took him from sight.

I leaned back against the cushioning, squeezed the bridge of my nose and closed my eyes. I felt oddly cheered. On the morrow, my tour of duty would be ended. They would crown a new May Queen, in Middlemarch; children would run to see me, their hair bedecked with flowers, and I would touch their hands.

I sat up, opened the file on Kitebase G15. A mile or so farther on though I tapped the glass screen in front of me and the chauffeur drew obediently to a halt. I watched back to where, above the shoulders of the hills, a Cody rig rose slowly, etched against the flaring yellow dawn.

NEIL FERGUSON
THE MONROE DOCTRINE

Milton Greene paused in the open doorway just long enough to give the scene framed in it a 250th at f5.6 through the Zeis lens in his mind's eye. The picture of the half-dressed movie star being groomed by her team of assistants was not one that audiences usually got to see. He regretted that for once he did not have a camera with him. But there had been times, looking at Marilyn, that Milton Greene regretted not *being* a camera.

Her wardrobe advisor, Agnes Flanagan, was calmly gathering up the articles of clothing that lay in colourful puddles over the floor, her practised eyes scanning each garment for split zips and seams. Marilyn had nothing but contempt for clothes. They simply got in her way. She might be seen in public — or in the syndicated newspapers, which isn't always the same thing — with a piece of waistline squeezing out of her dress, and not give a damn. Nobody did. If anything, people loved her all the more because it showed she was not just someone with a thousand dollars to spend on a French silk day-gown. Any woman with a thousand dollars could do that. Not many could wear one like Marilyn Monroe.

Agnes was keeping a cool head amid the contradictory instructions coming from Marilyn and her other assistants, all of whom, Milton Greene included, were there to reflect her whim. She was their sun, mooring them in the universe like lesser bodies around her. Without Marilyn, Agnes would not be holding up the just-above-the-knee powder-blue dress in the mirror of the vanity-table; Whitey Snyder and his assistant would not be working on her face with the care and despair of boxing seconds prettifying their contender between rounds.

Milton Greene glanced at his watch: almost ten. The plane was waiting on the runway and Marilyn was still in her nightgown tossing conversation over her shoulder like free money. 'Agnes, did you see those English girls? That Jean Shrimpton and that waif, Twiggy . . . Their dresses are so *short*! You gotta be *skinny* to wear them . . .'

'I'm not going to be wearing one.'

'Agnes! I'm talking about *me*! No one wants tits anymore!'

Agnes had to laugh but she did not contradict her.

'I'm such a fatty these days . . .'

'You're the same size you were ten years ago,' Agnes reminded her. Which was no lie. Marilyn's measurements were recorded as faithfully as the rainfall by the Weather Bureau, being matters of almost equal importance to the Nation.

'Well, I feel a lot fatter!'

Milton Greene had woken her up personally to give her the news but, from the way she was acting, nobody would have guessed whether it was the latest international crisis or some shock ball-game result: the Yankees whupped in an Okie fixture. Milton Greene, however, never underestimated Marilyn's picture of a situation. Having been married to Arthur Miller and to Joe DiMaggio, she knew the difference between a crisis and a ballgame.

'Short skirts are fine for the beach,' Agnes said, 'but for this you need some style.'

'Miniskirts *are* the style in England now.'

'Who cares? We're not going to England!'

'Sure we are! We stop over there.'

'But it'll be the middle of the night when we do!'

Marilyn opened her mouth to speak.

'Will you shut your mouth,' quiet Whitey Snyder said. 'Please Marilyn, so I can get some kind of line. It's like painting the side of a ship!'

Agnes took the opportunity to put out of Marilyn's mind any notion that she could step off a plane in London or any other place with a skirt ten inches above her knee. 'Honey, you don't want to be showing the colour of your underwear to this bigshot you're meeting, whoever it is . . .'

Whitey made sure Marilyn was unable to answer so Milton Greene took another step into the room and said: 'Leonid Brezhnev, is who.'

'*Milton!*' Whitey Snyder's hands froze as Marilyn searched the mirror. 'Where've you been? Did you get the tickets?'

'You don't need tickets,' he reminded her. Marilyn still hadn't gotten used to the idea that she had an Air Force jet at her disposal any time she wanted one. At heart she was just another private citizen.

'You know what I mean. Is everything ready?' she said and let Whitey take up from where he left off.

'Westmorland and Bobby Kennedy are pacing the Conference Room in opposite directions,' Milton Greene told her. 'Waiting to give you the latest situation report. Naturally they have opposite ideas about what you should do about it.'

'What do you think, Milton?' Marilyn said, patting her hair in the mirror, either referring to her coiffure or to the crisis in hand. Milton Greene grinned at the first possibility and, to the second, said: 'Search me, honey.'

Wasn't this just what Bobby Kennedy ached after? None of the White House staff could walk into the President's bedroom while she was dressing and have their opinions asked for. Only her friends could do that and none of them, when it came to affairs of State, had any opinions. Milton Greene was happy just to take photos of her. Wasn't that enough to ask from life?

But Bobby Kennedy was downstairs eating his liver because he could not have Marilyn all to himself. The poor fool! No one could own her. She belonged to everyone. All Kennedy could do, the same as everyone else, was give her as much as possible of the vast quantities of love she got through as fast as some people do bottles of Johnnie Walker or Marvel comics.

General Westmorland was eating his liver for different reasons. His reaction to bad news — in this case the Russian invasion of Czechoslovakia — was always the same: to have the newly formed cavalry units — armed with Mr Gatling's self-breech-loading machine guns firing 360 shots a minute — burn up the motherfuckers' village while they were still asleep on their bows and arrows. Fortunately in Marilyn Monroe the country possessed a President who had never enjoyed Westerns. She had no interest in power. What drove her was a need to be loved, to be part of a family. It had driven her out of the Los Angeles Orphans' Home and across the tracks into the Columbia Studios. Nobody had taken seriously a Californian movie star's bid for the highest executive office while she was whistle-stopping across the country on a ticket that if no one else was going to stop that Dick Nixon then she would, but by the time her pink Caddy was driving through the gates of the White House they had learnt to love her. By then she had found her family. It was called America.

As soon as Marilyn ran into the Conference Room, Kennedy and Westmorland quit pacing and, to Milton Greene, looked as if they suddenly wanted the same piece of air. 'Morning Bobby,' she said breathlessly. 'General . . . Am I late?'

'They arrested Dubcek,' Kennedy said. 'As well as his Cabinet.'

'His cabinet?' Marilyn looked confused. 'What d'they do that for?' Milton Greene had to smile at the picture he imagined she had of soldiers stiff-arming some piece of drawing-room furniture. But with Marilyn you could never be sure. She had a sense of humour.

'That's his ministers,' Westmorland said helpfully. 'The Russians have twenty divisions in there.'

'What about the Czechs, how are they taking it?'

'Lying down.'

'You mean . . . *They don't care*?'

'They're lying down in front of tanks. And throwing rocks at them. They're setting fire to themselves in the street because they don't have twenty divisions to care with!'

Milton Greene waited for something to fill the emptiness in Marilyn's eyes. Finally Kennedy said: 'A student called Jan Pallach sat himself down in the main square in Prague, poured gasoline over himself and put a match to it. He took three minutes to burn.'

'To *himself*!' Marilyn's voice quivered. She might just have seen an auto accident.

'Nobody twisted his arm,' Kennedy said.

'Unless,' Westmorland corrected with a smile, 'you count a tank corps with infantry and air support.' He was loving this. 'M33 tanks with Kalashnikov anti-personnel cannons. What we must do . . .'

Milton Greene gazed through the open window at all air outside, imagining himself breathing some of it. Bright-coloured leaves lay here and there across the patch of mown lawn he could see, lying very still like the uniforms of soldiers after the charge, where they had fallen.

'C'mon, Milton,' Marilyn said, turning to him. 'We better hurry. The plane'll be waiting.'

Westmorland and Kennedy stopped bickering and looked at Marilyn as if suddenly remembering she was present. What the hell did she know about War or Diplomacy? She was a woman, an actress; not even that. A movie-star with big tits. The movement of an army across the face of Europe was not something that happened every day, couldn't she get that into her pretty little head?

'What goddamn plane? You can't take off to some movie premiere. Not now!' Westmorland said spitefully, aiming a look without any love in it at Marilyn's photographer.

'Where *are* you going Marilyn?' Kennedy asked.

'Why . . . Czechoslovakia of course. What did you think? I had Milton telephone the airport soon as he told me the situation. Didn't he tell you?'

This was the part Milton Greene enjoyed. He said nothing. Suddenly the General's big uniform looked a size too small for him. 'You intend flying into a Soviet war zone?'

'What else can I do?'

Westmorland said nothing and Bobby Kennedy said: 'Nothing!'

'Then it can't hurt any if I talk with Brezhnev,' Marilyn said as if the matter were settled.

'He isn't in Czechoslovakia. He's in Moscow,' Kennedy informed her.

'Telephone him then, Bobby honey. Ask him to meet me there.'

'In a bar?' Kennedy sneered. 'Or some movie theatre?'

Marilyn smiled. 'Oh I don't mind. I'll leave it to him.' To Milton Greene she said again: 'C'mon Milton. Let's go. Mustn't keep the Air Force waiting.' She blew a kiss in the direction of her two advisors — just one, so they would have to fight over it. 'Bye boys. Look after America for me while I'm gone.' Then she ran out of the door that Milton Greene was holding open for her.

'What do I tell Brezhnev?' A desperate Kennedy called after her.

'Tell him he has a date with Marilyn Monroe,' Milton Greene, following her out, said. 'So he better not be late!'

Aboard the President's jet Marilyn was reassuring Bobby Kennedy over the ground-to-air: 'Sure it's me, honey. What did you say?'

'What I would have said. The same.' Kennedy's more-American-than-thou voice amplified through the suite. 'They refused to believe me.'

'Why not? Brezhnev and me will meet and talk things over. In this kind of jam it's the only . . .'

Czechoslovakia seemed a long way off to Milton Greene. He would have preferred not to have been party to Marilyn's conversation. Below, through the portal, the dirty grey Potomac slowly receded, the morning sun decalled on its surface like a nice girl on the wing of an old bomber.

'They told me any alien aircraft in their air space would be in violation of internationally agreed air-conduct treaty and would be treated as hostile. They will intercept. Tell the pilot to turn back, Marilyn.'

'They would shoot us down!'

'Of course. We'd do the same. How do they know you aren't an ICBM?'

'Well . . .' Marilyn never liked to sound ignorant. 'And am I?' Milton Greene felt sure he could hear Kennedy's teeth grinding.

'No, Marilyn. You may be our secret weapon but you would never destroy a city the size of Prague. By the way, how's your Russian? Brezhnev speaks no English.'

'*Vchera*! That's Russian for today,' Marilyn said as if that was going to open doors for her.

'It's Russian for *yesterday*!'

'Oh well,' she giggled. 'I guess it'll be yesterday by the time we get there. If they shoot me down, promise me you'll look after Mitzou, Bobby.' Mitzou was Marilyn's cat. '*Dosfordania*!' she said lightly, but lowered the telephone into its cradle as carefully as if it had been a baby, as one does after the other party has replaced theirs without saying goodbye. She lay back and lowered her eyelids. Soon she was asleep.

After London, on the final leg of the journey, Milton Greene also got some sleep. At least, he dreamed he did. He dreamed there was a bump as if something was striking the fuselage from the outside. With a start his eyes opened onto Marilyn peering into

Whitey Snyder's portable mirror. So they were landing. This meant the Russians had not shot her down. They had decided the plane was not an Inter-Continental Ballistic Missile after all. Marilyn hadn't arrived yet and already she had them taking risks.

Outside the morning was as pale as the face of a sentry who has been on duty all night and doesn't care who knows it. The world looked flat and bloodless and about as much fun as the opening sequence of a European art movie. Milton Greene surveyed with alarm the army officers on the tarmac and the automatic weaponry in their hands while, beside him at the opening hatch, the President of the United States waved and smiled and blew kisses in their direction as she had learnt to do with men in uniform during her tour of Korea. Wide un-American faces stared back at her, blank as snow. Clearly this woman in a powder-blue silk day-dress who had stepped out of the sky like a goddess was not a contingency they had been briefed for at the Academy. Their automatic guns rattled with embarrassment. Marilyn disarmed them.

'They'd be a lot happier with a few Pentaxes,' Milton Greene murmured to Agnes as they descended the ramp, although what he meant was that he, Milton Greene, would have been happier.

Marilyn had starred in so many movies that by now reality followed her around like an expensive studio camera. Her presence transformed the dismal grey airport into a location erected solely for her performance. She breathed life into it.

The big lighted foyer they stepped into could have belonged to an interstate bus depot in Galveston during the Depression. The décor was not what a connoisseur would have called rococo. A platoon of generals with faces as expressive as taxidrivers escorted Marilyn's party in. At least, Milton Greene assumed they were generals; their uniforms had nothing in common with the hotel livery which the US big brass wore. No gold lace or sign of rank. They might all have been corporals. He had no idea who was who and he felt pretty sure Marilyn hadn't either.

'Say fellas, I'm really sorry to put you to all this trouble . . .' she was saying as Milton Greene became aware of a posse of civilians lined up across the foyer, standing perfectly still, chests out like brave men in front of a firing squad. They must have been brave; none of them was carrying a gun. Abruptly all the soldiers came to attention behind them. Agnes Flanagan took hold of Milton Greene's arm. Whitey Snyder looked no whiter than he usually did. Marilyn was trying to make herself understood by the dignitary who might have been Chief of Staff or the person who checked your ticket and asked to see your visa. Not having either, Marilyn was giving him a smile you could have opened a bank account with. Maybe he was a customs officer listening to whether she had anything to declare but from the way he shook his head it didn't look as if he could make up his mind whether or not to believe her story. No one could have called her smile exactly innocent.

'Boy!' Marilyn's voice piped, her arm linked inside the arm of the Chief of Staff. 'Couldn't I do with a drink!'

The overcoats and the uniforms closed in, eyeing her like rival horse-traders. Milton Greene found himself being addressed by a civilian who spoke English — as opposed to the kind of American he spoke himself — with a British accent. Obviously the Reds still thought the British counted for something. 'Good morning. Did you have a good flight? You are President Monroe's interpreter, I presume?'

'No, I dreamed you shot our plane down. And I don't speak a word of Russian,' Milton Greene said. 'Who are you?'

The man made a good stab at looking friendly. 'Uri Gregorovitch.'

'Pleased to meet you, Uri.' They shook hands. 'Milton Greene.'

'May I ask what your position is?'

Translating his question into American, Milton Greene said, 'You mean, what do I do? I'm a photographer.'

'You are security personnel. I understand.'

'The hell you do. I'm just a friend of Marilyn. I take pictures of her. None of us speaks Russian. Or Serbo-Croat. We have an appointment with President Brezhnev.' Milton Greene grinned. 'Take me to your leader!'

Uri Gregorovitch let that one go. 'He is the comrade whom Miss Monroe is talking to,' he said.

'Ah ha. Well, first: Marilyn is no Miss. And second: how good does the President speak English?'

He let the interpreter drag him over to where Marilyn and Agnes were surrounded by the cream of the Red Army. He was beginning to feel better. This was just like a cocktail party only without the cocktails.

'Say, Milton!' Marilyn cried out to him. 'Agnes and me were just trying to explain to this nice waiter here what a Coke is . . .'

'This nice waiter,' Milton Greene said. 'Is Leonid Brezhnev.'

'He is? How did you find out?'

'Uri Gregorovitch here told me. He's an interpreter.'

Marilyn turned to him. 'Uri, d'you think you could rustle us all up something to drink? With plenty of ice. I'm so goddarn thirsty I could spit cotton balls!'

While Uri gave instructions everyone tried on their best smile. The way those old warriors smiled you might have been forgiven for thinking they had once been young, had once felt soft fingers stroke their skin and nothing else under the moon had had any importance for them. 'Sorry Marilyn,' the interpreter reported. 'No ice.'

'What!' Marilyn said in her dumb Sugar Kane voice: 'Is there some kind of thaw on?'

If there wasn't, that cracked whatever ice there was still around; the Russians were chuckling! Genially they propelled the Americans towards a large empty bar behind which a forlorn barman stood polishing glasses. He was, everyone realized as soon as the soldiers gave their orders, a Czech. It was a sticky moment until Marilyn called to him: 'Sweetheart, make mine a scotch,' smiling. 'Forget the ice!'

The scotch had the bouquet of an operating theatre; it had Milton Greene panting for air and the Russian President slapping his back. 'Not so fast! This is good vodka!' — so good, apparently, it gave Milton Greene the gift of tongues. Brezhnev laughed the laugh of the proprietor of a liquor able to lick his rivals. It was developing into quite a party. If Marilyn could make these big Russians laugh, he could relax. Even the barman was beginning to cheer up.

Smiling like a father-in-law, the President of the Soviet Republics touched Marilyn's glass with is own: 'Prosit!'

'Vchera . . .' she replied.

'Niet!' Brezhnev corrected her. 'Prosit!'

'Prosit! is Russian for "Your health",' Uri Gregorovitch said. 'Vchera means Yesterday.'

'I know . . .' Marilyn continued. 'Vchera dosfordania . . .'

'Yesterday goodbye . . .?'

'A-ha. Vchera dosfordania Jan Pallach.'

The interpreter looked helpless.

'Or as we say in pictures, he got dead.'

'Who?'

'Jan Pallach!' Milton Greene chorused with Agnes and Marilyn. Brezhnev, he noticed, had stopped laughing.

At that moment the barman said something in Russian that had all the soldiers jerking their eyes in his direction. Milton Greene wondered whether they were about to order a Jan Pallach from him. If that was the case he felt sure it wouldn't have tasted like a Tom Collins. Another sticky moment. Marilyn waited; she had said her lines. There was a silence a baby could have fallen asleep in. Milton Greene could hear the interpreter breathing. Or maybe it was just a floorboard creaking somewhere. Finally Brezhnev spoke.

'The President,' Uri relayed, 'is sorry. He has not been informed about any Mata.'

'Any what?'

He said it again, pronouncing 'martyr' as the British say 'tomArto' when they mean 'tomato' but in Marilyn's LA-suburb-so-near-Hollywood-it-makes-no-difference it sounded like how a Britisher thinks a Bronx New Yorker pronounces 'Mother?'

'Mother?' the interpreter echoed, sweat on his brow. Communication was breaking down. Boy was he earning his money!

'You are cowards! All of you! Cowards . . .'

So Marilyn had decided to raise the temperature. Even by now Milton Greene could not always be certain when she was acting. Nor, he suspected, could she herself. Her method of acting tapped the root of something painful inside her and when it happened she became a piece of live wire; she needed an audience just to earth all the electricity she gave out.

'. . . What d'you think Czechoslovakia is feeling — that's if it's got any feelings left! — you big men with nothing to justify being here except more tanks?' She let them think about that for a while. When nobody said anything she told them. 'Like Jan Pallach's *mother* is how, whose kid just set fire to himself on account of the M33 tank up his back yard!' The interpreter was murmuring in fast Russian, his voice soaking up Marilyn's performance. He sounded good, but not as good as she did. 'You invade a small country the size of Texas with twenty divisions that all the Czechs can do is throw rocks at. You put Dubcek and his cabinet in jail . . .'

'You said something about Texas,' Gregorovitch said. 'The President would like to know if you remember the Alamo.'

'Sure I do. It was a lousy picture.'

Whether at that moment the barman made a sharp move, something shiny in his hand, or he didn't, no one will ever know for sure because just as he did — or didn't — Brezhnev went to slug Marilyn — or maybe to take her in his arms — who screamed as a pistol cracked and a bullet from nowhere buried itself in Milton Greene's chest, the reflection of it in the bar mirror in front of him, narrowly missing the barman who had already fainted, still holding onto the cocktail shaker.

Nobody moved. Milton Greene's heart fluttered like a clay pigeon. Finally Brezhnev — his arm still around the President of the United States — hollered, and the generals grabbed one of the civilians — some jumpy secret service man — and took away his gun; obviously he couldn't be trusted with it. The tension had snapped, a spark had passed between opposite poles. It had not proved fatal but Milton Greene wished the barman would wake up; his mouth was dry as an empty barrel, one he could still taste the cordite in. Who said Hollywood was the only place that could make pictures?

Next day Milton Greene woke up somewhere and quickly looked around to see where it was. A bit too quickly. With a lot of respect for whatever the Russian is for a cracking hangover, he lowered his head back onto the carpet. Where was he? And why? His recollection of the previous day was blank. Gently, behind closed lids, he removed with mental fingers the piece of film in his mind's eye, expertly imagined each step in the developing process, then waited for something to appear on the paper floating in his memory. Eventually he began to make out Marilyn at her vanity-table, framed in the doorway; then the grey Potomac seen from the air; then the deserted foreign airport; the reception party and the gun going off; the drive out of the city, tanks in the streets; the huge old chateau out of a fairy tale; more vodka; finally the two most influential people in the world not talking the same language but dancing together. Cheek to cheek! No wonder his head hurt!

After that he tried again. This time he made it as far as the bed, a nice cool friendly-looking bed that someone had recently not slept in. Milton Greene had a hunch he knew who it was. Instead of getting into the bed, however, he headed for the door, curious about where he would find his reason for being there.

She was sitting in a kitchen the size of a ballroom, leaning back in a chair explaining something to Leonid Brezhnev who at that moment was sliding a fried egg from the skillet in his hand onto the plate in front of her, a white apron around his big belly and such a look on his face you could have believed Marilyn's egg was his only care in the world. A big grin spread over Brezhnev's face — he'd done it! — as he looked up and saw Milton Greene standing in the door.

Uri Gregorovitch was seated at the other end of the table with his head over a chessboard as if he had not noticed Milton Greene's arrival. The low obbligato of Russian words coming from him, however, suggested his mind was not entirely on his game.

'Hi!' Marilyn called out while Brezhnev, still grinning, made a gesture with the skillet which an Eskimo could have interpreted. 'Sleep well?'

'Like a piece of lead,' Milton Greene replied. 'In my own heart.'

'Comrade Brezhnev,' Gregorovitch said, looking up, 'would like to know if you'd like eggs for breakfast, Milton.'

'You bet!' Milton Greene said but he had already made an unambiguous nod towards the Comrade in question. He was beginning to feel better already. No one seemed to mind that he had lurched off in the middle of the party. Had they been up all night? Or had they been lucky and found their beds? 'Sunny side up please, Leonid,' he said.

Brezhnev chuckled. 'With respect, Milton,' Uri Gregorovitch moved one of the chess pieces. 'He knows how to cook an egg.'

'He does?' Milton Greene began to understand why Brezhnev was President of the Soviet Republics. 'In that case, tell him I'll start filing for a divorce as soon as I get back to the States!'

Brezhnev laughed like a big friendly bear. 'Comrade Brezhnev regrets to inform you but he's already engaged.' The interpreter moved another piece. 'To Marilyn!'

'Not so fast!! I can't marry *you*!' Marily piped, just keeping the panic out of her voice. 'This egg's cooked so darned well I can hardly bear to eat it!' The way the words quaked, anyone would have thought she had been asked to stab a baby chicken; her fork hovered over the yolk as if she could not bring herself to do it. When she did — suddenly — the three men laughed with relief. But for a moment she had them shucked.

Milton Greene knew Marilyn could make people laugh but the interpreter wasn't bad either. On his chessboard the red and white pieces were set out from left to right as if he were not playing a game but plotting the progress of a battle: translating the conversation into chess moves. If this was the case, so far things looked pretty even. 'You're good, Uri,' Milton Greene said while Brezhnev cooked and Marilyn started into her egg.

'How good is that, Milton?'

'Better than just OK, I guess.'

'Is that all?'

'Well . . .' Milton Greene paused to think.

'Do you mean "well" as an interjectory adverb, or as a qualifying one?'

'As in "Well I'll be damned".'

Uri looked up from his board. 'I do my job well which is better than just good.'

'Well and good, what's the difference?' This was such an obvious thing to say Milton Greene knew it had to be dumb. He regretted having started this. Clever conversation wasn't his department.

'A great deal. Adjectives — good, bad, American, drunk — say something about *nouns*, of course. But adverbs are in tow to *verbs* which are stronger, more versatile, as a bishop' — he laid a finger on the piece — 'is stronger than a knight.'

'That's a matter of opinion,' Milton Greene was not certain he followed the language-wizard's drift but he was damned if he was going to allow this foreigner to tell him how to speak. Something told him he was being made to take sides in the conversation that

Neil Ferguson

was being played out, as if Brezhnev was pitching his strong verbs against Marilyn's concrete nouns. 'You don't want to under-estimate nouns,' he said. 'Earth, tanks, America, vodka . . . things you can take photographs of.'

From the cast-iron stove, Brezhnev said something which Gregorovitch reprocessed: 'Marilyn, the President understands when you say you felt abused and exploited during your early career. As a woman and as an employee you were doubly cheated. That's why you left the Fox Studio. *To gain the means of pro-duction!*'

'*Me*? I never produced a thing in my life,' Marilyn said, as if this fact had occurred to her before.

'He means the production of films.'

'Oh, you mean *movies*!' Marilyn laughed, her throat white as a truce flag. '*I* never controlled a movie-production yet! Thousands of men run the industry. Not me!'

'Not the President of the United States?'

'Look, to most Americans the President is just someone who looks good on TV. It could be any poor fool.'

'No one is suggesting you're a fool, Marilyn,' Gregorovitch said gravely.

'I never said I was — ' Marilyn began to pour out coffee into four cups — 'intelligent. I look better on TV than Nixon, is all. That wouldn't be difficult.'

Gregorovitch's hand hung over the board as if he could not make up his mind which piece to move next. Brezhnev placed an egg in front of Milton Greene — sunny side up but with no more interest than any roadside short-order cook. His mind was else-where, on this beautiful American film star. Was he learning that communicating with her required areas of his psyche he had probably not used since he was in short pants? She was no fool, merely a woman who reasoned with her heart. Her beauty did not lie in the cosmetic stereotype she manipulated with such dialectic skill; her presence was greater than all the things that could be said about it. Marilyn may not have been the first international leader who was a woman but she was maybe the first who did not attempt to compete with men in terms of those clever right-handed skills with which men for centuries had ordered the universe: logic, language, ideology. Marilyn had Brezhnev bothered. He was no different than other men.

'Put it this way,' Brezhnev plodded on. 'The American people elected you, someone trying to gain the means of production . . .'

'Me? No more than anyone else is. No more than Jan Pallach! Anyone who pours gasoline over himself and sets fire to it must feel desperate but at least he's going to produce the spark. That's what he's saying to you Russians. With your tanks in his streets, that's the only goddamn freedom he's got!'

'Comrade Brezhnev,' the interpreter sighed, his face as grey as the line between truth and fiction, 'is sorry to hear about his story.'

'Who's talking about history? It only happened yesterday!'

All Milton Greene could hear was his own knife cutting his egg. Yet another communication breakdown.

'By committing suicide, Jan Pallach opted out of history,' Gregorovitch said. Suddenly Milton Greene understood what the game was about. Verbs are agile and clever; they toss nouns around as strong men do sacks of cement, humping and dumping them, changing them into something else. It was verbs mobilized tanks to cross Europe, that set fire to Jan Pallach, that sent Gatling guns into sleepy Indian villages. Brezhnev was no different than Westmorland but in Marilyn Monroe they were coming up against a woman they could not change. To Marilyn everything was a noun — a *thing*, not a process — including everything Westmorland or Brezhnev could do or say to her. History was a noun. The World was one. In the end.

'In the end,' Milton Greene heard himself say, 'Jan Pallach did not commit suicide. He was sentenced to death.'

Uri Gregorovitch made a minute smile and moved a pawn. 'Check?' he murmured.

'Well,' Milton Greene, with egg in his mouth, said. 'He sure as hell wasn't Russian!'

Leaving Brezhnev with the washing up, Marilyn led Milton Greene out of the room and into the extensive garden in back of the building, put his arm around her and hugged into his body. The cold smoked their breath in the clear air. Under Gregorovitch's greatcoat, Milton Greene held her silk-covered arm and waited for her to speak. In silence they followed the path in and out of sculptured laurel trees until the big eighteenth-century chateau became a piece of fairy cake. He felt oppressed by the tired elegance of Europe, its subtleties of mood no camera he owned could ever capture.

'Marilyn. What Brezhnev said in there . . . About you two being married.' Her eyes, hooded within the collar of the greatcoat, opened. 'What did he mean?'

'Oh that! Leonid thinks he wants to marry me.' Her voice seemed to bruise on the effort of saying the words.

'He was serious!'

'Oh sure. He's the old-fashioned sort. Likes to do everything kosher.'

'But you can't marry Brezhnev!'

'I can't? Why? Is he married already?'

'Probably. But he's a communist! President of the Soviet Union! Try explaining that to Westmorland. It would be like Night marrying Day.'

'Sounds to me like a good reason for giving it a try.'

Milton Greene — he knew he was going to burst into tears or laughter, but which? — said 'When did you decide?'

'Last night. This morning.' Marilyn shrugged. 'It just decided itself. Leonid likes me. I make him feel good.'

'YOU SLEPT WITH HIM!'

'Why sure, Milton. You disapprove?'

Of course he damn well disapproved! 'Marilyn, you know who you sleep with is none of my business. I just think . . .' Suddenly he burst into laughter. 'It's one helluva way of conducting diplomacy!'

'I was never very diplomatic.'

'You're doing fine, Marilyn. I'm sure no-one negotiated a peace like this. But where do we go from here? The tanks are still in Prague. If your . . . union with Brezhnev is to have political results . . .'

'Political? You don't understand, Milton. We're getting married. We'll have children.'

For a moment Milton Greene felt what Bobby Kennedy must have to go through all the time. 'I guess you might,' he said.

'No might can stop it. I *know* we will. Sometimes a woman knows when it's happened. I know. I'm going to have Leonid's baby!'

'Hey, Duchess!' Milton Greene called down the length of the bar to where a girl was hunched over a paperback book. 'Two more of the same!' The young woman closed her book and turned to draw the beer while Milton Greene continued his disquisition with Uri Gregorovitch. 'From what I hear Westmorland is doing his darndest to have her impeached but he can't swing that, not after all Marilyn has done for the blacks and women in the Senate. They won't walk out on her now,' he said. 'And Bobby Kennedy has been in tears since he arrived, trying to change her mind. The way he talks you'd think the Girl Next Door was marrying the Garbage Collector. That's the kind of reaction it has brought.' Without a word the girl placed two fresh quarts of pilsner beer in front of them. Milton Greene batted her an eyelid as he took a bite out of the beer, grateful to lay hands on a drink that was not 100% potato juice. 'Have one yourself kid,' he said, a thin moustache of foam on his top lip, grinning. Now that the emergency had all but passed he was learning to like Prague, its marbled skies churning the light over a joyous architecture, birds and silences hidden inside the human curve of its Baroque. He liked the dignity of the Bohemian woman behind the bar who had a name as long as a Sunday afternoon and spoke English as if it were blank verse.

'Thanks,' she told him. 'I will.'

'. . . But if you're asking me what kind of reaction it has bought in America, Uri, I'd have to tell you people are wetting themselves. Americans are like kids at a Christmas party when it comes to a celebration. You wait till the rodeo bands start arriving, the cheerleaders . . . Uri, you ain't seen nothing yet! These planes coming in every day, each one full of Yankee razzmatazz, cowboys, baseball teams, rock and roll, sex, plus all the bad taste Hollywood can ship over here. You don't think it's going to pass up an opportunity like this? The way Hollywood sees it, they're just making a return on what it cost them to put Marilyn in the White House.'

Gliding towards them, the bar person put her own glass on the bar and lounged discreetly into the conversation. White hands of an aristocrat, Milton Greene surmised. Or maybe from having washed too many glasses in cold water.

'What's the news from your camp? How come the Russians are putting up with it?'

'How do you stop kids?' Gregorovitch said. 'They find it hard enough trying to keep pace with Europeans. How d'you think they can cope with pretty girls in mini-skirts, red indians . . . Their guns are made for shooting people.'

'Relax! The sight of fifty teenage crowd warmers for the Arkansas Warriors will melt the heart of a tank captain.'

'You think so?'

'If it doesn't, there's always Detroit Thunderbirds, Texas beef, New York style. The Czechs may not get happier, but they sure as hell are going to get richer!'

'Maybe that's what's eating me, as you would say,' Gregorovitch said. 'In all this fuss over Marilyn, we seem to be forgetting Czechoslovakia.'

'So is that such a bad thing? At least Marilyn has got the tanks off the street!' Milton Greene then turned to the Czech girl. 'What do you think, Duchess? Let's have your two cents worth.'

She said nothing. Milton Greene began to think she had not followed the drift. Then, as if reciting words learned by heart, she said: 'The game is finished that you gentlemen have been playing with us. There is not Czech or Slovak, no America or Russia. These are words, names of peoples for kings and generals. Are we not all one under the same sun? Human love is the womb of history. Unless the strong can touch the weak within itself, our dreams of heaven will destroy the earth. Unless we make army generals laugh and cry, lay hands gently on soldiers' sleeves, we are no better than the frightened dog that bites its own tail.'

Milton Greene raised his glass. The Russian interpreter and the Czech bar person did the same, touching their glasses together. 'I'll drink to that,' he said.

RACHEL POLLACK
ANGEL BABY

The angel came at me in the IBM parking lot, the huge double football field of concrete behind the long grey factory. Like I did every day in summer I'd gone there to pick up my mother's car. Every afternoon she would drive to work, and an hour or two later, after I'd cleaned up my dinner, I could go get the car and visit my friends or go to the shopping centres or the movies. At a quarter to twelve Mrs Jacobi, who lived across the street and worked a couple of departments down from my mother, would take Mom home, telling the same old pumpkin jokes year after year. My mother could have gone to work with Mrs Jacobi too, and saved me the twenty minute walk to the parking lot down by the river, but my mother claimed Mrs Jacobi sometimes came late and it made her nervous that her work record should depend on someone else.

The angel came over the river away from the mountains. I remember thinking, crazylike, that it must have come from one of the Catskill hotels, one of the resorts where rich people went to get away from the city.

I saw the eyes first. I don't know how, but I did. You'd think I'd see the wings before anything, but no, I looked up, I don't know why, it wasn't like anything called me or anything, I just looked up with the car keys in my hand, and I saw — they looked like small shiny bits of metal floating towards me. I stared at them. I didn't feel faint or nauseous, just weird, like my skin or something was sliding off into those horrible cold eyes.

Then I saw the wings. I guess he was coming straight towards me, because I first saw a wavy line of white, dipping down in the centre, then coming up again. I squinted and shook my head, and then he must have shifted, because suddenly the wings filled the whole sky, like a long white cloud pointed at both ends, and narrow in the middle. Very slowly it moved, up and down, up and down. Christ, how slowly those wings beat, they took over my breath, forcing my lungs to open and close so slow that my chest burned. They made me want to cover myself, like *I* was somehow naked, and not him.

I managed to look around in the parking lot, and I saw, I guess maybe five or six or seven people, walking to their cars and looking tired, like they'd worked overtime and hadn't finished whatever they had to do. A couple were running and checking the big clock over the door, some guy with a big black leather brief-case. And none of them saw. I didn't cry out, I didn't even think of it. My eyes went back to the angel.

The wings looked like they could cover the whole parking lot, like they'd sweep the cars right off the concrete and just smash the whole row of trees separating the front and back lots. And in between, the legs sticking out, the arms hanging down, his hard naked body.

He was very thin, kind of stretched out, I even thought I could see his ribs. His skin shone. Not much, not as much as the wings. It made me think of the radium watch my father had had when I was a little kid and he let me take it in the closet and shut the door so I could see it glow. The angel's skin shone a lot like that, except it wasn't green but white, like watery milk, so that for a moment I thought of an old movie I'd seen on TV, where they've got this radioactive milk and the scientists are trying to find it and they keep showing it moving around until it ends up on someone's table, pale and glowing. But of course I only thought that for a moment. Later, when I tried to remember his skin, I thought of the way snow looks under a full moon. Even now, I sometimes can't stand to look at snow at night, and I won't even let Jimmy out of the house after dark in winter.

I don't think I realized the angel was coming for me until the last moment. He just came closer and closer, getting larger, and in a funny way *smaller*, as I could see he wasn't really so big, his body no longer, I mean no taller than Bobby Beauhawk, the basketball player who kept breaking things in my bio class. (I wrote 'longer' because once my mother took me on a vacation, she said we could both use a rest, but she meant me, and we went to Florida and I saw this alligator lying in the mud, and I started to scream because it was just as long, exactly as long as the angel.) The wings weren't short, they could have stretched over two or three cars easy, but nothing like as long as I thought when I saw them far away.

I never saw — his thing. I know that sounds really crazy, but I just didn't see it. I have some picture of it in my head as bright red and pointy, so maybe I saw it unconsciously or something, but I don't remember anything about it. Even as I realized he was coming right at me and I should run or something, I went back to looking at his eyes. I felt like I could look inside them, not into his head, but into all the things he'd seen, his own world. I saw it like a place where the sky filled up with lightning all the time, where nothing ever stayed in one piece, where the ground kept melting and turning into water, or even huge fires that jumped up —— Except it always stayed cold. Cold like you can't possibly imagine, like no one ever even thought of heat, even knew what it was.

One of the wings knocked me to the ground — I screamed, afraid I'd hit my head — and then his long fingers started fumbling at my clothes, stiff and clumsy like he didn't know what he was doing. I thought of Mary Tunache, who made out with that exchange student and later told us all he didn't even know how to get her bra off.

He didn't mean to knock me over, not like he wanted to force me or anything like that, he just couldn't use his hands very well, our world was too clumsy for him. I know that, because once he'd got my clothes off he just started stroking me, long strokes with his fingers all spread out, like the way my piano teacher used to hold her hands over the keys before she began. At first his fingers seemed horribly cold, and it wasn't until I saw the lines of blood down my breasts and stomach that I realized they weren't fingers at all, but claws, long and thin, a pale gold that picked up reddish highlights from the sun, like my friend Marie's hair that everyone envies so much.

The claws just touched my skin but they reached into me too, and they stirred up something all the way down. I started making noises, they sounded like animal imitations, but they weren't. I was talking his language, his people's talk, not talk but shrieks and whistles that didn't mean anything like our words do, they just said everything they needed to say. Everything.

I want to get this right, put it down just like it happened, but I can't. It's not fair. I know what to say, but I don't know the words. Whatever I saw makes it something else. How can I use human words to describe angel language? If I could only speak that again I wouldn't have to describe.

The funny thing was, nobody heard me, the one or two people I could see in the lot didn't even turn, some woman walked past only an aisle away, in the middle of my screams I could hear the click of her heels. But she didn't hear me, she couldn't even see the angel spread over me, with his wings curving over the tops of the cars.

Reading this it strikes me how crazy it sounds. If no one else saw it, then it didn't happen, right? Well, I think that no matter how crazy a person is, he's got to know, secretly anyway, when he's made something up. Maybe that's what makes them unhappy and violent, because inside they know it's not true, yet outside they can't get away from it.

But the angel was real all the way down, so much that for weeks afterward my mother and my friends looked and sounded fake to me, like people on television saying words that someone else has written and no one cares about.

I don't really know when the angel . . . entered me. I know he did because later when I checked I wasn't a virgin any more, but I don't remember. It doesn't matter. Can you understand? What really counted was speaking the angel's language.

I don't even know when it ended. Suddenly I was lying alone, between my mother's car and some Cadillac, my body all scratched, as much by the pebbles under me as by the claws, and in the sky I could see the angel, his back and legs incredibly bright, getting larger and larger until they covered the whole sun and sky. And then they were gone.

I grabbed up my clothes, found the car keys on the ground, and scrambled inside. I lay there on the back seat, still not excited or frightened or happy or sad, or anything like that. What the angel did, what he showed me, made me, you can't find any feelings to go with it. I've got a kind of thing about feelings. I think they make up a sort of language we use, just like words, to tell ourselves what's happened to us. They explain things. Happiness says, this was a good experience, you enjoyed it, sadness says, this one was crummy, you didn't like it.

But the angel didn't need any explanations. I'd spoken his

language. If I could have I would have given up feelings, and words, forever. But you try to do that without the angel's language and you just become fake.

But that came later. Lying there on the back seat I tried to hold on to what the angel had given me. I tried making those sounds again, only they came out stupid so I stopped right away. I tried to remember the things I'd seen in his eyes and that came a little clearer, except it was only a memory.

One thing real remained. The angel's message. His promise. The angel wanted a child. No, the angel never wanted anything. He was going to have a child. And he'd chosen me as the mother. That's not right either. He didn't choose, didn't find me worthy or anything like that. In the angel's world nothing gets chosen or picked out. You'd think I would wonder why he picked me. But I'd seen that world, I'd talked it, and I knew you didn't need any reason for anything.

I was going to have the angel's child. Except I couldn't do it right away. My human body couldn't hold his angel seed. It wouldn't burn up or anything, the two things just wouldn't fit together. So the first time he came just to prepare me. What he did would change me, not all at once, but slowly, over years until I was ready for him. The only thing I had to do was allow it to work. That meant no husband or lovers, no human disturbing that slow movement all the way through me. Lying there in the car I had to laugh a little. It reminded me of my mother telling me that 'virginity still matters. No man wants soiled goods, no matter what he says.'

Well, the angel had certainly soiled me, and whatever any man might want I was going to make sure that dirt soiled me all the way down. The angel had promised me a child and I planned to get it.

The strange thing was, I knew that wanting the angel's child already cut me off from him. Wanting things, that's what makes us people and not angels. But I couldn't help it.

I lay there for a while, breathing the hot stuffy air of the car but not wanting to open the windows, watching the sky darken. Finally I heard a couple of men laughing and hid on the floor while I pulled my clothes on. When they'd gone I got up and drove home.

For the next few days I tried, like I said, not to feel anything. I thought it would help me hold on to the angel language. But that was gone. Finished. The angel had dropped me back in the human world and I had to teach myself all over how to work in it. Besides, I could see my mother was getting suspicious.

At first her job and the summer heat kept her so wrapped up she didn't notice anything. I was really glad of that. I'd spent hours scrubbing the blood stains off my clothes and the back seat of the car. But the next evening, when I called my mother after she'd driven to work, she just went on about the heat and the men in her department wanting a young secretary with big tits instead of someone who could type and cared about her work, and how I shouldn't forget to water the lawn before it got dark.

For a few days it went like that, but then she started to ask did I feel okay, why didn't I go visit my friends or go to a movie, get away from the heat. I didn't say anything, just made a face and moved away when she tried to touch me. One day she told me of a dance the Lutheran Center was giving at Speckled Lake, and all my friends were going, why didn't I go, maybe I'd meet someone there, if I sat at home every night I'd just get depressed.

I could see her watching me closely, and it took me a minute to realize the test she'd set up. She didn't care about the dance, well, she did, but more, she wanted to see how I'd react to her interfering. Almost too late I shouted, 'You called all my friends? Jesus, how could you do that? Didn't I tell you I hate it when you butt in like that?' She had to fight not to smirk as she apologized and went on to say, even so, maybe I should go to the dance anyway, now that the damage was done, no sense in my denying myself.

The funny thing was, she was playing a part just as much as I was. It made me wonder how much she knew. For just a second the crazy idea hit me that an angel (or the angel, maybe there was only one, except it made no difference how many there were, they were all the same), maybe the angel had come to her, to everybody, and everyone kept it hidden, thinking no one would understand, so that if I told the truth, everyone else would want to.

But no, I could see in my mother's face, and later, in other people's faces when I looked at them in the street, she'd never seen those eyes. I could tell by looking at hers. You could go a certain way into them and then they stopped.

Later, after my mother had apologized again, I lay up in my room with the fan on, and thought about my feelings, like anger or sadness, and how they only described things, but how, without the angel talk, I couldn't do anything else. It's all fake, I thought, no matter which way I go. If I acted like other people, that wasn't real, but if I tried not to, if I tried to act like the angel, that made me even more fake. The best I could do, I decided, was act like ordinary people but at least remember the truth. I got up and went to the mirror and looked at my eyes. I thought they looked different than they used to, but how could I tell without seeing them from before at the same time, I thought they went all the way down, but I could only see them in the glass which made everything flat and dull. If only I could really look in my own eyes. The angel can, I thought. He can look at himself from the outside and in at the same time.

The next day I went into town, to Woolworth's, and bought a diary, one of those blue plastic things with thick gold edged paper and a lock on the cover. If I couldn't act like the angel, I thought, I should at least write it all down so I wouldn't forget. I planned to write something every day, all my thoughts and feelings, even if I had to use human language, so when the angel came back I'd have stayed close to him.

The first couple of days I must have filled up half the book. I imagined ending up with a whole stock of diaries and giving them to the angel or maybe saving them for the baby. But then my daily writing started getting shorter. I found myself trying to think of things to say, or writing about my mother or people I saw or something like that, just to fill up the pages. So I told myself I didn't need to write every day, I would just put things in when they came to me, like if I remembered something about the wings or the claws then I could put it down with the date.

For a few weeks I kept doing it, then I just sort of forgot. I've still got it. I read it recently, while Jimmy was out playing with his toy cars. I thought I'd hate it, thought it would sound stupid. But it said so much, so many beautiful things, almost like some little piece of angel language translated into English. Why didn't I keep doing it, I thought, and began to cry, angry at the same time, because tears, and even anger, had nothing to do with it, they pushed aside the angel voice, leaving nothing but human talk in its place.

Around the time I got the diary I also made the claw. I got some clay (at first I thought of papier mâché, but decided I wanted something better and besides, I couldn't remember how to make papier mâché) and spent hours bending, twisting, pinching, sometimes screaming and throwing it at the wall (I waited till my mother went to work) because I couldn't get it right.

Finally I told myself I'd never get it right, and settled for a version that didn't try to look just like it, but instead gave me a kind of memory of it. I'd bought a little book on clay which told me how to bake it, and then I painted it, gold with a bit of red glitter, but afterwards I was sorry because the paint took away from the memory. It looked too fake. I thought of using turpentine but decided I'd better leave it alone.

I kept the claw in my drawer, underneath my underwear. Sometimes, sitting in school, or watching television, I imagined the claw inside my clothes, touching me, and I'd get so excited I couldn't stand it. I'd feel like I could burn right through my skin. One time Mrs Becker called on me in English class, to say what some character in Shakespeare said to his mother or something, and I just stammered at her, my mouth half hanging open, while everybody tried not to laugh, whispering things back and forth, until finally Mrs Becker called on Chris Bloom, who always knew everything.

Other times, if my mother or the kids at school were bothering me, I would go home and take out the claw and hold it against me or make it stroke my body, just like his had done, sometimes hard enough to make blood come out. Or else I would just put it next to me while I slept.

My mother kept after me a lot. She wanted me to date more, to go to dances, have lots of boy friends, she wanted all the girls to envy me, and she was scared they pitied me instead. She couldn't stand that.

The funny thing was, I didn't really mind dating. I thought at first that I could never do it again because I had to keep myself clean for the angel, for the baby. And I thought that all the boys would look so clumsy and stupid and thick, their voices all hard and ugly. I thought any time they'd ask me I'd want to laugh or gag. But then I discovered they didn't touch each other at all, boys and the angel. They had nothing to do with each other, despite my being in the middle, like a kind of bridge connecting them. I saw it almost as two different mes, the one that belonged to the angel, and the one that went to the movies with Billy Glaston or Jeffrey Sterner.

But if I didn't mind dating, I didn't care either. I made no effort, and like my mother told me, the bees'll fly around a pot of warm honey, not a glass of cold water. It wasn't like I dressed sloppy or didn't use makeup, that would have made more trouble than it was worth, it was just that I paid no special attention to what boys said, and didn't try to laugh in a nice way, or give boys any special looks, things like that.

But I got dates anyway, sometimes with boys too ugly or dumb or just clumsy to try for the popular girls, boys who automatically looked for someone in their range. I didn't care. If someone asked me to the movies and I wanted to see the picture I went. I knew I couldn't let any boys do anything with me, so what difference did it make who took me? Only, I avoided the really ugly boys, not for myself, but so people wouldn't make fun of me.

One boy got to me, at least a little. His name was Jim Kinney, though around that time he told everyone to call him James, figuring it sounded more adult or intellectual or something. Jim — James — knew more about computers than half of IBM. In fact, when he was just a junior in high school he got permission to use the big computers down in the factory and wrote some program or other that IBM bought for a huge pile of money. He planned to use some of it, he said, to publish a book of his poetry. Poetry and science, Jim said, were 'two horses pulling the same chariot'. He often talked like that. He even showed me some of his poems. He didn't write about nature or love or stuff like that. Jim wrote about truth and knowledge and God, though he said he didn't mean God like in the church.

What he did mean was what got me excited about him. When I read his poems carefully, getting around the fancy words, like 'the sheer blank wall of mortal ignorance', I saw he was writing about the difference between human talk and angel language. He knows, I thought, and got goosepimples, almost like when I could feel the angel claw under my clothes.

But how could an angel visit him? Did they visit boys? The thought upset me the same time it excited me. Maybe a woman angel needed a human man to make her pregnant. Maybe he was also waiting. Out of breath I looked up at him. And saw it wasn't true. He should have been looking at my face, my eyes, testing me the way I would have done him. Instead, he was reading his own poem over my shoulder. 'Should I explain it to you?' he said, when he should have waited for me to say something. I could see he really cared about the human words, whatever he pretended.

That day I gave him back his poems and told him I didn't feel well, and ran home. (Later he told me he thought his poems had made me sick, and we both laughed.) But over the next few days I kept thinking about him.

I'm not sure what made Jim interested in me. He wasn't ugly, and he sure wasn't stupid, he could even play sports pretty good, and for a while he had a car, but it broke down. You'd think he could have gotten any girl he wanted, and wouldn't look at someone like me who never made an effort. But maybe the other girls found him too weird, writing poetry and playing tricks with computers. Too smart. Anyway, his car was already gone by the time he started taking me out.

Once Jim and I got started my mother just about bounced off the walls with happiness. Not only was I acting more normal, but I was doing it with someone who had 'rich' written all over him.

Myself, I didn't really know why I was doing it. I liked being with Jim, I liked when he called me, when he helped me with my homework, or when we went to the movies (which he called 'cinema'), but it still confused me when I thought about the angel. One night Jim and I had gone to a carnival and got home late. I said goodnight to him, and then to my mother (she always waited up for me), and went upstairs laughing at the way some boy had looked so sick coming off the snap-the-whip.

I opened the drawer with my nightgown in it. And then suddenly I started to cry. I'd forgotten the angel. A whole night had gone by and I hadn't thought about him at all. I pushed aside my clothes and grabbed the claw, but then I just threw it down again.

I sat down on the bed and rubbed the tears away, feeling my eye makeup smear. Did I still care? Did I still believe? I opened my diary and stared at the last date. Two years ago. For two whole years I'd had nothing to say. I knew I didn't really stop believing. I couldn't. But I wondered — now that years had gone by, did it still mean anything? Anything more than Jim's poems? Maybe the angel had lied to me and would never come back. Or maybe it had meant what it said, but had forgotten as soon as it left me. Maybe only humans remembered things. How could memory exist in a sky full of fire?

The whole time Jim and I had gone around together I hadn't let him touch me. Well, sometimes we'd hold hands and he'd put an arm around me, but whenever he moved in for something more, even just a kiss, I pushed him away. I had to make up a whole story about how my mother hadn't kissed my father until they were almost engaged, and I really wanted to act different than that but I couldn't help it. I could tell a couple of times Jim was fed up and didn't want to see me any more, but I guess he liked me, or liked having a girlfriend, because he always came back.

But now I thought, if the angel's not coming back, why should I keep so clean for him? I decided the next time Jim tried to kiss me I would let him. The strange thing was, the next night he tried again — we'd gone to the movies and Howard Johnson's, and Jim stopped to show me some craters on the moon on the way home, though we both knew he didn't care about them any more than me — and still I pushed him away. I couldn't make myself do it.

Jim shrugged. 'I'm sorry,' he said in a voice that really meant 'Screw you'. He started walking away from me but I called him. In fact, I called him in a really strange voice, like I'd taken charge, which surprised me as much as him. He came back and held my shoulders and for a moment we looked at each other — not for any real reason, I think, but just because people in the movies always look at each other before they kiss. Part of me wanted to stop, to shove him really hard and run away, but I wouldn't let that happen. I made myself stand there, and when his mouth, already half open, came down towards mine I closed my eyes and kissed him.

I never felt such pain in my life. Like some burning knife coming right up my insides all the way to my face. I screamed, and then I did shove Jim, so hard he fell right on his backside. For a moment he lay there, all bent over, holding his stomach with his face all screwed up and wet with tears or sweat, and I knew the pain had hit him too. He kind of gagged and got to his feet. 'You're sick,' he said, 'you're really, really sick.' He had to keep himself from running as he got away from me.

I walked home slowly, making dumb whimpering noises. Inside I became like two people, one of them miserable that Jim had run off and now no one wanted me, and scared because he was right and they'd lock me up screaming in a straitjacket — and the other shaking with joy because the angel was real, the fire had come because his power had worked its way deep inside me and any day now the angel would come back and give me its baby. And I knew, too, that the first me, the unhappy one, was a fake, built up out of years of acting normal to satisfy my mother and the kids and teachers at school. I'd almost let it take over, convince me the real one had never existed. But the angel had saved me.

Graduation came soon after, saving me from my mother as well, and her constant asking what had happened with me and 'James'. I'd applied to college, mostly because everyone else did, and when the fall came I went off to Albany State. I didn't stay long. The stuff there didn't mean anything more than the stuff in high school. Maybe the other kids got something out of it. But I was waiting for the angel to come back.

I moved down to New York. No reason really. I got a job in the city tax department, sorting forms, making spot checks on people's income tax returns, things like that, and I found an apartment on Queens, one of those streets with six-storey apartment houses where rich people used to live. (My building had a big lobby with even a picture made of tiles on the floor, but the tiles were too faded or broken for me to make it out. The elevator never worked.) And I waited.

Months went by, almost two years really. I'm not sure what I did all that time, how I managed to use up the days. I watched TV, read the paper, sometimes went to people's houses, or movies, or even parties. It didn't make any difference. Now and then one of the men, one of the shy or ugly ones, asked me out, or even made a pass. I never got nasty or aggressive, but none of them ever tried anything again.

Then one weekend I went for a walk in Greenwich Village. I'd taken to walking a lot, all around, though mostly Manhattan. I liked looking at the buildings, sometimes staring up just like a tourist. I liked the way they were so big, so heavy. That day in the village, they were having one of those sidewalk art shows, with the painters standing alongside trying to look relaxed while they watched everybody passing by. I thought of Jim and his poems.

Then, on Bleecker Street, I came to an exhibit of photos. Most of them showed buildings or people bent over in funny ways, or tricks, like a cat jumping out of someone's chest, but one of them — I almost didn't see it, or maybe I saw it subconsciously, because I walked right past it at first, then stopped just like a hand had grabbed my shoulders and turned me around. The picture wasn't large, 8″ by 11″ I later found out. It showed nothing by light. Wavy sheets of light with slivers of dark buried inside them.

I just about grabbed the woman standing beside the photos. 'That picture,' I said. 'Did you take that?'

'No,' she said, frightened I was going to attack her, or the exhibit. 'No, they're all by different people. I'm just taking a turn —'

'How much is it?'

'Fifty dollars.'

I checked my wallet though I knew I'd only brought fifteen. 'Shit,' I said, then I did grab her jacket. 'I'm going home to get some more money. Don't sell that picture to anyone else. Do you understand?' She nodded, her mouth hanging open.

I had to meet the person who'd taken the picture, but first I had to get the thing itself. I couldn't stand the idea of someone else buying it. Someone who didn't know. It would have taken too long to go home, but I knew someone who lived pretty close, on East 6th Street. I pushed through the crowds, begging God to make Joan be at home. She was, and loaned me the money. I think she was scared not to.

When I got back the photo was still there, but the woman had put a little sign next to it saying 'Sold'. I must have scared her too. I gave her the money and stood shifting from one leg to the other while she carefully wrapped it for me.

'Listen,' I said to her once I had it in my hand, 'the person who took this, where can I find her?'

She looked scared, her eyes moving away from me to see who might help her if I got really crazy. 'How do you know it's a woman?' she said.

'Please,' I told her. 'You've got to help me.'

'Well,' she said, 'I guess it's okay.' She gave me a name and an address near Wall Street. I nearly knocked over some people looking for a cab. The building turned out to be an old office building reaching some twenty storeys above the dirty luncheonettes and cheap clothing stores. I stood there staring at it, thinking the goddamn woman had lied to me, until I looked in the lobby and saw the doorman sitting on a wooden stool and reading the *Post*. Then I realized it must be one of those places where they'd converted some of the empty offices into apartments.

The doorman didn't wear a uniform or anything like that, just jeans and a dirty sweater, but he still wouldn't let me up until he'd checked with the woman. I didn't know what I'd do if she didn't answer. I had planned to sit by her door if she wasn't there but the doorman wouldn't let me do that, I knew, and I didn't want to have to stand on the street.

She was there. When the doorman asked who I was I told him, 'Just say I want to ask about her picture. Her photo.' He made a face and repeated it. It seemed like a whole minute before the scratchy voice said to come up.

When I got off the elevator she was already standing in the faded yellow hall, looking a little sick in the fluorescent light. She was tall, much taller than me, with a wide face and straight dull brown hair that didn't help it any. I only noticed these things, and her loose blue cotton dress and white plastic sandals, because it's the kind of thing my mother used to point out. But really I watched the way her hands jumped about looking for a relaxed way to hold themselves, while her eyes, looking very glary behind blue tinted glasses, jumped onto the package I held. 'You said photo,' she said. 'Just one? Which one do you mean? Where did you get it?'

I tore off the wrapping and held it up. Her breath sounded like something jumping down her throat. 'Where did you get this?' I said. 'Tell me what it is.'

She started telling me all sorts of things, about light, and filters, and double exposures, all sorts of things, talking very fast, like she didn't want me to interrupt. But I said nothing, just held the photo, refusing to give it up to her hands that kept clutching at it like she didn't even know they were doing it. And she wouldn't look at me, not for more than a second, except she kept doing that, looking at me, then jumping her eyes away again. And suddenly she stopped all the stuff she was saying, because she knew, and I knew, she could have taken that picture with a snapshot camera, with an old Brownie like the one my mother kept in her bedroom because my father had used it as a kid.

I said, 'It's him, isn't it? It's him.'

And suddenly she started saying how she shouldn't have sold it, she never meant to sell it, she still kept the negative, she just needed money so bad, she never thought anyone would *know*.

I don't know who grabbed who first, but somehow we were holding each other and kissing, and couldn't stop, and crying. And the fire didn't hurt, or not so much as that other time, with Jim. It hurt, it hurt her too, she made a kind of choked sound, but it hurt more like lowering yourself into a hot bath where it comes up first around your legs and then your groin and finally your breasts. And then the fire is gone because you've made it all the way in, and it feels so good, so strong, stronger than anything, with the sweat pouring off your face and the steam beating the breath out of you.

Her name was Jo, short for Josephine I thought, but she said no, it was always Jo, and we sort of moved in together, even though we both kept our own places. You'd think I would have worried about us being, you know, both girls, but that never bothered either of us, it was the angel that brought us together, not anything else. When I touched her, her breasts or below, it felt really nice, very soft and warm, but also I saw it as somewhere the angel had touched. Sometimes one of us would make claws with our hands and run it down the other's stomach, but we always stopped that right away, like it embarrassed us. I never showed her the claw I'd made.

The really strange thing was, neither of us ever talked about it. We just kept copies of the photo up in each of our apartments, facing the bed in mine, over the refrigerator in hers because even though she wasn't fat she said the kitchen was her favourite room, and sometimes we'd sit or lie together, staring at it, even make love after looking at it. But we could never make ourselves talk.

We wanted to. At least I did. Sometimes, usually at breakfast for some reason, like the morning gave me a new start, I would try to think of how to begin, and Jo would also look like she wanted to say something. Then one of us would talk about the weather or the brand of orange juice or someone at work, and that was it for another day. I never even found out when the angel had come to her or where.

Maybe if we could have talked about the angel we would have stayed together longer. I don't know. In everything else we were so different. Jo was very artsy. She did television things, not programs or stories, just pictures of her moving very slowly or even standing completely still, all wrapped up in aluminium foil. She did it herself of course, she'd gotten her own camera, and then she sent tapes to art galleries, where I guess they showed them instead of pictures. And she used to wear those old saggy dresses she got in some filthy shop on St Mark's Place, not just because they were cheap, I offered to give her money for real clothes, but because she liked them.

Her friends were artsy too, doing things like writing stories that made no sense, and they had to publish them themselves on really cheap paper because no regular magazine wanted to buy them. Her friends all thought of me as weird or funny or something, because I worked in an office and didn't wear torn clothes, and they didn't understand how Jo and I had gotten together. But that didn't matter. I knew that Jo didn't care about her 'friends' any more than I cared about mine. It was just a game she was playing while she waited for the angel to come back.

For the first few months we were very careful with each other, very polite, except when we looked at the picture or made love. But after a while, we started to fight. About clothes, or where to go to eat, or people we knew, never anything that mattered. Because only the angel mattered. And we didn't talk about that.

So we started fighting, and then making excuses not to see each other, and finally one night I went to her place after work and let myself in with the key, and there over the refrigerator door was a note saying she'd gone to San Francisco for some 'video festival' and didn't know when she was coming back. She'd taken the picture.

I got angry. I called up her friends and asked for her address but they said she didn't have one yet and of course she'd send it to me. I got really depressed too, thinking of how to kill myself without any pain. Yet at the same time I knew it didn't matter. I still had my copy of her picture. That's what really counted.

I don't mean my anger or depression were nothing or they went away just like that. As far as I can tell it hit me as hard as anyone else's who'd gotten dumped like that, and it lasted almost longer than the actual time we'd spent together. The thing is, for other people those sorts of feelings are all they've got. But I was waiting for the angel, and anything else just got added on top of that.

The experience with Jo did have one big effect on me. I didn't want to be alone any more. Like when I decided I couldn't give up feelings if I couldn't keep the angel language, now I knew I wanted people, lovers, at least if the angel wasn't coming back. I didn't forget my promise and keeping myself clean. I just figured that if I didn't really care, if I remembered I was only doing it 'until', then it wouldn't change anything.

So I began to date, not just to pass the time or see a movie, but for the person. The first time some guy tried to kiss me, a divorced guy named Bobby, I didn't know what to do. Would the pain hit me? Maybe it went all right with Jo only because the angel had also come to her. But no. Being with Jo had already changed me. I could kiss or let someone touch me — or more — and nothing happened. I mean no pain.

One thing — I made sure not to get pregnant. I used a diaphragm but I also took the pill, secretly, so people wouldn't know I did both and once some guy discovered my pills and he called me sick, like Jim had done, and said I should see a shrink. I told him to go to hell and it was worth any trouble not to get anything of *his* growing inside me.

Sometimes I wondered, what if the angel came back and the pills made it so I couldn't get pregnant with him either? But I didn't think a bunch of pills could stop the angel.

I didn't really live with anybody, though I sort of went steady a few times, once with another girl, a typist from work named Karen. Karen worried a lot about people at work or her family finding out about us. Once we went away to a hotel for the weekend and she brought along her cousin who lived with a guy, so we could make it look like two normal couples, even registering that way, then sneaking into the right rooms when no one was looking. I didn't really mind, though it bothered me that I had to watch the way I looked at her in restaurants or places like that. I knew how to hide things myself.

One guy even wanted to marry me. His name was Allen and I met him in my cousin Jack's house. He'd spent some years in the navy which was why he'd never gotten married, he said. He liked to show slides of all the countries he'd visited, and sometimes he imitated the funny way the people talked. He said it amazed him how many languages there were. Without thinking I said, 'They're all just human languages.' He looked at me funny and asked what I meant. I told him nothing.

When Allen said we should get married I didn't know what to do. I really liked him a lot, he was the only person I knew who enjoyed walking around the city as much as me, he could even show me things I'd missed. And I was sick of my crummy apartment.

But I didn't know what marriage would mean. Did it count in some way that dating and sex didn't? Allen wanted to get married in a church. His brother Michael was a minister and Allen liked to joke about Mike needing the business. Would that mean more than marriage by a judge? I didn't think so. Marriage was still something two humans did, whatever the church said. Why should the angel care about marriage any more than he cared about two people riding the subway together? Nothing humans did meant anything. Or maybe the other way around. Everything humans did had to mean something because humans couldn't stand it otherwise. Only the angel did things that didn't mean something else, something explained in words or feelings.

Still, when Allen insisted I give him an answer I said no. He got really angry, said I had to tell him why. Give him a reason. I told him I didn't have one and that was the truth. Refusing to marry Allen was the closest I ever came to angel talk, because after I'd gone through everything in my mind, I ended up saying no, for no reason at all.

Of course Allen didn't understand that. He'd go back and forth between begging me and screaming at me, sometimes calling me up late at night and just about biting through the phone. He got my mother on his side and the two of them went after me so much I sometimes thought of going out to San Francisco like Jo and leaving a note on the refrigerator. Later, when I got pregnant,

Allen figured I'd said no because I was already screwing someone else, and he sent letters to everyone calling me a prostitute in about six or seven languages. 'Prostitute' was the one word he'd learned in all the countries he'd visited.

The angel came on Saturday morning when I couldn't sleep. Sometimes I wonder, if I'd stayed in bed would the angel have broken through the window, or would he have flown right past the house, and I'd never have seen him again? But the rash had stopped me from sleeping, and maybe the angel made the rash in some way.

The thing was, the night before the angel came, I'd spotted some funny red bumps all over my stomach and backside. They didn't itch, but I still spread Calordryl all over, and I guess I didn't wait long enough for it to dry because the sheets got all sticky. That, and thinking about Allen, woke me really early. When I couldn't get back to sleep I decided to go for a walk. It was late May and sunny, very pretty with all the trees full of leaves, especially a few blocks away where the houses got much fancier, with regular lawns, almost like Long Island.

That's where the angel came for me, right in front of a grey brick split level with a Cadillac in the driveway and probably another one in the garage. Maybe the angel liked Cadillacs. I didn't see it coming at all this time. I was looking at some flowers with really pretty colours and little coloured rocks spread all through them.

Suddenly I turned — maybe I heard the wings — and saw him, almost right up against me, his blank eyes, the huge wings, one of them almost brushing the house's picture window. His mouth hung open, really wide, but I didn't hear anything. I didn't see any teeth, only a long tongue that kept flicking back and forth. Then he pushed me to the ground.

I had trouble getting off my clothes. I was only wearing a light jacket, but his claws kept getting in the way until I almost shouted at him to let me do it. Then I lay back, trying to stare in his eyes, see his world again, while I waited for his claws to stroke me, for my voice to explode in his sounds, his perfect language.

Instead, he just shoved himself at me, pushing me into the wet dirt, his wings thumping the lawn and the street, his tongue slapping my cheek, my neck, my forehead, burning the skin. I wanted to scream, or cry, or beg, but I couldn't. I wouldn't. If he wouldn't let me speak angel language, I wasn't going to give him the satisfaction of hearing anything human coming out of me.

At the same time I thought, it's my fault, I betrayed him. I ruined myself. I became too human. But now, I wonder, maybe it just happened that way and would have been the same if I'd never gone with Allen or Jo or anyone.

I didn't watch him leave. I just lay there on the ground, curled up and hitting the grass with my fist. Finally, I got scared someone would see me, naked and crazy like that, and lock me up. I got my clothes and ran home.

Five times the next week I almost tore up the picture, the one Jo had left. Ten times in the next month I almost tried to call Jo herself and ask if the angel had come back to her too. I ended up doing nothing. What difference could any of it make now that the angel had come back and shut me out?

When I found out I was pregnant I didn't know what to do. I almost went to get an abortion. I didn't know if I could, if whatever they did would work any better than the pills had. I was wild. I walked up and down the streets in midtown, waving my arms in a pouring rain and stopping every now and then to make a noise like a roar or a shriek. I couldn't figure out if I was afraid or angry or thrilled, but all the choices sounded pretty rotten, all of them feelings, talk. I wanted to see the angel world and all I could see was my goddamn belly getting bigger and bigger.

One thing I knew. I didn't want any doctor to deliver the baby. I wanted to do it myself. I'd never even seen a baby being born, outside of the movies they showed the girls in high school, and of course they only showed ordinary babies. This one I didn't even know how long it would take, the regular nine months, or ten, or six, or what. But I just decided if the angel was using a human woman then probably it wouldn't run that different from a regular birth. And I didn't want any doctors near me.

So I read books and took courses and did exercises, and when I figured the time was getting close I rented a house by a lake — it was someone's summer house but they had it insulated for winter too — and stocked it with lots of food and any medicine I could get without a prescription. Then I set everything up — I'd gotten some books on midwifing so I knew pretty much what I needed. And I waited.

It was horrible. The pain filled the whole room, it rolled off the walls at me, it went on for hours and hours so that I thought the kid must have braced itself inside and would never come out. I was scared I was going to die. The angel was killing me because I'd betrayed it. If only I could phone a hospital, tell them I needed a caesarean. But I'd torn out the wires in case I'd get scared and want an ambulance, and now, when I really needed one, I couldn't call anywhere. I wondered if I could somehow drive my car, at least down to the snowmobile centre down the road. But when I tried to walk I couldn't even get out of bed.

It went on for so long I started seeing things. I imagined myself outside, with snow all around, and the angel circling way over my head.

When the baby did come out it came so quickly I didn't know it had happened. I went on pushing, with the kid lying there on the soaking wet sheets. When I realized I'd done it I lay back, shaking so much the whole bed made this awful squeaking noise. Probably it had squeaked like that for hours, and I was cursing and crying so much I never noticed. I picked up the kid and cut the cord and cleaned him off as best as I could. I had to get rid of the afterbirth and get him breathing and everything, and I knew I better do it all at once, because if I stopped I'd just fall asleep. At last I held him up so I could look at him.

A haze or something must have covered my eyes because it took awhile before I could actually see him, what he really looked like. When I did see I just stared at him. Wings grew on his back, small, dirty white, not feathers but sort of rough, almost like cheap leather, the kind you get on pocketbooks bought at one of those downtown discount stores. For the first time I realized the angel's wings were like that, leather and not feathers at all. Even while I stared at him his sad little wings fluttered a couple of times and then came right off. They fell on my leg. I screamed and knocked them onto the floor. When I looked for them a couple of days later they were gone. Crumbled right into dust, maybe.

His hands did the same thing. I don't mean they fell off, but they changed, from claws to ordinary baby hands, the hard curved claw fingers shrinking to stubby human ones.

There's nothing left, I thought. All that pain for nothing. But I was wrong. He had his father's eyes, cold, very hard, and empty. Even now you can see it, not all the time, but sometimes he'll put down his truck or his cap gun, or else he'll just stand there when some other kid throws the ball to him. Then you can see that metal coldness take over his eyes, and you know he's looking right past you, into a world of lightning, and fire that jumps into the sky, a world where the sounds say everything, and not just words.

He's going to find it hard, much harder than I ever did. I only saw it, only spoke to it once. But he's got to look at that world all the time. And live in this one.

DAVID REDD
ON THE DECK OF
THE FLYING BOMB

First Evening

As a stowaway, hidden like an unseen parasite, I can use the lifeboat cameras to observe the workings of the Flying Bomb and its crew. My lifeboat is one bead in the necklace of three hundred lifeboats strung along the rim of the upper deck: no inquiring crewman will think to examine my little hermit cell until I lift it from the deck and glide away. This is a strange behemoth that I shall be leaving: a creature so vast that on its deck there is no sensation of motion. The Flying Bomb is four miles long and two miles wide, and its curving underbelly is over a mile deep. On its upper deck the buildings form a large town where the crewmen live and work. On the lower deck the maintenance staff move like pale ants in caverns, tending the machines which keep this artificial world airborne. And further below is the unstable cargo which will explode novalike when the Flying Bomb reaches its target.

I shall reconnoitre through the nearby buildings like an enemy spy — not that I am an enemy — and through my espionage learn the best moment to escape. The lifeboat supplies include several one-size uniforms, so I can imitate the chameleon and change my disguise to suit my surroundings. However, on this first day exploration in person would be too dangerous. I have studied the deck through the monitors. These well-spent hours have rewarded me with a full knowledge of the nearer buildings — the sick bay, kitchens, dormitories and married quarters, recreation rooms, chaplain's cabin, and so on. Tomorrow, armed with this knowledge, I shall venture out.

Second Evening

Today I learned the location of the bridge, the nerve centre from which information and commands radiate to all parts of the Flying Bomb. Emerging from my lifeboat, I walked through a sector appropriate to the hour and to the uniform I wore. The buildings were like holiday chalets, with timber panels and shining windows in standard metal frames. The brown decking planks were solid under my boots: the polished sun-darkened bones of an entire forest.

Crewmen passed me about their business, or came to life momentarily behind windows, but they did not query my presence. One man seen in the lifeboat would have demanded attention: one man seen in the crowd was nothing. I followed an unsuspecting officer who might lead me to the bridge, but he entered a restricted zone and only my careful researches of yesterday saved me. Turning away, I wondered how the crewmen could avoid the myriad pitfalls inevitable in so complex an organisation. In my journey I had passed signs, notices, training halls, even a squad on a shed construction exercise, but although I had seen these things I had learned nothing. My learning began when I watched a private take something from a wall dispenser labelled INFORMATION. I followed him and picked up three colourful booklets. An adjacent poster reminded me: DO YOUR DUTY. THE PENALTIES ARE SEVERE. I retreated.

In the sanctuary of a nearby recreation room I examined the booklets. LOCATION. ORGANISATION. PROCEDURE. So this was how each crewman of the Flying Bomb was kept fully aware of his part in the system. All men had to keep themselves informed of their rights and restrictions: failure was punished by loss of benefits or worse. These booklets gave me a complete knowledge of the basic organisation. Every crewman, however newly recruited, was given the same knowledge, and theoretically could make himself master of the Flying Bomb.

By studying these guides I have prepared my route towards the bridge, the captain and the navigational data I require. I am amazed that this information is freely available. Most amazing of all, the booklets describe the Enemy which the Flying Bomb will destroy.

Third Evening

Today I gained admission to the bridge. At first I roamed the adjoining corridors as a waiter, bearing beakers of coffee from one room to another. In this role I watched the rituals of relationship among the superior officers, and I memorised their undocumented gestures and procedures until I could mimic the symbols of power. In an empty washroom I became a lieutenant.

On this stage there were set formulae for entrances and exits: the cues which I had to learn. I found a lecture theatre opposite the bridge, and by joining some officers for a training session I obtained a window seat overlooking the glass-sided central control room. While the other students took notes on the control of subordinates, I took notes on the bridge and its inhabitants. The navigating officers were extremely busy. During the session I also studied the lecturer and officers: they appeared unconcerned about their approaching doom when the Flying Bomb will destroy itself and its target. Perhaps they too were actors.

The lecture, on projection of authority, aided my entry to the bridge. Outside the hall I noticed a private at the door of the bridge, struggling to trigger the door release while holding six coffee cups. I smiled and approached him like a true lieutenant, lifting three cups from his hands. 'I'll take these, private. You open the door.' He obeyed swiftly and gratefully. 'Couldn't find a tray, sir.'

'Next time, improvise something or make two trips.' I followed him inside, my eyes busy as I set down the cups on the tabletop. The captain was instantly recognizable by his uniform and his authoritative bearing. Beyond him I saw two navigators at a display panel. But any delay here would arouse suspicion. 'Remember what I told you, private.'

'Yes, sir. Thank you, sir.' And though it hurt me to go I walked unhesitatingly out of the bridge. The incident had been excellent preparation for tomorrow.

I returned to my lifeboat via the lower deck: curiosity took me down to see the assembled power units, levitatory devices, and battle weapons. As usual the crewmen were working with apparent indifference to their final destiny: one group of maintenance men had invented a new coupling lubricator. I was not sure whether to pity or to admire their pointless endeavour. I then examined the cargo through a viewer, but the screen showed only more machinery, with camouflage nets and inspection ladders leading downwards. The cargo itself was hidden further below.

In all my travels I was unchallenged. My outward conformity ensured my acceptance.

Fourth Evening

The dream this morning upset me. I was in a metal coffin, floating within a greater emptiness: beside me were two human skulls shining in the darkness, one still wearing ancient earphones. I ached with sympathy for these lost creatures, but I could not help them. A voice whispered: 'All dark past the terminator . . . what have they done?' Then I awoke. I would never help them now.

I walked to the bridge still depressed by the dream. With little hope of success I carried in some data sheets borrowed from the maintenance deck, and said that a manual check was required. To my surprise the officers were very helpful, even demonstrating the operation of the display units. 'And if you want more checks any time, come in again.'

The bridge was crowded, and I had no chance to obtain the co-ordinates. Nevertheless, my time was not wasted: I overheard an argument between the captain and a senior officer. The officer wanted the captain to inspect our cargo, which served as both payload and fuel. The captain refused: 'It's safer left alone.' — 'It needs watching, but it's harmless in itself.' — 'Not when we're burning it up!' Listening to this, my previous admiration for the captain lessened swiftly. He was a slave to his orders. The flight was scheduled to take ten days: a slow journey, exposing the Flying Bomb to many outside dangers. Faster flight, to reduce these risks, would have increased the danger from the cargo. The captain mentioned this and said he was glad his orders had decided his flight pattern for him. I was sickened: a captain should make his own decisions. Even I, a stowaway, could do that. I was right in wishing to leave.

Taking the data sheets back to the lower deck, I said the next batch would need checking tomorrow. Those papers would be my passport to escape.

On the upper deck, a corporal stopped me. 'Away from your post, private? Where are you going?'

Confused, I indicated my lifeboat. 'Just on my way back, sir!'

'Then jump to it! If I see you off limits again I'll report you!'

I hurried away, thankful the encounter had gone no further. But why had the ambassador of Order questioned me? The booklets are silent.

Soon it will not matter. The Flying Bomb soars on, a shadow in the sunset, over plains of rippling wheat, through the smoke of burning cities, onward to its doom. I am a temporary resident, and will soon depart.

Fifth Afternoon

It began perfectly. I collected the papers, went up to the bridge, and spent the coffee break with the navigators. I obtained both our position and the route to safety. But while I was still on the bridge, the captain called us all to the main vision panel. 'It's happened, men. We were afraid of this.' I saw the image of a distant Flying Bomb, dark against the orange sky. 'Collision course. We'll have to fight.' While he alerted the crew, I raced back to my lifeboat. Inside, I sealed the hatch and began the separation sequence. I cut the external power supply: to my horror the internal power died also. I reversed the switch and power returned. I wept. The lifeboat drew its power from the Flying Bomb: its independent reserves were a sham. I could never leave.

But other than that, my escape went perfectly.

I am staying in the lifeboat: there is nothing else to do. On the monitors I watch the approaching enemy. It could be a mirage, an atmospheric reflection of our own Flying Bomb, except that I can see the weapons of its lower deck puffing smoke, and can feel the detonations of shells bursting against our hull.

The corporal just opened my hatch. 'Don't you know your battle station? Get down and guard the payload!' He shouted his orders and disappeared. He is under the illusion that I am a member of the crew. I shall remain here and watch the battle until —

Corporal returns: 'Get down there!'

I go.

JOHN SHIRLEY
WHAT CINDY SAW

The people from the clinic were very nice. Of course, they lived on the shell, and people who lived on the shell often behaved nicely, and with uniformity of purpose, like the little magnetically-moved toy players on an electric football game. They seemed very sincere, and they had a number of quirky details making them ever so much more realistic. The way Doctor Gainsborough was always plucking things from the corner of his eye, for example. And the way Nurse Rebeck was forever rubbing her crusty red nose and complaining of allergies.

Doctor Gainsborough admitted, with every appearance of sincerity, that, yes, life was mysterious and ultimately Cindy might well be right about the way things were under what she called 'the shell'. Doctor Gainsborough couldn't be sure that she was wrong — but, Cindy, they said, we have our doubts, serious doubts, and we would like you to consider our doubts, and our reasoning, and give our viewpoint a chance. Doctor Gainsborough had known Cindy would respond to his pretence of politely considering her ideas. Cindy was, after all, fairminded.

And she simply refused to respond at all when people told her she was crazy and seeing things.

Yes, Cindy, Doctor Gainsborough said, you could be right. But still, we have severe doubts, so it's best that we keep up the treatments. All right?

All right, Doctor Gainsborough.

So they'd given her the stelazine and taught her how to make jewellery. And she stopped talking about the shell, after a while. She became the clinic's pet. It was Doctor Gainsborough himself who took her home, after 'just three months this time, and no shock treatments'. He let her off in front of her parents' house, and she reached in through the car window to shake his hand. She even smiled. He smiled back and crinkled his blue eyes, and she straightened, and took her hand back, and stepped onto the kerb. He was pulled away down the street; pulled away by the car he drove. She was left with the house. She knew she was turning toward the house. She knew she was walking towards it. She knew she was climbing the steps. But all the time she felt the pull. The pull from the shell was so subtle that you could think: *I know I'm turning and walking and climbing*, when all the time you weren't. You were being pulled through all those motions, so it wasn't you doing it at all.

But best you think it's you.

She had practised it, that steering amongst the obstacle course of the mind's free associations. She did it now, and she managed to suppress her sense of the pull.

She felt fine. She felt fine because she felt nothing. Nothing much. Just . . . just normal. The house looked like a house, the trees looked like trees. Picture book house, picture book trees. The house seemed unusually quiet, though. No one home? And where was Doobie? The dog wasn't tied up out front this time. She'd always been afraid of the Doberman. She was relieved he was gone. Probably gone off with the family.

She opened the door — funny, their not being home and leaving the door unlocked. It wasn't like Dad. Dad was paranoid. He even admitted it. 'I smoke Paranoid Pot,' he said. He and Mom smoked pot and listened to old Jimi Hendrix records and screwed listlessly on the sofa, when they thought Cindy was asleep.

'Hello? Dad? Mom?' Cindy called, now. No answer.

Good. She felt like being at home alone. Playing a record, watching TV. Nothing to cope with. No random factors, or scarcely any. And none that weren't harmless. Watching TV was like looking into a kaleidoscope: it was constantly shifting, going through its motions with its own style of intricacy, but there was never anything really unexpected. Or almost never. Once Cindy had turned it on and watched a Japanese monster movie. And the Japanese monster movie had been too much like a caricature of the shell. Like they were mocking her by showing what they knew. What they knew she knew.

Now, she told herself. Think about *now*. She turned from the entry-hall to the archway opening into the living room.

In the living room was what looked very much like a sofa. If it had been in the rec-room of the clinic she'd have been quite sure it was a sofa. Here, though, it sat corpulent and dusty bluegrey in the twilight of the living room, scrolled arm-rests a little too tightly wound; it sprawled ominously in the very centre of the room. There was something unnatural in its texture. It had a graininess she'd never noticed before. Like one of those ugly, irregular scraps of jelly-fish at the seashore, a membranous thing whose stickiness has given it a coating of sand.

Even more disorienting was the sofa-thing's ostensibly familiar shape. It was shaped like a sofa. But there was something bloated about it, something tumescent. It was just a shade bulkier than it should have been. As if it were swollen from eating.

So that's their secret, she thought. It's the sofa. Normally I don't notice anything unusual about it — because normally I don't catch it just after it has eaten.

She wondered who it had eaten. One of her sisters? The house was silent. Maybe it had eaten the whole family. But then Mother had said that they wouldn't be home when she got there: she remembered now. One of the nurses had told Doctor Gainsborough. Sometimes the stelazine made Cindy forget things.

They had gone out to dinner. They wanted to go out to dinner, probably, one last time before Cindy came home. It was embarrassing to go out to dinner with Cindy. Cindy had a way of denouncing things. 'You're always denouncing things, Cindy,' Dad said. 'You ought to mellow out. You're a pain in the ass when you do that shit.' Cindy would denounce the waitress, and then maybe the tables, the tablecloths, the folds in the tablecloth. 'It's the symmetry in the checker-pattern on the table that reveals the deception,' she would say earnestly, like a TV commentator talking about communist terrorism. 'This constant imposition of symmetrical pattern is an attempt to delude us into a sense of harmony with our environment that isn't there at all.'

'I know you're precocious, Cindy,' her Dad would say, brushing crumbs of French bread from his beard or maybe tugging on one of his ear-rings, 'but you're still a pain in the ass.'

'It could be,' Cindy said aloud to the sofa, 'that you've eaten one of my sisters. I don't really mind that. But I must hastily and firmly assure you that you are not going to eat *me*.'

Still, she wanted to find out more about the sofa-thing. Cautiously.

She went to the kitchen, fetched a can-opener and a flashlight, and returned to the living room.

She shone the light on the thing that sat on the polished wooden parquet floor.

The sofa-thing's legs, she saw now, were clearly fused to the floor: they seemed to be growing out of it. Cindy nodded to herself. What she was seeing was a kind of blossom. It must have roots far underground.

It quivered, self-consciously in the beam of her flashlight.

With the flashlight in her left hand — she could have turned on the overhead light, but she knew she'd need the flashlight for the caverns under the shell — she approached the sprawling, bluegrey thing, careful not to get *too* close. In her right hand was the can-opener.

All the while, she seemed to hear a backseat driver saying: This isn't part of the programme. You should go upstairs and watch TV and move from moment to moment thinking safely, steering around the obstacles, turning the wheel away from the dangerous clumps of association, pretending you don't know what you know.

But it was too late, her stelazine was nearly worn off and the couch had startled her into a wrong turn, and now she was on a side road in a foreign suburb and she didn't know the route back to the familiar highway. There were no policemen she might ask, no mental cops like Doctor Gainsborough.

So Cindy crept toward the sofa-thing. She decided that the sofa couldn't hurt her unless she sat on it. If you sat on it, it would curl up, enfold you. Venus flytrap.

She knelt by its legs. Sensing her intent, it bucked a little, dust rising from its cushions. It contracted, the cushions humping. It made an awful sound.

She began to work on its legs, where they joined the floor. For thirty-eight minutes she worked busily with the can-opener.

The sofa-thing made a series of prolonged, piteous sounds. Her arm ached, but the can-opener was surprisingly sharp. Soon she had the cavity under the sofa partly exposed; you could see it under the flap-edge of the shell. Cindy took a deep breath, and prised the flap so it opened wider. It was dark in there. Musky smell; musky and faintly metallic, like lubricant for a motor. And a faint under-scent of rot.

By degrees, working hard, she rolled back the skin of the floor around the sofa. Nature was ingenious; the skin had looked like a hardwood parquet floor till now. It had been hard and solid and appropriately grained. Marvellous camouflage. The skin was hard — but not as hard as it looked. You could peel it back like the bark of a tree, if you were patient and didn't mind aching fingers. Cindy didn't mind.

The sofa-thing's keening rose to a crescendo, so loud and shrill Cindy had to move back and clap her hands over her ears.

And then, the sofa folded in on itself. Its sirening folded too, muffled like a scream trying to escape from a hand clamped over a small child's mouth.

The sofa was like a sea anemone closing up; it deflated, shrank, vanished, sucked down into a dark wound in the centre of the living room floor. The house was quiet once more.

Cindy shone the flashlight into the wound. It was damp, oozing, red flecked with yellow. The house's blood didn't gush, it bled in droplets, like perspiration. The thick, vitreous underflesh shuddered and drew back when she prodded it with her can-opener.

She tucked the can-opener into her boot, and knelt by the wound for a better look. She shone the flashlight's beam into the deepness, into the secret, into the undershell. . .

The house supposedly had no basement. Nevertheless, beneath the living room floor was a chamber. It was about the same size as the living room. Its walls were gently concave and slickly wet — but not organic. The wetness was a kind of machine lubrication. In the centre of the cable was a column, the understem of the creature that had masqueraded as her house. The column, she reflected, was actually more of a stalk; a thick stalk made of cables. Each cable was thick as her Dad's forearm, and they wound about one another like the strands in a powerline. The sofa must have been sucked into its natural hiding place, compressed within the stalk.

She wondered why the house hadn't struck till today . . . Why hadn't it got them all while they were sleeping? But probably the

undershell people, the programmers, hadn't bred it to be a
ravenous, unselective carnivore. It was there for the elimination of
select people — she realised this must be the explanation for
the disappearance of their houseguests. Mom had brought four
houseguests home in the last two years, bedded each one on the
sofa, and each of them hadn't been there for breakfast. Awfully
curious, awfully coincidental, Cindy had thought, every house-
guest deciding to leave the house before breakfast. Now Cindy
knew that they hadn't left the house at all. They'd become part of
it. Probably that was what had happened to Doobie — Mom
usually wouldn't let him sleep in the house, and never allowed him
up on the sofa. But her sister Belinda sometimes let Doobie in after
Mom had gone to bed; the dog must have snuck onto the sofa for
a nap, the sofa's genetically programmed eating hour had come
around, and it had done to Doobie what a sea anemone does to a
minnow. Enfolded, paralysed, and digested him.

Cindy didn't mind. She'd always hated Doobie.

She lay face down, peering into the gap in the house's skin. The
under-floor was about fourteen feet beneath her. She considered
dropping to the sub-world, to explore. Cindy shook her head.
Best go for help. Show them what she'd found.

A funny feeling in her stomach warned her to look up . . .

The living room archway was gone. It had sealed off. The
windows were gone. A sort of scar tissue had grown over them.
She had alarmed the creature, cutting into it. So it had trapped
her.

Cindy made a small, high, 'Uh!' sound in her throat. The walls
were bending inward. She stood, and went to the nearest wall,
pressed her hands flat against it. It should have felt like hard
plaster, but it depressed under her fingers, taking her handprint
like clay. Softening. The house would ooze in on her, collapsing
on itself like a hill in an L.A. mudslide, and it would pulp her and
squeeze the juices from her and drink.

She turned to the gap she'd made in the floor. Its edges were
curling up like paper becoming ash. But it was closing, too. She
got a good grip on the flashlight, knelt, and wriggled through the
opening, dropping to the floor below. The impact stung the balls
of her feet.

Cindy straightened, breathing hard, and looked around.

Tunnels opened from the chamber on both sides, stretching as far as she could see to the right and left. She stepped into the right-hand tunnel. The ceiling was just two feet overhead; it was curved and smooth. She walked slowly, feeling her way with one hand, shining her flashlight beam at the floor. The darkness was rich with implications, and Cindy felt her nerve falter. She had a vice-squeezing sensation at her temples and a kind of greasy electricity in her tongue. She tried to picture the flashlight's beam as a raygun's laser, straight and brightly furious, burning the darkness away — but the light was weak, and set only a small patch of the darkness afire. Gradually, though, her eyes adjusted, and the darkness seemed less dense, less oppressively pregnant, the flashlight beam no longer important. At intervals the oblong of light picked out what looked like transparent fishing lines passing from floor to ceiling. The plastic wires came in irregularly-spaced sheaves of eight or nine. Sometimes there was hardly room to squeeze between them. Then, she'd sidle through, twisting this way and that. When she brushed a wire, it would resonate like a guitar string, but with an overtone to its hum that was like the call of a desert insect. She sensed, somehow, that the wires had to do with events in the upper world. They certainly weren't installed by the utility company, she said to herself.

She came to a place where the wall was transparent in a patch big as her two hands put together. It was a little cloudy, but Cindy could see through it into another chamber; two men sat in the chamber at a metal card-table. They were playing cards, the little white rectangles in their hands marked with mazes and mandalas instead of the usual kings and queens and jacks and spades. Each man was hunched over his hand, deep in concentration. One sat with his back to her. He was the smaller man; he had grey hair. The other was a round-faced man; stocky, a little overweight, his brown beard streaked with white. The bigger man wore a rumpled jacket and trousers of a contemporary cut; the other wore a threadbare suit many decades outdated. The room looked like a jail cell. There were two bunks, a toilet, trays of half-eaten food, empty beer-cans lying about under the table. 'It's your bid, Mister Fort,' said the bearded man, with humorous formality. 'Right you are, Mister Dick,' said the other man lightly. He slapped a card face-up on the table and said, 'M.C. Escher against

Aztec Maze,' The other man sighed. 'Ah, you've locked again. You win. It's not fair: you had decades to practise, playing against Bierce . . . Dammit I wish they'd let us smoke . . .'

Cindy banged on the glass, and shouted, but she couldn't make them hear her. Or perhaps they pretended not to. She shrugged, and went on.

Another ten strides onward, something glimmered on the left, reflecting her flashlight's beam. It was a long, vertical, rectangular mirror, set flush into the wall. The mirror distorted Cindy's reflection, making her seem ludicrously elongated. She reached out to touch it, and accidentally brushed one of the wires; the transparent wire thrummed and her image in the mirror shimmered, vibrating in and out of visibility in a frequency sympathetic to the wire's quivering. She struck the wire again, harder, to see what it would do to the image in the mirror. Her reflection fluttered and vanished, and in its place was a flickering image of the upper world. A mundane street scene, children walking home from school, cars honking impatiently behind a slow-moving Volkswagen Rabbit driven by an elderly lady . . .

On a hunch, a hunch that became an impulse, Cindy struck the tunnel wires repeatedly, as hard as she could.

The mirror — really a kind of TV monitor — showed the traffic careening out of control, the VW Rabbit backing up at great speed, ploughing into the others, the children losing control of their limbs and flapping haphazardly at one another.

Cindy tittered.

She took the can-opener from her boot and slashed at the wires, watching the 'mirror' all the while. The strings parted with a protesting *whang*. And in the upper world: children exploded, cars began to wrap around one another, suddenly becoming soft and pliable, tying themselves round telephone poles . . . a great invisible current swept the street, washing the buildings away . . .

Cindy smiled and went her way down the tunnel, randomly snipping wires.

Every few hundred yards she came to an intersection of tunnels; three opening to the right, three to the left, her own continuing on ahead. Sometimes Cindy changed direction at these subworld crossroads, following her intuition, vaguely aware that she had a specific destination.

At length the tunnel opened out into a circular room in the centre of which was another thick, red-yellow stalk; a corded, man-thick stalk, grown up to merge with the ceiling. But here, the walls swarmed with what looked like oversized aphids. Mechanical aphids, each big as her hand, and the colour of a blue-metal razor blade. They clung to the walls in groups of twenty or thirty, only a hand's width between each group; the aphids crawled methodically on small metal legs thin and numerous as the bristles of a hairbrush; on the right-hand wall they swarmed between banks of TV monitors. She switched off her flashlight; there was enough light from the TV screens. Standing at the monitors, spaced more or less evenly, were a score of dusty blue fellows, vaguely human, wearing jumpsuits of newspaper. Looking closer, Cindy could see that the newspaper-print was in some kind of inscrutable cipher, quite unreadable. And the newsphotos showed only half-recognizable silhouettes.

For the first time, real uneasiness shivered up in her, and bits and pieces of fear, like irregular hailstones, rattled down through the chill focal-heart of her sensations.

Fear because: the men at the monitors were entirely without mouths, without noses, without ears. Each had only large, blinking, watery grey eyes. And fear because: with Cindy's arrival in the room, the aphids, if that's what they were, began to move feverishly — but somehow purposefully — in mandala patterns over the walls, rustling through a thick coating of shag-rug cilia; the cilia, she saw now, covered the walls everywhere. It was the colour of a throat with a bad cold.

The mouthless men used three-fingered hands to manipulate knobs on the frames of the TV monitors. Now and then one of them reached up and brushed an aphid; something in the touch galvanized the creature so that it scurried furiously up the wall, parting the cilia and altering the symmetrical patterns made by the collective motion of the other aphids.

The TV pictures were black-and-white. The floor was alabaster, patterned with inset silver wires; the wires were arcanely configured, and occasionally sparked at the touch of the metal shod feet of the almost-people.

Cindy had decided to call them almost-people.

Her eyes adjusted to the dim light, and she saw that in the small of each almost-person's back was an umbilicus. The long, atten-tuated black umbilicus drooped, then rose to attach to the base of the thick red-yellow stalk in the centre of the chamber, much as a May Day reveller's ribbon attaches to a maypole. Cindy supposed that the umbilici made mouths and noses unnecessary for the almost-people.

Cindy was afraid, but that always put her on the offensive. Take control she told herself.

So just to see what would happen, she went about the room and — with her can-opener — methodically clipped the umbilici severing the almost-people from the stalk.

The almost-people stopped what they were doing; they turned and looked at her.

Cindy wondered how they felt. Were they alarmed or surprised or outraged or hurt? She couldn't tell.

One by one they fell, clutching their spindly throats. They writhed and twitched, making the wire-patterns on the floor spit blue sparks, and Cindy supposed that they were choking to death.

She felt a little sorry this time. She even said so. 'Oh. I'm sorry.'

After a few minutes, they stopped moving. Their big eyes shut. Breathing shakily, Cindy stepped over the corpses and went to one of the TV screens. She was careful not to step on the silver wires in the floor; she was sure she'd be electrocuted if she did.

The TV screens monitored life on the upper world. Reticulating charcoal-and-chalk video images of houses and motels and traffic and dogs. Junk-yards. Traffic lights changing. Farms, Seaside resorts. Canadian hikers. Rock singers. A teenage boy with stringy blond hair and a thin chest shakily trying to fill a syringe from a rusty spoon. Jazz players. Masturbating children. Mastur-bating women. Masturbating monkeys. She gazed for a while at a TV showing two people copulating in a hotel room. They were both middle-aged and rather doughy. The man's hair was thinn-ing, and his paunch waggled with his hip motions; the woman's hair was as defined and permanent in shape as a hat. A bell-shaped hat.

Impulsively, Cindy reached out and twiddled the monitor's unmarked black-plastic knobs. The picture shimmered, changed: the woman's head warped, bent out of shape, reified — it had become the head of a chimpanzee. The man screamed and disengaged and backed away. The woman clawed at herself.

Cindy made a moue with her lips, and tilted her head.

She reached up and prodded a number of the metallic aphids with her can-opener. They scurried, frightened at the unfamiliar touch, and set the others to scurrying more frantically, till the thousands of aphids clinging to the rounded ceiling were re-shaping in the cilia in swarming hysteria, their symmetry of pattern obliterated.

Cindy looked at the TV monitors. Now they showed only crowd scenes. People at football games, looking confused and distressed, as if they'd all gone blind and deaf; they staggered into one another, arms flailing, or tripped, went tumbling down the grandstands, upsetting other people — but, as Cindy watched, the people began to move cohesively down toward the playing field. They streamed onto the field, crowding it, and began to arrange themselves according to the dictates of a spontaneously recon-ceived psychic schema: people wearing white or yellow shirts moved together, people with dark shirts congregated, till the bird's eye view of the stadium showed the crowd spelling out words with their re-ordered colour scheme. They spelled out:

ZEITGEIST

and then

LOVE TIMES DEATH EQUALS ACTION

and then

LACEWORK REBELLION

Cindy turned away. She approached the stalk in the centre of the room. With the can-opener stuck in her teeth, she began to climb. The going was slippery, but she was determined, and soon reached the ceiling. Arms and legs aching, she clung there and, with one hand, began to carve an opening.

The skin parted more easily from the underside. Ten minutes of painful toil and the gap was wide enough to climb through. Cindy dropped the can-opener and wormed her way upward, through the wound in the ceiling.

She broke through a second layer, gnawing with her teeth, coming up through the skin of another seeming-floor.

She found herself under what looked like an ordinary four-legged wooden table. Around her were four empty wooden chairs, and a white floor-length tablecloth.

She dragged herself out of the wet, shuddering gap, and onto the floor. Gasping, she pressed aside the tablecloth, which had so far concealed her from those outside, and crawled into the upper world, once more atop the shell.

She was in a restaurant. Mom and Dad and Belinda and Barbara sat at the next table.

They stared at her, open-mouthed. 'What the hell have you got all over you, Cindy?' her father asked. The girls looked a little sick.

Cindy was coated with the wetness, the stickiness, the half-blood death essence of underplace things.

Still breathing hard, her head pounding, Cindy reached down and lifted the tablecloth aside, revealing the ragged, oozing wound she'd crawled out of. This time, her family saw it too.

Her father got up from the table rather convulsively, so that he nearly upset it, and his wineglass splashed Mom's dress. He turned away and, fumbling for his pot-pouch, staggered toward the exit. Her sisters had covered their eyes. They sobbed. Her Mother was staring at her. Mom's face was changing; the eyes growing bigger, the lips vanishing, her skin going dusty-blue. So, then. Her mother was the one they'd planted in the family. 'They're not under every house,' Cindy tried to explain to her sisters. 'They aren't always there to find. You might dig under our house and not find it — you have to know *how* to look. Not *where* to look. They keep us blinded with false symmetries.'

Her sisters followed their father outdoors.

Cindy turned away. 'Fuck them all, then,' she said. She felt her Mother's subworld eyes on her back as she fell to her knees and crawled back under the table. She slid feet-first into the wound, and dropped into the room below. She searched through the monitors, and found a screen showing her Dad and her sisters getting into the car. She turned the knobs, and laughed, seeing the car rising into the sky like a helium balloon with the string cut, turning end over end, Belinda spilling out of it and falling, her father screaming as the car deliquesced, becoming a huge drop of mercury that hung in the air and then burst into a thousand glittering droplets falling to splatter the parking lot with argent toxicity.

J.G. BALLARD

THE OBJECT OF
THE ATTACK

**From the Forensic Diaries of Dr. Richard Greville,
Chief Psychiatric Adviser, Home Office**

7 June 1987. An unsettling week — two Select Committees; the
Biggs trial with its vindictive sentence (Ipanema and its topless
beaches were clearly a more desperate hell than Parkhurst will
ever seem); the failure of mother's suspect Palmer to reach its
reserve at Sotheby's (I suggested that they might re-attribute it to
Keating, which doubly offended them); and wearying arguments
with Sarah about our endlessly postponed divorce and her over-
reliance on ECT — she is strongly for the former, I as strongly
against the latter . . . I suspect that her patients are suffering for
me.

But, above all, there was my visit to The Boy. Confusing, ugly —
the stench of purines in the excrement smeared on his cell walls
indicates huge overdoses of largactil — and yet strangely inspir-
ing. Inviting me to Daventry, Governor Henson referred to him,
as does everyone else in the Home Office, as 'the boy', but I feel he
has now earned the capital letters. Years of being moved about,
from Rampton to Broadmoor to the Home Office Special
Custody Unit at Daventry, the brutal treatment and solitary confinement have failed to subdue him.

He stood in the shower stall of the punishment wing, wearing
full canvas restraint suit, and plainly driven mad by the harsh light
reflected from the white tiles, which were streaked with blood
from a leaking contusion on his forehead. He has been punched
about a great deal, and flinched from me as I approached, but I felt
that he almost invited physical attack as a means of provoking
himself. He is far smaller than I expected, and looks only 17 or 18

(though he is now 29), but is still strong and dangerous — President Reagan and Her Majesty were probably lucky to escape.

Case notes: missing caps to both canines, contact dermatitis of the scalp, a left-handed intention tremor, and signs of an hysterical photophobia. He appeared to be gasping with fear, and Governor Henson tried to reassure him, but I assume that far from being afraid he felt nothing but contempt for us and was deliberately hyperventilating. He was chanting what sounded like 'Allahu akbar', the expulsive God-is-Great cry used by the whirling dervishes to induce their hallucinations, the same over-oxygenation of the brain brought on, in milder form, by church hymns and community singing at Cup Finals.

The Boy certainly resembles a religious fanatic — perhaps he is a Shi'ite Muslim convert? He only paused to stare at the distant aerials of Daventry visible through a skylight. When a warder closed the door he began to whimper and pump his lungs again. I asked the orderly to clean the wound on his forehead, but as I helped with the dressing he lunged forward and knocked my briefcase to the floor. For a few seconds he tried to provoke an assault, but then caught sight of the Sotheby's catalogue among my spilled papers, and the reproduction of mother's Samuel Palmer. That serene light over the visionary meadows, the boughs of the oaks like windows of stained glass in the cathedral of heaven, together appeared to calm him. He gazed at me in an uncanny way, bowing as if he assumed that I was the painter.

Later, in the Governor's office, we came to the real purpose of my visit. The months of disruptive behaviour have exhausted everyone, but above all they are terrified of an escape, and a second attack on HMQ. Nor would it help the Atlantic Alliance if the U.S. President were assassinated by a former inmate of a British mental hospital. Henson and the resident medical staff, with the encouragement of the Home Office, are keen to switch from chlorpromazine to the new NX series of central nervous system depressants — a spin-off of Porton Down's work on nerve gases. Prolonged use would induce blurred vision and locomotor ataxia, but also suppress all cortical function, effectively lobotomising him. I thought of my wrangles with Sarah over ECT — psychiatry cannot wait to return to its dark ages — and tactfully vetoed the use of NX until I had studied the medical history in the

Special Branch dossier. But I was thinking of The Boy's eyes as he gazed on that dubious Palmer.

The Assassination Attempt

In 1982, during the state visit of President Reagan to the United Kingdom, an unsuccessful aerial attack was made upon the royal family and their guest at Windsor Castle. Soon after the President and Mrs Reagan arrived by helicopter, a miniature glider was observed flying across the Home Park in a north-westerly direction. The craft, a primitive hang-glider, was soaring at a height of some 120 feet, on a course that would have carried it over the walls of the Castle. However, before the Special Branch and Secret Service marksmen could fire upon the glider it became entangled in the aerials above the royal mausoleum at Frogmore House and fell to the ground beside the Long Walk.

Strapped to the chest of the unconscious pilot was an explosive harness containing 24 sticks of commercial gelignite linked to NCB detonators, and a modified parachute ripcord that served as a hand-operated triggering device. The pilot was taken into custody, and no word of this presumed assassination attempt was released to the public or to the Presidential party. HMQ alone was informed, which may explain Her Majesty's impatience with the President when, on horseback, he paused to exchange banter with a large group of journalists.

The pilot was never charged or brought to trial, but detained under the mental health acts in the Home Office observation unit at Springfield Hospital. He was a 24-year-old former video-games programmer and failed Jesuit novice named Matthew Young. For the past eight months he had been living in a lock-up garage behind a disused Baptist church in Highbury, north London, where he had constructed his flying machine. Squadron Leader D.H. Walsh of the RAF Museum, Hendon, identified the craft as an exact replica of a glider designed by the 19th century aviation pioneer Otto Lilienthal. Later research showed that the glider was the craft in which Lilienthal met his death in 1896. Fellow-residents in the lock-up garages, former girl-friends of the would-be assassin and his probation officer all witnessed his construction of the glider during the spring of 1982. However, how he launched this antique machine — the nearest high ground is the Heathrow control tower five miles to the east — or remained airborne for his flight across the Home Park, is a mystery to this day.

Later, in the interview cell, The Boy sat safely handcuffed between his two warders. The bruised and hyperventilating figure had been replaced by a docile youth resembling a reformed skinhead who had miraculously seen the light. Only the eerie smile which he turned upon me so obligingly reminded me of the glider and the harness packed with explosive. As always, he refused to answer any questions put to him, and we sat in a silence broken only by his whispered refrain.

Ignoring these cryptic mutterings, I studied a list of those present at Windsor Castle.

President Reagan, HM The Queen, Mrs Reagan, Prince Philip, Prince Charles, Princess Diana . . .

The U.S. Ambassador, Mr Billy Graham, Apollo astronaut Colonel Tom Stamford, Mr Henry Ford III, Mr James Stewart, the presidents of Heinz, IBM and Lockheed Aircraft, and assorted Congressmen, military and naval attachés, State Department and CIA pro-consuls . . .

Lord Delfont, Mr Eric Morcambe, Mr Andrew Lloyd-Webber, Miss Joanna Lumley . . .

In front of Young, on the table between us, I laid out the photographs of President Reagan, The Queen, Prince Philip, Charles and Diana. He showed not a flicker of response, leaned forward and with his scarred chin nudged the Sotheby's catalogue from my open briefcase. He held the Palmer reproduction to his left shoulder, obliquely smiling his thanks. Sly and disingenuous, he was almost implying that I was his accomplice. I remembered how very manipulative such psychopaths could be — Myra Hindley, Brady and Mary Bell had convinced various naive and well-meaning souls of their 'religious conversions'.

Without thinking, I drew the last photograph from the dossier: Colonel Stamford in his white space suit floating free above a spacecraft during an orbital flight.

The chanting stopped. I heard Young's heels strike the metal legs of his chair as he drew back involuntarily. A focal seizure of the right hand rattled his handcuff. He stared at the photograph, but the gaze of his eyes was far beyond the cell around us, and I suspected that he was experiencing a warning aura before an epileptic attack. With a clear shout to us all, he stiffened in his chair and slipped to the floor in a *grand mal*.

As his head hammered the warders' feet I realized that he had been chanting, not 'Allahu akbar', but 'Astro-naut' . . .

Astro-nought . . . ?

Matthew Young: the Personal History of a Psychopath

So, what is known of The Boy? The Special Branch investigators assembled a substantial dossier on this deranged young man.

Born 1958, Abu Dhabi, father manager of Amoco desalination plant. Childhood in the Gulf area, Alaska and Aberdeen. Educational misfit, with suspected *petit mal* epilepsy, but attended Strathclyde University for two terms in 1975, computer sciences course. Joined Workers Revolutionary Party 1976, arrested outside U.S. Embassy, London, during anti-nuclear demonstration. Worked as scaffolder and painter, Jodrell Bank Radio-Observatory, 1977; prosecuted for malicious damage to reflector dish. Jesuit novice, St. Francis Xavier seminary, Dundalk, 1978; expelled after three weeks for sexual misconduct with mother of fellow novice. Fined for being drunk and disorderly during 'Sculpture of the Space Age' exhibition at Serpentine Gallery, London. Video-games programmer, Virgin Records, 1980. Operated pirate radio station attempting to jam transmissions from Space Shuttle, prosecuted by British Telecom. Registered private patents on Video-games 'Target Apollo' and 'Shuttle Attack', 1981. Numerous convictions for assault, possession of narcotics, dangerous driving, unemployment benefit frauds, disturbances of the peace. 1982, privately published his 'Cosmological Testament', a Blakean farrago of nature mysticism, apocalytic fantasy and pseudo-mathematical proofs of the non-existence of space-time . . .

All in all, a classic delinquent, with that history of messianic delusions and social maladjustment found in regicides throughout history. The choice of Mr Reagan reflects the persistent appeal of the theme of presidential assassination, which seems to play on the edgy dreams of so many lonely psychopaths. Invested in the President of the United States, the world's most powerful leader, are not only the full office and authority of the temporal world, but the very notion of existence itself, of the continuum of time and space which encloses the assassin as much as his victim. Like the disturbed child seeking to destroy everything in its nursery, the assassin is trying to obliterate those images of himself which he identifies with his perception of the external universe. Suicide would leave the rest of existence intact, and it is the notion of existence, incarnated in the person of the President, that is the assassin's true target.

The Dream of Death by Air

'. . . in the Second Fall, their attempt to escape from their home planet, the peoples of the earth invite their planetary death, choosing the zero gravity of a false space and time, recapitulating in their weightlessness the agony of the First Fall of Man . . .'

Cosmological Testament, Book I

The Dream of Death by Water

'. . . the sea is an exposed cerebral cortex, the epidermis of a sleeping giant whom the Apollo and Skylab astronauts will awake with their splashdowns. All the peoples of the planet will walk, fly, entrain for the nearest beach, they will ride rapids, endure hardships, abandon continents until they at last stand together on the terminal shore of the world, then step forward . . .'

Cosmological Testament, Book III

The Dream of Death by Earth

'. . . the most sinister and dangerous realms are those devised by man during his inward colonising of his planet, applying the dreams of a degenerate outer space to his inner world — warrens, dungeons, fortifications, bunkers, oubliettes, underground garages, tunnels of every kind that riddle his mind like maggots

through the brains of a corpse . . .'
Cosmological Testament, Book VII

A curious volume, certainly but no hint of a dream of death by fire — and no suggestion of Reagan, nor of Her Majesty, Princess Diana, Mrs Thatcher . . .?

The Escape Engine: the Ames Room

14 October 1987. The Boy has escaped! An urgent call this morning from Governor Henson. I flew up to Daventry immediately in the crowded Home Office helicopter. Matthew Young has vanished, in what must be one of the most ingenious escape attempts ever devised. The Governor and his staff were in a disoriented state when I arrived. Henson paced around his office, pressing his hands against the bookshelves and re-arranging the furniture, as if not trusting its existence. Home Office and Special Branch people were everywhere, but I managed to calm Henson and piece together the story.

Since my previous visit they had relaxed Young's regime. Mysteriously, the Samuel Palmer illustration in Sotheby's catalogue had somehow calmed him. He no longer defaced his cell walls, volunteered to steamhose them himself, and had pinned the Palmer above his bunk, gazing at it as if it were a religious icon. (If only it were a Keating — the old rogue would have been delighted. As it happens, Keating's reputation as a faker may have given Young his plan for escape.)

Young declined to enter the exercise yard — the high British Telecom aerials clearly unsettled him — so Henson arranged for him to use the prison chapel as a recreation room. Here the trouble began, as became clear when the Governor showed me into the chapel, a former private cinema furnished with pews, altar, pulpit, etc. For reasons of security, the doors were kept locked, and the warders on duty kept their eyes on Young by glancing through the camera slit in the projection room. As a result, the warders saw the interior of the chapel from one perspective only. Young had cunningly taken advantage of this, re-arranging the pews, pulpit and altar table to construct what in effect was an Ames Room — Adelbert Ames Jr., the American psychologist, devised a series of trick rooms, which seemed entirely normal when viewed through a peephole, but were in fact filled with unrelated fragments of furniture and ornaments.

Young's version of the Ames Room was far more elaborate. The cross and brass candelabra appeared to stand on the altar table, but actually hung in mid-air ten feet away, suspended from the ceiling on lengths of cotton teased from his overalls. The pews had been raised on piers of prayer books and Bibles to create the illusion of an orderly nave. But once we left the projection room and entered the chapel we saw that the pews formed a stepped ramp that climbed to the ventilation grille behind the altar table. The warders glancing through the camera slit in the projection room had seen Young apparently on his knees before the cross, when in fact he had been sitting on the top-most pew in the ramp, loosening the bolts around the metal grille.

Henson was appalled by Young's escape, but I was impressed by the cleverness of this optical illusion. Like Henson, the Home Office inspectors were certain that another assassination attempt might be made upon Her Majesty. However, as we gazed at that bizarre chapel something convinced me that the Queen and the President were not in danger. On the shabby wall behind the altar Young had pinned a dozen illustrations of the American and Russian space programmes, taken from newspapers and popular magazines. All the photographs of the astronauts had been defaced, the Skylab and Shuttle craft marked with obscene graffiti. The Boy had prayed to the astronauts, but I could guess his prayers. He had constructed a Black Chapel, which at the same time was a complex escape device that would set him free, not merely from Daventry, but from the threat posed by the astronauts and from that far larger prison whose walls are those of space itself.

The Astro-Messiah

Colonel Thomas Jefferson Stamford, USAF (ret). Born 1931, Brigham City, Utah. Eagle scout, 1945. B.S. (Physics), Caltech, 1953. Graduated US Air Force Academy, 1957. Served Viet Nam,

1964–69. Enrolled NASA 1970; deputy ground controller, Skylab III. 1974, rumoured commander of secret Apollo 20 mission to the Moon which landed remote-controlled nuclear missile station in the Mare Imbrium. Retired 1975, appointed Vice President, Pepsi-Cola Corporation. 1976, script consultant to 20th Century Fox for projected biopic *Men with Fins*.

1977, associated with The Precious Light Movement, a California-based consciousness-raising group calling for legalisation of LSD. Resigned 1978, hospitalised Veterans Administration Hospital, Fresno. On discharge begins nine months retreat at Truth Mountain, Idaho, inter-denominational order of lay monks. 1979, founds Spaceways, drug rehabilitation centre, Santa Monica. 1980–81, associated with Billy Graham, shares platform on revivalist missions to Europe and Australia. 1982, visits Windsor Castle with President Reagan. 1983, forms the evangelical trust COME Incorporated, tours Alabama and Mississippi as self-proclaimed 13th Disciple. 1984, visits Africa, S.E. Asia, intercedes Iraq/Iran conflict, addresses Nato Council of Ministers, urges development of laser weapons and neutron bomb. 1986, guest of Royal Family at Buckingham Palace, appears in Queen's Christmas TV broadcast, successfully treats Prince William, becomes confidante and spiritual adviser to Princess Diana. Named Man of the Year by *Time Magazine*, profiled by *Newsweek* as 'Space-Age Messiah' and 'founder of first space-based religion.'

Could this much-admired former astronaut, a folk hero who clearly fulfilled the role of a 1980s Lindbergh, have been the real target of the Windsor attack? Lindbergh had once hobnobbed with kings and chancellors, but his cranky political beliefs had become tainted by pro-Nazi sentiments. By contrast Col. Stamford's populist mix of born-again Christianity and anti-communist rhetoric seemed little more than an outsider's long shot at the White House. Now and then, watching Stamford's rallies on television, I detected the same hypertonic facial musculature that could be seen in Hitler, Gaddafi and the more excitable of Khomeini's mullahs, but nothing worthy of the elaborate assassination attempt, a psychodrama in itself, that Matthew Young had mounted in his Lilienthal glider.

And yet . . . who better than a pioneer aeronaut to kill a pioneer astronaut, to turn the clock of space exploration back to zero?

10 February 1988. For the last three months an energetic search has failed to find any trace of Matthew Young. The Special Branch guard on the Queen, Prime Minister and senior cabinet members has been tightened, and several of the royals have been issued with small pistols. One hopes that they will avoid injuring themselves, or each other. Already the disguised fashion-accessory holster worn by Princess Diana has inspired a substantial copycat industry, and London is filled with young women wearing stylized codpieces (none of them realize why), like cast members from a musical version of *The Gunfight at the OK Corral*.

The Boy's former girl-friends and surviving relatives, his probation officer and fellow programmers at Virgin Records have been watched and/or interrogated. A few suspected sightings have occurred: in November an eccentric young man in the leather gaiters and antique costume of a World War I aviator enrolled for a course of lessons at Elstree Flying School, only to suffer an epileptic seizure after the first take-off. Hundreds of London Underground posters advertising Col. Stamford's Easter rally at Earls Court have been systematically defaced. At Pinewood Studios an arsonist has partially destroyed the sets for the $100 million budget science-fiction films *The Revenge of R2D2* and *C3PO Meets E.T.* A night intruder penetrated the offices of COME Inc. in the Tottenham Court Road and secretly dubbed an obscene message over Col. Stamford's inspirational address on the thousands of promotional videos. In several Piccadilly amusement arcades the Space Invaders games have been reprogrammed to present Col. Stamford's face as the target.

More significant, perhaps, a caller with the same voiceprint as Matthew Young has persistently tried to telephone the Archbishop of Canterbury. Three days ago the vergers at Westminster Abbey briefly apprehended a youth praying before a bizarre tableau consisting of Col. Stamford's blood-stained space-suit and helmet, stolen from their display case in the Science Museum, which he had set up in a niche behind the High Altar. The rare blood group, BRh, is not Col. Stamford's, but The Boy's.

The reports of Matthew Young at prayer reminded me of Governor Henson's description of the prisoner seen on his knees in that illusionist chapel he had constructed at Daventry. There is an eerie contrast between the vast revivalist rally being televised at this moment from the Parc des Princes in Paris, dominated by the spotlit figure of the former astronaut, and the darkened nave of the Abbey where an escaped mental patient prayed over a stolen space suit smeared with his own blood. The image of outer space, from which Col. Stamford draws so much of his religious inspiration, for Matthew Young seems identified with some unspecified evil, with the worship of a false messiah. His prayers in the Daventry chapel, as he knelt before the illusion of an altar, were a series of postural codes, a contortionist's attempt to free himself from Col. Stamford's sinister embrace.

I read once again the testimony collected by the Special Branch:

Margaret Downs, systems analyst, Wang Computers: 'He was always praying, forever on his confounded knees. He even made me take a video of him, and studied it for hours. It was just too much . . .'

Doreen Jessel, health gym instructress: 'At first I thought he was heavily in to anaerobics. Some kind of dynamic meditation, he called it, all acrobatic contortions. I tried to get him to see a physiotherapist . . .'

John Hatton, probation officer: 'There was a therapeutic aspect, of which he rather convinced me against my better judgement. The contortions seemed to mimic his epilepsy . . .'

Reverend Morgan Evans, Samaritans: 'He accepted Robert Graves's notion of the club-footed messiah — that peculiar stepped gait common to various forms of religious dance and to all myths involving the Achilles tendon. He told me that it was based on the crabbed moon-walk adopted by the astronauts to cope with zero gravity . . .'

Sergeant J. Mellors, RAF Regiment: 'The position was that of a kneeling marksman required to get off a lot of shots with a bolt-action rifle, such as the Lee-Enfield or the Mannlicher-Carcano. I banned him from the firing range . . .'

Was Matthew Young dismantling and reassembling the elements of his own mind as if they were the constituents of an Ames Room? The pilot of the Home Office helicopter spoke graphically of the spatial disorientation felt by some of the special category prisoners being moved on the Daventry shuttle, in particular the cries and contortions of a Palestinian hijacker who imagined he was a dying astronaut. Defects of the vestibular apparatus of the ear are commonly found in hijackers (as in some shamans), the same sense of spatial disorientation that can be induced in astronauts by the high-speed turntable or the zero gravity of orbital flights.

It may be, therefore, that defects of the vestibular apparatus draw their sufferers towards high-speed aircraft, and the hijack is an unconscious attempt to cure this organic affliction. Prayer, vestibular defects, hijacking — watching Col. Stamford in the Parc des Princes, I notice that he sometimes stumbles as he bows over his lectern, his hands clasped in prayer in that characteristic spasm so familiar from the newsreels and now even mimicked by TV comedians.

Is Col. Stamford trying to hijack the world?

28 March 1988. Events are moving on apace. Colonel Thomas Jefferson Stamford has arrived in London, after completing his triumphal tour of the non-communist world. He has conferred with generals and right-wing churchmen, and calmed battlefields from the Golan Heights to the western Sahara. As always, he urges the combatants to join forces against the real enemy, pushing an anti-Soviet, church-militant line that makes the CIA look like the Red Cross. Television and newspapers show him mingling with heads of state and retired premiers, with Kohl, Thatcher and Mitterand, with Scandinavian royals and the British monarch.

Throughout, Col. Stamford's earlier career as an astronaut is never forgotten. At his rallies in the Parc des Princes and Munich's Olympic Stadium these great arenas are transformed into what seems to be the interior of a gigantic star-ship. By the cunning use of a circular film screen, Col. Stamford's arrival at the podium is presented as a landing from outer space, to deafening extracts from *Thus Spake Zarathustra* and Holst's *Planets*. With its illusionist back-projection and trick lighting the rally becomes a huge Ames Room, a potent mix of evangelical Christianity, astronautics and cybernetic movie-making. We are in the presence of an Intelsat messiah, a mana-personality for the age of cable TV.

His thousands of followers sway in their seats, clutching COME Inc's promotional videos like Mao's Red Guards with their little red books. Are we seeing the first video religion, an extravagant light show with laser graphics by Lucasfilms? The message of the rallies, as of the videos, is that Col. Thomas Stamford has returned to earth to lead a moral crusade against atheistic Marxism, a Second Coming that has launched the 13th Disciple down the aisles of space from the altar of the Mare Imbrium.

Already two former Apollo astronauts have joined his crusade, resigning their directorships of Avis and the Disney Corporation, and members of the Skylab and Shuttle missions have pledged their support. Will NASA one day evolve into a religious organisation? Caucus leaders in the Democratic and Republican Parties have urged Col. Stamford to stand for President. But I suspect that the Great Mission Controller in the Sky intends to bypass the Presidency and appeal directly to the U.S. public as an astro-messiah, a space ayatollah descending to earth to set up his religious republic.

The First Church of the Divine Astronaut

These messianic strains reminded me of The Boy, the self-sworn enemy of all astronauts. On the day after the Colonel's arrival in London for the Easter rally, to be attended by Prince Charles, Princess Diana and the miraculously cured Prince William, I drove to the lock-up garage in Highbury. I had repeatedly warned the Home Office of a probable assassination attempt, but they seemed too mesmerised by the Stamford fever that had seized the whole of London to believe that anyone would attack him.

As Constable Willings waited in the rain I stared down at the oil-stained camp bed and the sink with its empty cans of instant coffee. The Special Branch investigators had stripped the shabby garage, yet pinned to the cement wall above the bed was a post-card that they had inexplicably missed. Stepping closer, I saw that it was a reproduction of a small Samuel Palmer, 'A Dream of Death by Fire', a visionary scene of the destruction of a false church by the surrounding light of a true nature. The painting had been identified by Keating as one of his most ambitious frauds.

A fake Keating to describe the death of a fake messiah? Pinned to the damp cement within the past few days, the postcard was clearly Matthew Young's invitation to me. But where would I find him? Then, through the open doors, I saw the disused Baptist church behind the row of garages.

As soon as I entered its gloomy nave I was certain that Matthew Young's target had been neither President Reagan nor the Queen. The bolt cutters borrowed from Constable Willings snapped the links of the rusting chain. When he had driven away I pushed back the worm-riddled doors. At some time in the past a television company had used the deconsecrated church to store its unwanted props. Stage sets and painted panels from a discontinued science-fiction series leaned against the walls in a dusty jumble.

I entered the aisle and stood between the pews. Then, as I stepped forward, I saw a sudden diorama of the lunar surface. In front of me was a miniature film set constructed from old *Star Wars* posters and props from *Dr Who*. Above the lunar landscape hung the figure of an astronaut flying with arms outstretched.

As I guessed, this diorama formed part of yet another Ames Room. The astronaut's figure created its illusion only when seen from the doors of the church. As I approached, however, its elements moved apart. A gloved hand hung alone, severed from the arm that seemed to support it. The detached thorax and sections of the legs drifted away from one another, suspended on threads of wire from the rafters above the nave. The head and helmet had been sliced from the shoulders, and had taken off on a flight of their own. As I stood by the altar the dismembered astronaut flew above me, like a chromium corpse blown apart by a booby trap hidden in its life-support system.

Lying on the stone floor below this eerie spectacle was Matthew Young. He rested on his back in a scuffle of dust and cracked flagstones, his scarred mouth drawn back in a bloodless grimace to reveal the broken teeth whose caps he had crushed. He had fallen to the floor during his *grand mal* attack, and his outstretched fingers had torn a section of a *Star Wars* poster, which lay across him like a shroud. Blood pooled in a massive haematoma below his cheek-bone, as if during the focal seizure of his right hand he had been trying to put out his eye with the telescopic sight of the marksman's rifle that he clasped in his fist.

I freed his tongue and windpipe, massaged his diaphragm until his breath was even, and placed a choir cushion below his shoulders. On the floor beside him were the barrel, receiver, breech and magazine of a stockless rifle whose parts he had been oiling in the moments before his attack, and which I knew he would reassemble the instant he awoke.

Easter Day, 1988. This evening Col. Stamford's rally will be held at Earl's Court. Since his arrival in London, as a guest of Buckingham Palace, the former astronaut has been intensely busy, preparing that springboard which will propel him across the Atlantic. Three days ago he addressed the joint Houses of Parliament in Westminster Hall. In his televised speech he called for a crusade against the evil empire of the non-Christian world, for the construction of orbital nuclear bomb platforms, for the launching of geosynchronous laser weapons trained upon Teheran, Moscow and Peking. He seems to be demanding the destruction not merely of the Soviet Union but of the non-Christian world, the reconquest of Jerusalem and the conversion of Islam.

It is clear that Col. Stamford is as demented as Hitler, but fortunately his last splashdown is at hand. I assume that Matthew Young will be attending the Earl's Court rally this evening. I did not report him to the police, confident that he would recover in time to reassemble his rifle and make his way to one of the empty projection booths beneath the roof of the arena. Seeing Col. Stamford's arrival from 'outer space', The Boy will watch him from the camera window, and listen to him urge his nuclear jihad against the forces of the anti-Christ. From that narrow but never more vital perspective, the sights of his rifle, Matthew Young will be ready once again to dismantle an illusionist space and celebrate the enduring mysteries of the Ames Room.

CHERRY WILDER
SOMETHING
COMING THROUGH

Wheeler was alone in a strange city; a glance out of the eastern windows of his small apartment told him, morning and evening, that it was one of the strangest cities on the face of the earth. Deskar was very white. The sun at noon was flung back at the brazen sky from white walls of plexiglass, stucco, concrete and white-washed brick. The savage glare of the streets produced a painful equivalent of snow-blindness.

The local designers favoured the ramp and the covered way: they were partial to helices. At last, in the evening, when sunset turned the walls to rose and gold, Wheeler knew where he had seen Deskar. It was that 'city of the future' drawn by Twentieth Century artists. There it was at last, soaring impossibly, full of pointless pinnacles and staircases that went nowhere.

Wheeler had been placed by Intourist and the Department of Justice in a half-completed white apartment block a kilometre from the centre of the city. Roberta Nyass, the attorney, his only contact, assured him that it was not a tourist ghetto. He began to note down conscientiously all the persons he met in the apartment block. 'Two Africans on the stairs, ? staff; German prospector, elevator three; M. Dupont, manager, terrace; African woman, western jeansuit, lower lobby.'

His own apartment was on the top floor, the third; beyond the elevators was a makeshift partition of white and gold laminated metal. Through the cracks one could see the raw sides of the west wing plunging downwards and the workmen in djibbahs and white rags toiling on its construction.

Wheeler's journal was written very small on sheets of rice paper and hidden in the lining of his Macduff overcoat hanging in the wardrobe. He had intended to record interviews with Judi and

Raoul and any of the proceedings he was permitted to witness. After the first interview he was driven back to his apartment in a state of abject terror and frustration. He wrote it all down with a shaking hand then remained wide awake for twenty-four hours, prowling the four white rooms.

Roberta Nyass had briefed him thoroughly before he entered the Imperial Prison. He wore a white shirt and white duck trousers specially purchased for the occasion and carried photocopies of all his documents attested and sealed with red wax by two attorneys. He bore in his left hand a paper carrying bag from the tourist supermarket containing two bottles of orange juice, four melons, a round of bread, a tin of herring and a plastic basin. He was passed quickly through the outer wards into the search area where he had a huge black man in a robe of Imperial purple all to himself.

Wheeler spread his documents on the bench; the giant rose up slowly, flicking a fly-whisk, and smiled.

'Business is slack,' he said in velvety Oxford English. 'Relax, Mr Wheeler . . .'

He ripped off the ring-pull top of the herring can and deposited the contents in the plastic basin. He dipped a finger in the herring brew and tasted a morsel of the fish.

'The tins must be discarded,' he explained, 'because of the suicide risk.'

He slashed open the four melons, selected two and put them aside.

'For supper,' he said. 'Do you know the cheese bar at the supermarket?'

'Sure . . .'

'The camembert is very good.'

'I'll remember that,' said Wheeler.

'Now the part you've been dreading,' continued the guard. 'Quite painless and not in the least humiliating.'

He gestured Wheeler towards the shining metal search cabinet. Wheeler removed his trousers, handed them to the guard, stepped into the tall padded box and adjusted the chin rest. He was slightly off balance and had the sensation of falling forward. The guard searched the trousers quickly then moved to the control panel of the cabinet somewhere beyond Wheeler's left ear. The X-ray hummed.

'How did you fracture your thigh, Mr Wheeler?' asked the guard.

'Ski-ing accident.'

For a minute or so Wheeler concentrated on his memories of Sun Valley while invisible fingers probed and prodded his anatomy.

He left the search area for interrogation laden with the food in its disintegrating bag, the bowl of herring and, in his right hand, his documents. The Inquisitor was a spare, light-skinned man of about fifty, Wheeler's contemporary. His accent was unclassifiable. The examination lasted half an hour with the Inquisitor returning several times to his first questions.

'What is your relationship to the prisoners?'

'I am Judi Crane's stepfather. She is the daughter of my wife by a previous marriage.'

'Do you have children with this wife?'

'We have one son, Jon . . . fourteen years old.'

'Where does the mother live?'

'We live in the United States of America — California—'

'There is no such place as the United States of America.'

'I mean, of course, the United States of North America, the USNA.'

'You are aware the prisoners are wanted by the police in Toronto in the state of Ontario?'

'Yes.'

'Are you aware of the charges against them?'

'Not exactly. They are Canadian Separatists who opposed mergence.'

'I suggest that they are terrorists and fall into the category of stateless outlaws against which every hand must be raised.'

'That is incorrect. You . . . that is, the Imperial Government knows about these charges from local news printouts carried by the young man, Raoul Martin,' said Wheeler. 'They are Separatists wanted in connection with a street demonstration.'

'Well, it doesn't matter,' said the Inquisitor. 'We have them so far only on the drug charges: Tobacco and Alcohol.'

He made a note on his clipboard and returned Wheeler's documents.

'They risk the garotte for the alcohol but it is complicated by the tobacco. The two together may add up to the guillotine which is public.'

'I protest!' said Wheeler, trying to keep his voice level. 'This is a savage and inhuman penalty!'

'The guillotine?' asked the Inquisitor sadly. 'Yes, it upsets the families, especially those of certain tribes.'

'The death penalty for carrying alcohol and tobacco is hideously unjust!'

'Our Imperial reformed religion forbids alcohol, and the tobacco is a prohibited substance, specifically proscribed by the World Health Organisation.'

'They didn't mean to enter your country!' burst out Wheeler. 'They crossed an unmarked border zone by accident.'

'They are here,' said the Inquisitor.

'I protest!' said Wheeler.

'There is little hope,' said the Inquisitor. 'We may ask for a clarification from the USNA embassy in Tanzania. If they are declared to be terrorists the penalty is almost the same: firing squad.'

He waved a hand and Wheeler scooped up his horrible possessions. He went through two more checkpoints and found himself suddenly confronting Judi and Raoul through the bars of chromed steel. The sight of them, unharmed, clean and healthy, filled him with relief. He went forward grinning foolishly, and handed the food through the bars to Judi. A guard in magenta battledress on her side of the bars did not stir in his chair.

'Judi!'

He had recognized her at once even down to the pouting underlip. Raoul, whom he had never met, lounged in another chair chewing at a green leaf and scowling.

'Judi, how are they treating you?'

'Are you from the Embassy or something?' she asked solemnly.

Wheeler paused, waiting for her to identify him. He saw the whole structure of the visit falling to the ground if she really failed to recognize him. 'You claim to be the girl's stepfather,' murmured the Inquisitor in his mind. Judi wiped her hands on her jeans.

'This fish is kind of sloppy.'

'Herring,' said Wheeler.

'You're Griff Wheeler, right?' she said, without a smile. 'Is Mom here?'

'No. She's not well. I made the journey. Are you comfortable, Judi?'

'Sure. We got busted.'

'Judi, it is very serious.'

She was a small girl with a pale, high forehead. Wheeler had always found her rather plain. Now her ragged short hair and slender neck put him in mind of Carl Dreyer's Joan of Arc.

'You better talk to Raoul if it's anything about extradition,' she said.

She went and whispered to Raoul and the young man sprang up.

'You don't have to worry!' he said in a loud harsh voice. 'We're fine. Tell those guys in the embassy that extradition won't work!'

'There is no embassy,' said Wheeler. 'Raoul, I was saying to Judi . . .'

'Pig!' said Raoul. 'Stupid yankee pig! Why don't you go back home on the first plane!'

He was swarthy, handsome; his muscles bulged under a white T-shirt printed with a red maple leaf. Wheeler shuddered, looking at the somnolent guard.

'Your situation is serious, Raoul!'

'Get my name out of your mouth, pig!' said Raoul. 'Judi, why the hell are you talking to this guy?'

He walked around the tiled enclosure making faces at Wheeler.

'Excuse him,' grinned Judi. 'He's high.'

Wheeler jumped. The guard avoided his eye, took a green leaf from his pocket and began to chew methodically.

'We get a ration of this *neo-vert* — new green. It is kind of like coca,' she explained. 'Makes you feel better.'

'New green?' asked Wheeler stupidly.

'Yeah . . .' She glanced at Raoul who was squatting on the seat of his chair and whistling. 'Seems crazy. To be busted for tobacco, you know, and then given this ration. Some guys burn the new green . . . inhale the fumes . . .'

'Judi, do you know the penalty for carrying tobacco or alcohol?'

'Yeah, well, so it's five years or even ten. We're never going back. You serve the time somewhere else. We spoke to a guard who had French and he told Raoul you go to either the Ring or the Basket. If these places up country are half as good as this Imperial pen we will do fine. We get to share a cell, Griff; honestly, where else could you do that? The food is okay. We don't want to be extradited. They can't . . . the Yank Invaders have no treaty with the Empire.'

Raoul came up to the bars again panting, his eyes rolling in his head.

'You don't have to worry,' he said. 'I've heard, I've had a message. We'll be out of here. We'll bust right out again.'

Wheeler felt as if he were choking.

'We'll do everything we can,' he whispered. 'Your mother sends her love, Judi.'

He turned away. As he hurried down to the nearest checkpoint he heard Raoul laughing: Judi called after him something that might have been 'Thanks for the herring.'

Outside the prison gates kindly Madame Nyass bundled him into the official Merc Electra and they were driven through the blanched streets back to the apartment. Wheeler saw the tourist bazaar, the sparse, darting electric cars and mopeds, the gates of the Imperial palace, he saw all these things and did not see them. He sat numb and silent while the attorney recited ways and means, avenues of approach, things that might put off the evil day.

'Never lose hope, Mr Wheeler,' she said.

A pair of swallows sliced across their path, twisted in mid-air so close to the windshield that Griff Wheeler saw the glitter of their eyes. The driver swerved, clever and quick as the birds themselves. Wheeler roused himself a little.

'What is *neo-vert* — new green?' he asked.

Madame Nyass smiled.

'It is from the agave,' she said. 'Oh, it spread out very quickly. The plains by Hirondel were covered with the green leaves in no time.'

'Is it a stimulant?'

'A mild one, apparently.'

They were already at the apartment block. Wheeler was so eager to be alone that he climbed the stairs to the third floor for fear that he might meet someone in the elevator. He began straight away to write down his minute account of the first prison visit. Half-way through he remembered that, if it were not a dream, he had passed a woman crouched down weeping on the stairs; the smart African woman in western dress whom he had seen earlier in the lobby.

He gritted his teeth and began a letter to Sara, his wife, rehearsing in his mind a second and truer account of things. The letter would be censored. He threw down his pen suddenly when the real letter became too difficult and the letter in his head became angry and desperate. It seemed certain that Judi and Raoul were going to die and he was powerless.

Wheeler prowled the four white rooms, lay down to sleep and rose up again, aching and unrefreshed. His discomfort was profound, a cerebral irritation, the more agonising because he regarded it as selfish. He could not think of Sara and young Jon; he could not think of Judi and Raoul. He sat motionless, his eyes unfocussed until he was aroused by a thump or cry within the building, the sound of a dripping tap, a bird on the balcony, a whiff of resinous perfume.

He cringed at the thought of his next prison visit. His visa would last six weeks; this encompassed three visits to the prison. He did not leave the apartment for several days but at last his mood changed. His apathy gave way to a furious activity. He exercised in the bathroom, travelled up and down the elevators, jogged around the terrace behind the building.

When Roberta Nyass came to restock his refrigerator he talked greedily of ways and means. He examined the texts of his two petitions to the Emperor, inscribed in French on imitation parchment. The first begged for clemency for the prisoners; the second begged for an extension of his own visa so that he might witness their execution. He asked silly questions.

'There is no presumption of innocence,' said Madame Nyass, shaking her magnificent green and gold turban, 'and no appeal against sentence.'

The day before his second visit he rode in elevator three with the German prospector who was in a talkative mood. He introduced himself to Wheeler: 'Schwalbe, Gottfried!' and shook him warmly by the hand.

'I have been ordered home,' said Herr Schwalbe. 'I have something you might like . . . a book in English.'

Wheeler was enthusiastic; they met in the same elevator next morning and transferred the book from Schwalbe's briefcase to Wheeler's airline satchel. That afternoon the Inquisitor's first question made Wheeler tremble.

'Now, about your books . . .'

'Books?'

'Your firm, Pegasoid Press.'

'It is a small specialty publishing company,' said Wheeler, relieved.

This was a true description which suggested pornography to most strangers he met in the States.

'We print books,' he continued, 'no cassettes. Even a number of hard covers. We print, for instance, books in Braille and collectors' editions of English classical authors. In fact many of our customers are collectors.'

'The paper shortage must have affected you,' said the Inquisitor.

'We use a little of the new pliokraft,' said Wheeler, 'and a range of rare, high-grade papers — willow paper from Japan, for instance.'

'We have no problem with paper,' said the Inquisitor, smiling. 'Our forestry projects replenish our needs with excellent speed. Especially in the region of Hirondel.'

Wheeler was allowed to gather up his groceries and before he came to the visiting room he realized that the Inquisitor had taken him momentarily into his confidence. He had made an ironic reference to the regime. Hirondel? Then he was confronted by Judi and Raoul, the chromed bars, the sleepy guard in magenta battledress.

They knew the truth. Wheeler was not sure if this was good or bad. Judi crouched shivering on a chair, Raoul approached and solemnly shook Wheeler's hand.

'She is depressed,' he murmured. 'Excuse my former behaviour, Mr Wheeler.'

'We are doing all we can.'

Wheeler felt afterwards that he had repeated nothing but this phrase throughout his visit. Raoul, on the other hand, talked a good deal about ways and means. Judi came forward once, white-faced, and sent love to her mother. Before the time was up Raoul said to him earnestly:

'Mr Wheeler . . . Griff . . . what I told you earlier was true.'

'What . . .?'

'I have no religion except perhaps the Work, you know, the Cause, but I have received a message of hope. I can't explain . . . I feel . . . something coming through . . .'

Wheeler could see Judi slumped in her chair, hopeless, stricken with the fear of death. As Wheeler turned to go Raoul held up a hand with two fingers spread in a V. In Wheeler's lifetime this had meant a couple of things and he knew it must have an even longer history. Raoul said with the firmness of habit:

'*Canada Séparé!*'

Wheeler was alone in his pearl-grey official auto this time and he had the driver set him down on the top of a long, spiral ramp about half a kilometer from the apartment block. It was late afternoon, not unbearably hot; the ramp was so high that he felt a breeze as he walked down. Foreigners were perfectly safe in the clean, uncrowded streets of Deskar.

He felt no anger after this visit but the beginnings of a sickening resignation. A long, silver shadow crept up beside him and Wheeler drew back against a white-washed wall. Then he noticed the diplomatic plates.

'I'm off!' called Herr Schwalbe, nursing his hand luggage. 'Auf Wiedersehen, Mr Wheeler!'

'Wait!' said Wheeler. 'Before you go, what is Hirondel?'

'Ssst!' said the prospector. 'It is — was — a fast-breeder up the country. Out of commission for months after an accident with the disposal of atomic waste. Top secret. The desert has blossomed . . . given the game away. Several new varieties of trees and plants. Does that answer your question?'

'Very well indeed!'

Wheeler stood waving until the auto whirled up to the top of the spiral. He walked on, brisk and gloomy, feeling the afternoon sun on the back of his neck. Three swallows darted into his line of vision above the curve of a roof and were joined by a fourth.

His revelation occurred when he was inside the white apartment block, inhaling its ill-conditioned air. He was on the stairs;

he had passed Dupont, the manager, in the lobby, wiping his face with what appeared to be a checked dish-towel. Wheeler steadied himself against the stair rail in case he fell down, then ran reeling along the hazy corridor to his four rooms.

He did not dare put it into words but the message was one of hope. There was a joyful synchronicity in everything that he did, in everything that happened. He laid out all his books on the low table of glass and imitation ebony and opened the new Pegasoid Press edition of Palgrave's *Golden Treasury* at random:

O swallow, swallow, flying south . . .

He opened the well-thumbed Pegasoid catalogue at random, in fact at Ransome, Arthur: *Swallows and Amazons*. He shut his eyes and felt a warm intelligence all about him. He took up Herr Schwalbe's book: an English paperback of *Anna Karenina*, rubber stamped 'Book Exchange for Cultural Freedom, 1957'. It was a relic of the Empire's long infiltration by the Communist front, enough to bring him five years in prison. The yellowed pages had to be pried apart. He opened the book at page 180 and read on the facing page: 'Four shots rang out and the snipe turned swiftly like swallows and vanished from sight'.

Wheeler stepped out onto the balcony and gulped the smoky air of sunset. The feeling of joyous certainty was sharpened, it was like chords of music. Something coming through. Suddenly the air before him was filled by clouds of swallows; they dipped and circled. If he narrowed his eyes the birds seemed to weave bright patterns in the air. Several birds flew right in under the roof of the balcony and out again, in sweet erratic flight, so close that he could see their plumage, darkest blue and black, and the creamy flash of their underbodies.

He went indoors again and switched on the television set. It had not been used for days; he had given up even on the news broadcasts. He found himself staring into the bearded face of the Emperor, leaving some public ceremony. He searched the face for a sign but this was not enough. He directed all his own hope, his own certainty at the young man.

The Emperor raised a hand in salute; he wore a sky-blue uniform of antique cut, heavily laced with gold and silver. Wheeler sat back on his heels on the carpet as the Emperor entered his palace gates; he felt drained of power. The newsreel ended with a filler, a few frames of the palace gardens; a string orchestra began to play and he recognized the melody. *La Golondrina* . . . the swallow.

Wheeler lay down on his bed still in his crumpled white prison visitor's suit. He slept deeply. He felt himself sinking swiftly down through layers of downy unaccustomed sleep. He slept, exhausted, for hours, then dreamed sweetly, without pain, of Sara and Jon. He experienced with delight the garish colours and sounds of that ugly section of the great metropolitan seaboard where they spent their holidays. In his dream he looked with aching relief upon hamburger stands and the grimy, sluggish ocean.

He remained asleep and presently he saw in his dream the city of Deskar, still and silent under the moon. The whorled streets were empty; the glass bubble that carried the muezzin to his perch hung glittering on its tower. Yet he knew that the citizens were merely sleeping; the domes and ziggurats were packed with sleepers. In the Imperial Prison Judi and Raoul slept in each other's arms. As he watched from some vantage point a mist arose; planes of blue vapour unfolded among the night-cooled walls.

Soon after his dream Wheeler woke up; it was three o'clock in the morning. His euphoria had receded; it was a remembered warmth, like the dream of home. He wandered through the apartment, ate a banana, and stepped meditatively onto the balcony again. The image of the city from his dream was so strong that he was surprised to see no mist reaching through the streets.

Wheeler looked up and saw the stars. The sky fell down on him, it sank into his brain. The old certainty, that feeling of absurd good news grew and blossomed in and around him. He understood everything; he understood space and time; he understood and was absorbed into the totality of mankind. He saw that between the earth and the stars there stretched a web of intelligence, rarely perceived, benevolent and not impersonal. They were there. He personalized them as female. He felt his thoughts and the thoughts of countless billions of human beings living and dying and still living since the world began rising up to be absorbed into the net. He had no need to concentrate, to make any plea or supplication. Their understanding was complete. He hardly remembered going back to bed and falling asleep again.

He slept until nine o'clock and had a shower and shave and hid his copy of *Anna Karenina* in a hurry before the young cleaner arrived to do his rooms. He gave the boy Imperial currency and went down to the terrace to escape the roar of the vacuum cleaner. He breakfasted, as he often did, on half a melon and a can of mineral water. The morning had not become too hot; there was no wind; the view from the terrace was of the suburbs. Hectares of low, flat-roofed white houses, sprawled over low hills; there were trees, spindly palms and acacias, and rolling clumps of vines growing on to the roof-tops.

Wheeler did not know what to make of his mystical experience. He could not discount it but he could not discount the notion that it was a defence against the fear and stress he lived with in Deskar. He walked to the end of the terrace to throw his melon rind, but not his drink-can, into the tangle of vines below the iron railing. He stared, like a sidewalk superintendent, at the construction work on the new wing.

There were a great many earthen ramps that put him in mind of the building of the pyramids; the three upper floors were coming along slowly; the completed ground floor, somewhere below the level of the terrace, was the base for operations. The noise and clatter had not built up to its mid-morning crescendo which stopped abruptly about half-past eleven. Siesta lasted from this time until fifteen hundred hours; the workers withdrew to the shade of tents and awnings perched all over the site; the foremen slept in the roofed shell of the ground floor.

Coffee-breaks or their equivalent went on all the time; in shady places, under the awnings, there were always little groups of workers or hangers-on tending fires, cooking, offering pieces of fruit to the men toiling up the ramps with their barrows. In accord with the reformed religion of the Empire there were a few women with swathed heads who formed a work-group of their own; there were two female welders who worked in overalls like the other welders but seldom removed their helmets.

Wheeler stared at the busy scene; he realized that he didn't know enough about construction work to be shocked by primitive methods. The workers seemed happy and, in their own way, well-organized. Wheeler stared and felt his stomach lurch; he felt as if a tight band were being twisted around his forehead. He looked again, walking to the very edge of the terrace and leaning over the rail. He sighed and exhaled and began to laugh.

At every one of the small camp fires a man or a boy was feeding the iron brazier or cut-down oil-drum with bundles of half-dried leafy twigs. He could see no other fuel being burnt. Many of these small fires were close to the shady wall of the completed section of the building, the section where he lived. A haze of bluish smoke blanketed this wall; thicker puffs and tendrils were actually curling into the cracks and interstices of the wall. At two, three of the campsites he could see the faggots being prepared. He was so close to the lower level that he could see an old woman pluck off a still-green leaf and chew it before making a bundle of new green and prodding it into her fire. A rickety housing that was surely the air conditioning plant was half invisible in a cloud of the smoke.

Wheeler chuckled to himself; he felt bereft and lonely. He had his reasonable explanation. He remembered his dream of the city. An apartment house, a whole city zonked out. He suddenly knew the smell of new-green: a stale, resinous odour . . . The apartment block reeked of it. He wondered what the other residents had hallucinated, what feelings of strength and hope and certainty it had brought them. Raoul had had the same experience. Something coming through. Damn stuff must be dangerous to health. Smoke pollution could kill you! He turned, ready to find M. Dupont, drag him out on to the terrace if necessary and show that he managed a houseful of new-green heads.

'Mr Wheeler!'

It was an urgent, joyous shout. Madame Nyass came on to the terrace with her draperies flowing and her arms outstretched. She bore down on him and folded him into an embrace.

'Mr Wheeler! Mr Wheeler! They are free!'

'Judi and Raoul?'

'General amnesty,' she panted. 'They were turned loose at eight o'clock!'

'Good heavens!' was all that Wheeler could find to say. 'But why? Where are they? Can I see . . .?'

'General amnesty,' she repeated. 'You had better leave at once, this minute. The young people are waiting for you over the border at Checkpoint South.'

'Which border?'

'Checkpoint South gives on to the International Zone surrounding the Highway.'

'My plane ticket,' stammered Wheeler.

'No,' she said firmly. 'For God's sake go with them in their safari wagon, Mr Wheeler. I cannot guarantee your visa any longer. Go with the children and drive back to the beaches of Namibia Free State where they came from in the first place. Stick to the Highway this time.'

She helped him pack; they were out of the apartment in twenty minutes. Instead of an official car Madame Nyass was driving her own battered BMW Electra wagon; Wheeler gave her his Imperial currency to change for him. He sat in the back seat and wrote away twenty thousand dollars in travellers' cheques for his attorney's fee. M. Dupont had been nowhere about when they left; Wheeler had given no warning about the new-green pollution. Selfish, he reflected coldly, selfish to the last. But the kids were free, free.

They went swiftly spiralling up and down on the ramps and overpasses of the city, drove for some time on the long, beautiful avenue that led to the airport, then turned off through meaner streets. There was the border, complete with striped poles, pillboxes, and, at ten-thirty in the morning, a trickle of incoming traffic. African women with handcarts, boys on bicycles, several rattle-trap gas-burning trucks, packed with passengers, were entering as they approached. He realized that these folk were in fact Imperial citizens who had to cross the international zone surrounding the Highway in order to reach Deskar. The Imperial guards, in magenta battledress, with machine-guns easily balanced, seemed friendly and obliging. Wheeler stared past them and saw a sight that pleased him beyond words. Three tall black men strode up and down with *their* machine-guns easily balanced; they wore Khaki battledress and the blue helmets of the United Nations.

While Madame Nyass fixed things up, as she put it, at the guard house, Wheeler tried to catch sight of Judi and Raoul in their safari wagon. There were a few beehive huts and prefabricated sheds on both sides of the border. A party of children were playing with slingshots; a skinny cow, towed behind a bicycle, suddenly kicked up its heels, hit by a stone. Wheeler remained in a daze watching this peaceful Third World scene until Madame Nyass hustled him out of the car, pressed a few dollars upon him, and festooned him with his hand-luggage.

They walked forward, ducked under the corner of the raised, striped pole and passed into No-Man's Land. Wheeler was already stammering out his thanks, uttering farewells. Out of the corner of his eye he saw a little cloud of birds twisting around the vane of a silver windmill, the tallest structure beyond the border. At the same time he saw the wagon, parked in the shade of a beehive hut. Yes, they were there, extravagantly waving to him. Judi sat on the half-raised canopy of the wagon; Raoul, still in his maple-leaf T-shirt, was in the driver's seat. They were calling but he could not make out their voices. He wondered, seriously, if he were dreaming, if he would wake up in the apartment again.

'There they are!' said Madame Nyass. 'Goodbye again, Mr Wheeler.'

'But was there a reason?' he asked, trying to pull himself together. 'Why was there an amnesty?'

'Didn't I mention that? The Emperor had a dream.'

Wheeler could not speak; he looked back towards the city of Deskar, rising fantastic, dreamlike, in a haze of heat. He clutched his valise and strode out of the Empire; the smiling guard in his blue helmet stamped his documents and waved to Madame Nyass. Ahead Judi and Raoul still waved and shouted. He felt a smile grow on his face; the rule of reason was being re-established. As Wheeler passed beside the silver windmill he heard the voice of the children raised in a cry of triumph and a swallow fell dead at his feet.

KIM NEWMAN
DREAMERS

Elvis Kurtz was dreaming. He dreamed he was John F. Kennedy, former president (1960–Lee Harvey Oswald) of the former United States of America. The dream was a riot of pornography; involving enormous wealth, extreme power, intermittent ultra-violence, and sex with Marilyn Monroe. It was a pre-sold success. An inevitable Iridium Tape. An inescapable quinquemillion-seller.

Kurtz was dybukking, a passenger in the mind. Kurtz was aware of what John Yeovil thought it felt like to be John Fitz-gerald Kennedy in August 1961. He had access to a neatly arranged file of memories, plus a few precog glimpses carried over from waking life. He would have to pull out before Dallas. The JFK similie was not aware of Kurtz. Actually, the JFK similie hardly seemed to be aware of anything.

Yeovil had had JFK plump his mistress' bottom on the edge of the presidential desk, and penetrate the former Norma Jean Baker (1926–next year) standing up. A pile of authenticated contemporary documents were scrunched up beneath their spectacular copulation.

Kurtz trusted Yeovil had got the externals right. Through the JFK similie he was perceiving the Oval Office precisely as it had been. Marilyn's squeals were done in her actual voice, distilled from over three hundred hours of flatty sound-tracks and disc aurals. Yeovil would have had a computer assist handle that. Sometimes Kurtz envied the man's resources.

Marilyn and the president were sexing like well-oiled flesh robots. The dreamership liked their sexing pristine, with all the mess and pain taken out. Kurtz seared his overlay onto the dreamtape, burning a semi-apocalyptic series of multiple climaxes.

This was standard wet-dream stuff. The sort of thing Kurtz

could do in his sleep. Kurtz's dybbuk overmind left the internals to his experienced subconscious and skimmed through the similie's memory. He ignored the story-so-far synopsis and picked a few random sensations.

The Pacific, WW II: the smell of burning oil and salt water, all-over Sun heat, repressed fear, an aural loop of *Sentimental Journey*. His father throwing a tantrum: the usual mix of shame, terror and embarrassment. Prawns at Hyannis Port. The inauguration; January chill, tension, incipient megalomania: '. . . ask not what your country can do for you . . .'

Kurtz wondered who had written that speech. Yeovil did not know; all the question got out of the similie was a momentary white-out. Damn, an extraneous thought. It would bleed onto the tape. Yeovil would have to do a post-erase. With the scene getting near the finish, Kurtz took ego control again.

Yeovil had taken the trouble to insert a 1961 image: Kennedy ejaculated like an ICBM silo; a thermonuclear chain reaction inside Marilyn took her out.

Yawn. Kurtz was an orgasm specialist. He topped the metaphor (too literary, but what did he expect) with a jumble of cross-sensory experiences. He translated the aural stimuli of the *Saint Matthew Passion* into a mass of tactiles. The dream shadow could take it, although a real body would have been blown away.

Marilyn lay face down, exhausted, her hair fanned on the pile carpet. JFK traced her backbone with the presidential seal. Yeovil had Catholic guilt flit through JFK's mind.

'Jack,' breathed Marilyn, 'did you know there's a theory that the whole universe got started with a Big Bang?'

Kennedy parted Marilyn's hair and kissed the nape of her neck. Kurtz felt a witty reply coming. Something hard at the base of the president's skull. A white hot needle in his head. A brief skin-and-bone agony, then nothing.

Damn Yeovil. Oswald was early.

Like most of the *haut ton* that year John Yeovil was devoted to Victoriana. The tridvid sages said the craze was a reaction to the acid smogs that had taken to settling on London. Usually Yeovil affected to despise fashions, but this one suited him. Frock coats and stiff collars became his Holmesian figure, a beard usefully concealed his slash mouth, and the habitual precision of his gestures was ideal for consulting a half-hunter, taking a pinch of snuff, or casually slitting a footpad's nose with an iridium-assist swordstick.

At thirty-nine Yeovil was rich enough to indulge himself with opium-scented handkerchiefs, long case clocks and wax wreaths under glass. Three of his dreams were in the current q-seller listings. The *JFK* advance had accounted for the complete redecoration of his Luxborough Street residence.

Awaiting his guest, Yeovil adjusted the pearl pin in his gray cravat. Exactly right. Exact rectitude was all Yeovil asked of life. That and wealth and fame, of course. He sighted his one-sided smile in the mirror. The smile which, flashed during a tridvid interview or frozen on a dustjack, could cost him one million pounds *per annum* in lost sales alone. A definitive figure would have to take personal appearances, merchandizing, and graft into consideration.

The smile was Yeovil's little secret. The mark of the submarine part of his mind he rigidly excluded from his dreams. John Yeovil had come to terms with his character. He lived with himself in relative comfort, despite the fact that he was easily the most hateful person he knew.

He had the dreaming talent, but so did hundreds of others. He had the patience to research and the skill to concept, but any raw Dreamer with funding could buy access to the D-9000 for those. Success in the dream industry was down to depth of feeling. Any feeling.

Great Dreamers were all prodigies of emotion. Susan Bishopric: empathy; Orin Tredway: imbecile love; Alexis St Clare: paranoia. And John Yeovil had hate. It did not come through as such in the dreams, but he knew that it was his great reservoir of hate that gave weight to his conjuring of excitement, joy, pain, and the rest.

The doorbell sounded. Yeovil had sent an in to Elvis Kurtz. The Household admitted him. A few tendrils of smog trailed the guest. The Household dispelled them.

'Mr Kurtz?'

'Uh. Yes.' Kurtz was muffled by his outdoor helmet. He pulled out of it. His eyes were watering profusely. Yeovil was familiar with the yellowish stream of tears. 'Sorry about this. I have a slight smog.'

'My sympathies,' said Yeovil. 'You can leave your things with the Household.'

'Thanks.' Kurtz ungauntleted and de-flakjacked. Underneath he wore a GP smock. Yeovil led his guest through the hall. The Household offed the hallway lamps, and upped the gas jets and open fire in the drawing-room.

'You were difficult to find, Mr Kurtz.'

'I'm supposed to be.' He had a trace of accent. Possibly Lichtenstein. 'I've been out.'

'Of course.' Yeovil decanted two preconstituted brandy snifters. 'Piracy or pornography?'

'A little of both.' Kurtz accepted the drink, smeared his tears, and sagged into a heavy armchair. He was not at ease. As well he might be. Yeovil decided to hit him now, and cover later.

'Mr Kurtz, prior to your incarceration you produced bootleg editions of my dreams which made a sizeable dent in my income. I can now offer you the opportunity to repay me.'

'Your pardon?' Kurtz was trying not to look startled. Like most Dreamers he was rotten at that sort of thing. Most, Yeovil reminded himself, not all.

'Don't worry. I'm not going to tap you for money. I'll even pay you.'

'For what?'

'The use of your talent.'

'I don't think you understand . . .'

'I'm well aware of your limitations, Mr Kurtz. Like myself you are a Dreamer. In many ways you are more powerful than I. You are capable of taping sensations far more intensely than I can. Yet I am successful and well-regarded,' (by most at least) 'and you are reduced to aping my dreams. Or producing work like this.'

Yeovil indicated a stack of tapes. Inelegant under-the-counter dreams with clinical titles: *Six Women With Mammary Abnormalities*, *The Ten Minute Orgasm*. They were badly packaged, with lurid artists-imps on the dustjackets. There was no Dreamer by-line, but Kurtz recognized his own stuff.

'I'm too strong, Yeovil. I can't control my dreams the way you can. My mind doesn't just create, it amplifies and distorts.

I wind up with so many resonances and contradictions that the dream falls apart. That's an advantage with one-reel wet dreams, but . . .'

'I don't require of you that you justify yourself, Mr Kurtz. I am an artist. I have no capacity for moral outrage. We have that much in common. Our position is at odds with those of the judiciary, the critical establishment, and the British Board of Dream Censors. Come with me.'

The dreaming room was different. Most of the house was a convincing, dark, stuffy, and uncomfortable recreation of the 1890s. The dreaming room was what people in 1963 had expected the future to look like. All the surfaces were a glossy, featureless white.

Kurtz was impressed. He touched his fingertips, then his naked palm, to the glasspex wall. He started away, and a condensation handprint faded.

'It's warm. Is that eternity lighting?'

'Partly. I have the dreaming room kept at womb temperature.'

'You dream here?'

'Of course. The surroundings have been calculated exactly. Psychologically attuned to be beneficial to the dreaming talent. The recording equipment is substantially what you are familiar with.'

'You have computer assist?'

'My Household has a library tap for research. I don't use it much, though. I actually read books. I'm not one of the D-9000's troop of hacks. I don't think we should be the glorified amanuenses of a heuristic pulp mill.'

'I don't like the machines either. They hurt.' Kurtz was irritated. Good, that should keep him off balance. 'What is all this about?'

'Would you be surprised to learn that I am an admirer of your work?'

Kurtz cleared an unconvincing laugh from his throat. 'Would you be prepared to say that on the dustjack of *Sixth Form Girls in Chains*?'

Yeovil tapped his ID into the console. The Household extruded a couch from the floor. It looked sculpted. Out of vanilla ice cream.

'Beside yours my talent is lukewarm. I want to make use of your capacities to underline certain aspects of my work in progress.'

'Uh huh.'

'I am dreaming a historical piece, focusing on the character of John Kennedy, martyred president of the United States of America. Kennedy was known to be a man with a highly passionate nature. I think it not inapt that your touch with erotica be applied.'

Kurtz sat on the couch, trying to find the loophole. 'What about the certification?'

'I plan on sidestepping the BBDC. They have no real authority, and I am supported by my publishers and the vast public interest in my work. The Board owes its precarious existence to its claim that it represents the desire of the majority. Once that is disproved, they will fall. *JFK* has been concepted as a radical dream.'

'How is this going to work?'

'I've dreamed a guideline. The sequence you'll work on is fully scripted. The externals are complete. However the first person is blank.'

'Kennedy?'

'Yes. He is emerging as a very strong figure in the dreaming. But in this scene he's empty. I want you to amend the internals as he sexes with his mistress.'

'Same old wet dream stuff?'

'Essentially. But in this case the explicit material is crucial to the concept. The character of Kennedy is seminal to an understanding of the twentieth century. All of his drives must be exposed. The underlying . . .'

'Yeah. Right. Let's talk about the money.'

Yeovil balanced the newly-discharged needle gun on his fingertips as he walked across the room, and dropped the weapon into the Household Disperse. Kurtz lay face down on the dreaming couch with a three-inch dart in his brain. The tape was still running, although the Kurtz input was zero. Yeovil sucked his burned fingers. He would smear them better when he was finished with Kurtz.

He had never killed anyone before. He sadly discovered that

dream was better than actual. Like sex. He stored the minor rush of emotions for future use.

The tape clicked through. The Household offed the recorder. Yeovil picked the subcutaneous terminals out of Kurtz's head and dropped them into their glass of purple. The whirlpool rinse sucked particles of Kurtz out of its system.

Yeovil went through Kurtz's smockpocks. A few credit cards and a bunch of ins. A couple of five-pound bits. They all went into the Disperse, along with Kurtz's outdoor gear, porno tapes, and finger-printed brandy glass. Do it, then clear up afterwards — the secret of criminal success.

The Household presented Yeovil with his outdoor kit: a visored hat, and a padded Inverness. The tailors boasted that their garments were proof against a fragmentation charge. That was true: in the event of such an unlikely weapon being turned on the cape, it would be unmarked. Anyone inside it, however, would find his torso turned to jelly by the impact. Most footpads used needle guns, anyway.

Yeovil hauled Kurtz out to his armoured Ford. On the street he fitted an outmoded breather. It kept the smog out of his lungs as well as a more stylish domino, and disguised him.

Yeovil pressed his car in, and tapped his ID into the automatic. The smog lights upped. The streets were deserted.

Yeovil drove around central London for fifteen minutes before chancing upon a suitable dump. He slung the body over several twist-tie rubbish bags in the forecourt of a condemned high-rise. It would look like an ordinary waylaying. There were probably five similar corpses within walking distance. If the Black Economists got to Kurtz before the Metropolitans, the body would be stripped of any usable organs. The incident would not rate a mention on the local.

Back at Luxborough Street Yeovil reprogrammed his Household to forget Kurtz's visit. He fed in a plausible dull evening at home, and wrote off the energy expenditure to various gadgets.

Then he slept. The next stage was complicated, and he did not want to deal with it late at night after his first murder. He felt a twinge of insomniac excitement, which he countered by backgrounding a subliminal lullaby.

The Household woke him early with a call. It was Tony, Yeovil's chief editor at Futura. Tony looked harrassed.

'You've overreached another deadline, John. I wanted the *JFK* master back yesterday. We're committed to a production start. And we have marketing to consider. It's a q-seller on advance sales, and you haven't delivered yet.'

'Sorry.' Yeovil stretched his mind around the problem. 'I've still got a few more amendments.'

'You're a trekkiehead, John. Leave it alone. I told you it was finished last week. I'm satisfied as is. And I'm supposed to be a bastard tyrannical editor. We're all expletive deleted here. The copiers are primed.'

'You have my word as a gentleman that a definitive master will be on your desk tomorrow morning.'

'Tomorrow morning? I get into the office Kubricking early, John.' Tony looked dubious. 'Okay, you've got it, but no more extensions. No matter how many errors slip through the fine-tooth. You can have Oswald miss, and re-elect the randy bugger for all I care. The next John Yeovil hits the stands Friday. Does that scan?'

'Of course. I apologize for the delay. I'm sure you understand . . .'

'If that means: will I forgive you for being an iridium-plated prick, no-way. However, my slice of your sales buys you a lot of tolerance. Ciao.'

Tony over-and-outed. He was getting near termination. There were other publishers. Offers tapped up in Yeovil's slab every morning.

The Kurtz-assist master was still slotted. Yeovil pulled it, primed the duplicator, and cloned a copy. The master tape was too recognizable as such for his purpose. Too many splices and scribbles. Plus he would need it later. His plan did not include writing off the work done on *JFK*. The dream would be worth a lot of money. Yeovil doled himself out a shiver of self-delight.

He printed on the clone's spine: *JFK* by John Yeovil. And under that he scrawled: review copy.

Review copy. Yeovil backgrounded an aural of Richard Horton's review of his last dream. Just to remind himself what this was about.

'Yeovil is lucky that his publishers have the clout to buy off his heroine's heirs, 'cause *The Private Life of Margaret Thatcher* is quite as unnecessary and unsavoury as his previous efforts. Yeovil is genned up on period externals, and has an insidious knack for concepting his dreams so you zip through without being too annoyed. But once the headset is off, you know you've had a zilch experience. A few critics praise the man for his high-minded moral tone, but even they will find the lip-smacking prurience of *Margaret Thatcher* difficult to get their heads around. Yet again Yeovil bombards the captive mind with an endless round of sensuality — enormous state banquets, thrilling battles, ichor-drenched 'tasteful' sexing — and finally condemns all the excesses he has dragged us through with such gloating relish. He is at his worst when his heroine submits to what he has her anachronistically think of as 'a fate worse than death' under the well-remembered, much-maligned Idi Amin in order to save a planeload of hostages. One sympathizes with the feminist group who have petitioned for Yeovil's judicial castration under the anti-sexism laws. Finally, the man's dreams are a far less interesting phenomenon than his publicity machine. If you're out there taking a rest from adding up the profits, John, pack it in and join the Rural Reclamation Corps. With relief we turn to a new dream from Miss Susan Bishopric, who has made such an . . .'

Richard Horton was as smug a little shit as ever there was. Listening to his middle-aged parody of the adjectival overkill of a comput-assessor made Yeovil's fingers twist his watch chain into flesh-pinching knots.

Yeovil could not decide which made him hate Richard Horton more. The Carol business, or his tridvid defamations. Carol Horton had been Yeovil's mistress for three months. Before he had elected to sever the bond, Carol had taken it upon herself to return to her husband. Moreover she had instituted a civil lawsuit against Yeovil, alleging that he had drawn upon copyrighted facets of her personality for Pristine, the protagonist of his *The Sweetheart of Tau Ceti*. When he thought about her Yeovil still disliked Carol, but only to prove a point. Deep down it was Horton's insulting reviews that lifted Yeovil's loathing into the superhate bracket.

Before leaving the house Yeovil vindictively erased all his Horton tapes.

Richard Horton was dreaming. He dreamed that he was John F. Kennedy. Or, rather he dreamed that he was John Yeovil jacking off while dreaming that he was John F. Kennedy. If Kennedy had been like the similie no one would now be around to review the dream. The Ivans would have nuked the world in desperation.

So far it had been the typical John Yeovil craptrap. The man never missed a chance to be cheap and obvious.

In the Oval Office JFK was sexing Marilyn Monroe. Why was it always Marilyn Monroe? Every dream set in the mid-twentieth century found it obligatory to have the hero sex Marilyn Monroe. The girl must have had a crowded schedule. The semiologically inclined comput-assessors called her an icon of liberated sensuality. Richard Horton called her a thundering cliché.

It was the regulation wet-dream stuff, a little harder than Yeovil's usual hypocritical lyricism. At least there were no butterflies and gentle breezes here. Just heavy-duty sexing. Another depiction of woman as a hunk of meat. Kubrick knows what Carol ever saw in Yeovil.

Horton's attention strayed around the scene. Perhaps he should feed the dream through the British Museum Library's researcher. It might catch Yeovil out on an external. It was probably not worth it. Yeovil was the kind of Dreamer who got every wallpaper tone and calendar date right and then hit you with a concept that would make a computer puke.

Yeovil had peppered the sexing with memories. The lanky git was pathetically pleased with himself. Look how much research I did, screamed a mass of largely irrelevant facts. WW II, Holy Joe Kennedy, Hyannis Port.

Who wrote Kennedy's inaugural address? That was out of character. Horton's dybbuk flinched from the white-out. There was another mind crowding in, superimposed on the Kennedy similie. It was not Yeovil, he was working overtime on having JFK remember who was topping the bill at the Newport, Rhode Island jazz festival in 1960. There was someone else. A strong mind Horton could not place. It was a contributory Dreamer. Was Yeovil trying to pirate again? Eclipsing a collaborator on the credits was not beneath him.

Horton felt himself getting lost in the dream. The fiction was broken, and he was disconcerted. For an instant he thought he actually was sexing Marilyn Monroe. The woman was screaming in his ear. After all these years, the real thing.

Then it was cartoon time. The JFK similie body stretched impossibly. The return of Plastic Man. There was a playback fault. That was it. Whoever had last dreamed through this copy had left an accidental over-lay. Horton fished around for a name, but was dropped into a maelstrom of explosion imagery.

Was Yeovil experimenting with hard core? At least that would make a change.

Then the dream came together again, and Horton was locked in. Wedged between the minds of Yeovil, Kennedy and the mysterious Mr X.

Marilyn lay face down, exhausted, her hair fanned on the pile carpet. JFK traced her backbone with the presidential seal. Horton was disgusted to feel Catholic guilt flit through JFK's mind. Yeovil was piling cant upon cliché as per usual.

'Jack,' breathed Marilyn, 'did you know there's a theory that the whole universe got started with a Big Bang?'

Yeovil's dialogue was always the pits.

Kennedy parted Marilyn's hair and kissed the nape of her neck. Horton felt a trekkiehead reply coming. Something hard at the base of the president's skull. A white hot needle in his head. A brief skin and bone agony (what was that about Oswald?), then nothing.

Horton was not Horton any more. Horton was not anybody any more. His mind had been wiped. Completely, as an erase blanks a tape. Yeovil watched as the former Horton rolled on his side, retracting his arms and legs, wrapping himself into an egg.

The dreamtape was still running. Yeovil offed the machine, and pulled the clone tape. Elvis Kurtz had been unknowingly generous. He had shared his death.

Yeovil freed Horton from his headset, and gently popped his

contact lenses. They had been making him cry. No point in keeping up enmities from a previous incarnation.

Yeovil wondered how Carol would take to motherhood. She always had shown an inclination to sentiment over gurgling infants. Now she had a chance to be closely acquainted with one. Horton had a lot of growing up to do.

Yeovil dropped the tape into Horton's Disperse, and used the critic's in to gain access to his Household. He wiped the whole day. As an extra flourish, he wiped the entire Household memory. A little pointless mystification to obscure his involvement.

Now all he had to do was get back to Luxborough Street, wipe Kurtz off the master tape, give that to Tony, and wait for the returns. Do it, then clear up afterwards.

Tony had messaged in the Household tridvid.

'I had a merry hell of a time overriding your Household, you bastard. But we didn't lend you company programmes for nothing. So you were spending the day putting a few final touches to the masterpiece were you? If so, you must be doing it in another dimension because the master is here and you aren't. Where the Jacqueline Susann are you? Actually, don't bother to tell me. I don't give a damn. I now have the *JFK* master, and that fulfils your contract. You can start looking for a new publisher. By the time you play this back we'll have a million copies in distribution, with an expected second impression on Monday. Don't worry, though. You won't have to sue us to get what's coming to you. Ciao.'

MICHAEL BLUMLEIN

TISSUE ABLATION AND VARIANT REGENERATION: A CASE REPORT

At seven A.M. on Thursday Mr Reagan was wheeled through the swinging doors and down the corridor to operating room six. He was lying flat on the gurney, and his gaze was fixed on the ceiling; he had the glassy stare of a man in shock. I was concerned that he had been given analgesia, but the attendant assured me that he had not. As we were talking, Mr Reagan turned his eyes to me: the pupils were wide, dark as olives, and I recognized the dilation of pain and fear. I felt sympathy, but more, I was relieved that he had not inadvertently been narcotized, for it would have delayed the operation for days.

I had yet to scrub and placed my hand on his shoulder to acknowledge his courage. His skin was coarse beneath the thin sheet that covered him, as the pili erecti tried in vain to warm the chill we had induced. He shivered, which was natural, though eventually it would stop — it must — if we were to proceed with the surgery. I removed my hand and bent to examine the plastic bag that hung like a showy organ from the side of the gurney. There was nearly a litre of pale urine, which assured me that his kidneys were functioning well.

I turned away, and entering the scrub room, once more conceptualized our plan. There were three teams, one for each pair of extremities and a third for torso and viscera. I headed the latter, which was proper, as the major responsibility for this project was mine. We had chosen to avoid analgesia, the analeptic properties of excruciating pain being well known. There are several well-drawn studies that conclusively demonstrate the superior survival of tissues thus exposed, and I have cited these in a number of my own monographs. In addition, chlorinated hydrocarbons, which still form the bulk of our anesthetics, are tissue-toxic in extremely small quantities. Though these agents clear rapidly in the normal course of post-operative recovery, tissue propagation is too sensitive a phenomenon for us to have risked their use. The patient was offered, routinely, the choice of an eastern mode of anesthesia, but he demurred. Mr Reagan has an obdurate faith in things American.

I set the timer above the sink and commenced to scrub. Through the window I watched as the staff went about the final preparations. Two large tables stood along one wall, and on top of them sat the numerous trays of instruments we would use during the operation. Since this was the largest one of its kind any of us at the centre had participated in, I had been generous in my estimation of what would be needed. It is always best in such situations to err on the side of caution, and so I had ordered duplicates of each pack to be prepared and placed accessibly. Already an enormous quantity of instruments lay unpacked on the tables, divided into general areas of proximity. Thus, urologic was placed beside rectal and lower intestinal, and hepatic, splenic, and gastric were grouped together. Thoracic was separate, and orthopedic and vascular were divided into two groups for those teams assigned to the extremities. There were three sets of general instruments — hemostats, forceps, scissors, and the like — and these were on smaller trays that stood close to the operating table. Perched above them, and sorting the instruments chronologically, were the scrub nurses, hooded, masked, and gloved. Behind, and throughout the operating room circulated other, non-sterile personnel; these were principally nurses and technicians, who carefully avoided the sterile field being constructed about the perimeter of the operating table but otherwise roamed freely, thus functioning as the extended arm of the team.

For the dozenth time I scrubbed my cuticles and the space between fingernail and fingertip, then scoured both sides of my forearms to the elbow. The sheet had been removed from Mr Reagan, and his ventral surface — from neck to foot — was covered by the yellow suds of antiseptic. His pubic parts, chest, and axilla, had been shaved earlier, although he had no great plethora of hair to begin with. The artificial light striking his body at that moment recalled to me the jaundiced hue I have seen at times on certain dysfunctional gall bladders, and I looked at my own hands. They seemed brighter, and I rinsed them several times, then backed into the surgical suite.

A nurse approached with a towel, whose corner I grabbed, proceeding to dry methodically each finger. She returned with a glove, spreading the entrance wide as one might the mouth of a fish in order to peer down its throat. I thrust my fingers and thumb into it and she snapped it upon my forearm. She repeated the exchange with the other, and I thanked her, then stood back and waited for the final preparations.

The soap had been removed from his skin, and now Mr Reagan was being draped with various-sized linens. Two of these were used to fashion a vertical barrier at the mid-point of his neck; behind this, with his head, sat the two anesthesiologists. Since no anesthetic was to be used, their responsibility lay in monitoring his respiratory and cardiovascular status. He would be intubated, and they would make periodic measurements of the carbon dioxide and oxygen content of his blood.

I gave them a nod and they inserted the intracath, through which we would drip a standard, paralytic dose of succinylcholine. We had briefly considered doing without the drug, for its effect, albeit minimal, would still be noticeable on the ablated tissues. Finally, though, we had chosen to use it, reasoning — and experience proved us correct — that we could not rely on the paralysis of pain to immobilize the patient for the duration of the surgery. If there had been a lull, during which time he had chosen to move, hours of careful work might have been destroyed. Prudence dictated a conservative approach.

After initiating the paralytic, Dr Guevara, the senior anesthesiologist, promptly inserted the endotracheal tube. It passed easily for there was little, if any, muscular resistance. The respirator was turned on and artificial ventilation begun. I told Mr Reagan, who would be conscious throughout, that we were about to begin.

I stepped to the table and surveyed the body. The chest was exposed, as were the two legs, above which Drs Ng and Cochise were poised to begin.

'Scalpel,' I said, and the tool was slapped into my palm. I transferred it to my other hand. 'Forceps.'

I bent over the body, mentally drawing a line from the sternal notch to the symphysis pubis. We had studied our approaches for hours, for the incisions were unique and had been used but rarely before. A procedure of this scale required precision in every detail in order that we preserve the maximal amount of viable tissue. I lifted the scalpel and with a firm and steady hand made the first cut.

He had been cooled in part to cause constriction of the small dermal vessels, thus reducing the quantity of blood lost to ooze. We were not, of course, able to use the electric scalpel to cut or coagulate, nor could we tie bleeding vessels, for both would inflict damage to tissue. Within reason, we had chosen planes of incision that avoided major dermal vasculature, and as I re-traced my first cut, pressing harder to separate the more stubborn fascial layers, I was re-assured by the paucity of blood that was appearing at the margins of the wound. I exchanged my delicate tissue forceps for a larger pair, everting the stratum of skin, fat, and muscle, and continuing my incision until I reached the costochondral junction in the chest and the linea alba in the belly. I made two lateral incisions, one from the pubis, along the inguinal ligament, ending near the anterior superior iliac spine, and the other from the sternal notch, along the inferior border of the clavicle to the anterior edge of the axilla. There was more blood appearing now, and for a moment I aided Dr Biko in packing the wound. Much of our success at controlling the bleeding depended, however, upon the speed at which I carried out the next stage, and with this in mind, I left him to mop the red fluid and turned to the thorax.

Pectus hypertrophicus occurs perhaps in one in a thousand; Billings, in a recent study of a dozen such cases, links the condition to a congenital aberration of the short arm of chromosome thirteen, and he postulates a correlation between the hypertrophied sternum, a marked preponderance of glabrous skin, and a mild associative cortical defect. He has studied these cases; I have not. Indeed, Mr Reagan's sternum was only the second in all my experience that would not yield to the Lebsche knife. I asked for the bone snips, and with the help of Dr Biko was finally able to split the structure. My forehead dripped from the effort, and a circulating nurse dabbed it with a towel.

I applied the wide-armed retractor, and as I ratcheted it apart, I felt a wince of resistance. I asked Dr Guevara to increase the infusion of muscle relaxant, for we were entering a most crucial part of the operation.

'His pupils are fixed and dilated,' he announced.

I could see his heart, and it was beating normally. 'His gases?' I asked.

'0^2 85, CO_2 38, pH 7.37.'

'Good,' I said. 'It's just agony then. Not death.'

Dr Guevara nodded above the barrier that separated us, and as he bent to whisper words of encouragement to Mr Reagan, I looked into the chest. There I paused, as I always seem to do at the sight of that glistening organ. It throbbed and rolled, sensuously, I thought, majestically, and I renewed my vows to treat it kindly. With the tissue forceps I lifted the pericardium and with the curved scissors punctured it. It peeled off smoothly, reminding me fleetingly of the delicate skin that encloses the tip of the male child's penis.

In rapid succession I ligated the inferior vena cava and cross-clamped the descending aorta, just distal to the bronchial arteries. We had decided not to use our bypass system, thus obviating cannulations that would have required lengthy and meticulous suturing. We had opted instead for a complete de-vascularization distal to the thoracic cavity, reasoning that since all the organs and other structures were to be removed anyway, there was no sense in preserving circulation below the heart. I signalled to my colleagues waiting at the lower extremities to begin their dissections.

I isolated the right subclavian artery and vein, ligated them, and did the same on the left. I anastomosed the internal thoracic artery to the ventral surface of the aortic arch, thus providing arterial flow to the chest wall, which we planned to preserve more or less intact. I returned to the descending aorta, choosing 3–0 Ethilon to assure occlusion of the lumen, and oversewed twice. I released the clamp slowly: there was no leakage, and I breathed a sigh of satisfaction. We had completed a crucial stage, isolating the thoracic and cephalic circulation from that of the rest of the body, and the patient's condition remained stable. What was left was the harvesting of his parts.

I would like to insert here a word on our behalf, our in the larger sense of not just the surgical team but the full technical and administrative apparatus. We had early on agreed that we must approach the dissection assiduously, meaning that in every case we would apply a greater, rather than a lesser, degree of scrupulousness. At the time of the operation no use — other than in transplantation — had been found for many of the organs we were to resect. Such parts as colon, spleen, and vasculature had not then, nor have they yet, struck utilitarian chords in our imaginations. Surely, they will in the future, and with this as our philosophy we determined to discard not even the most seemingly insignificant part. What could not immediately be utilized would be preserved in our banks, waiting for a bright idea to send it to the regeneration tanks.

It was for this reason, and this reason alone, that the operation lasted as long as it did. I would be lying if I claimed that Mr Reagan was not in constant and excruciating pain. Who would not be to have his skin filleted, his chest cracked, his limbs meticulously dissected and dismembered? In retrospect, I should have carried out a high transection of the spinal cord, thus interrupting most of the nerve fibres to his brain, but I did not think of it beforehand and during the operation was too occupied with other concerns. That he did survive is a testimony to his strength, though I still remember his post-operative shrieks and protestations. We had, of course, already detached his upper limbs, and therefore we ourselves had to dab the streams of tears that flowed from his eyes. At that point, there being no further danger of tissue damage, I did order an analgesic.

After I had successfully completed the de-vascularization procedure, thus removing the risk of life-threatening haemorrhage from our fields, I returned to the outer layer of thorax and abdomen. With an Adson forceps I gently retracted the thin sheet of dermis and began to undermine with the scalpel. It was painstaking, but after much time I finally had the entire area freed. It hung limp, drooping like a dewlap, and as I began the final axillary cut that would release it completely, I asked Ms Narciso, my scrub nurse, to call the technician.

He came just as I finished, and I handed him the skin.

I confess that I have less than a full understanding of the technology of organ variation and regeneration. I am a surgeon, not a technologist, and devote the major part of my energies toward refinement and perfection of operative skills. We do, however, live in an age of great scientific achievement, and the iconoclasm of many of my younger colleagues has forced me to cast my gaze more broadly afield. Thus it is that I am not a complete stranger to inductive mitotics and controlled oncogenesis, and I will attempt to convey the fundamentals.

Upon receiving the tissue, the technician transports it to the appropriate room wherein lie the thermo-magnetic protein baths. These are organ specific, distinguished by temperature, pH, magnetic field, and substrate, and designed to suppress cellular activity; specifically, they prolong dormancy at the G1 stage of mitosis. The magnetic field is altered then, such that each cell will arrange itself ninety degrees to it. A concentrated solution of isotonic nucleic and amino acids is then pumped into the tank, and the bath mechanically agitated to diffuse the solute. Several hours are allowed to pass, and the magnetic field is again shifted, attempting to align it with the nucleic loci that govern the latter stages of mitosis. If this is successful, and success is immediately apparent for failure induces rapid and massive necrosis, the organ system will begin to reproduce. This is a macroscopic phenomenon, obvious to the naked eye. I have been present at this critical moment, and it is a simple, yet wondrous, thing to behold.

Different organs regenerate, multiply, in distinctive fashion. In the case of the skin, genesis occurs quite like the polymerization of synthetic fibres, such as nylon and its congeners. The testes grow in a more sequential manner, analogous perhaps to the clustering of grapes along the vine. Muscles seem to laminate, forming thicker and thicker sheets until, if not separated, they collapse upon themselves. Bone propagates as tubules; ligaments, as lianoid strands of great length. All distinct, yet all variations on a theme.

In the case of our own patient, the outcome, I am pleased to report, was bounteous; this was especially gratifying in light of our guarded prognostications. I was not alone in the scepticism with which I approached the operation, for the tissues and regenerative capacity of an old man are not those of a youngster. During the surgery, when I noticed the friability and general degree of degeneration of his organs, my thoughts were inclined rather pessimistically. I remember wondering, as Dr Cochise severed the humeral head from the glenoid fossa, inadvertently crushing a quantity of porotic and fragile bone, if our scrupulous planning had not, perhaps, been a waste of effort, that the fruits of our labour would not be commensurate with our toil. Even now, with the benefit of hindsight, I remain astonished at our degree of success. As much as it is a credit, I believe, to the work of our surgical team, it is, perhaps more so, a tribute to the resilience and fundamental vitality of the human body.

After releasing the dermal layer as described, I proceeded to detach the muscles. The adipose tissue, so slippery and difficult to manipulate, would be removed chemically, thus saving valuable time. As I have mentioned, the risk of haemorrhage — and its threat to Mr Reagan's life — had been eliminated, but because of the resultant interruption of circulation we were faced with the real possibility of massive tissue necrosis. For this reason we were required to move most expeditiously.

With sweeping, but well guided, strokes of the scalpel I transected the ligamentous origins of Pectoralis Major and Minor, and Serratus Anterior. I located their points of insertion on the scapula and humerus and severed them as well, indicating to Ms Narciso that we would need the technician responsible for the muscles. She replied that he had already been summoned by Dr Ng, and I took that moment to peer in his vicinity.

He and Dr Cochise had been working rapidly, already having completed the spiraling circumferential incisions from groin to toe, thus allowing, in a fashion similar to the peeling of an orange, the removal in toto of the dermal sheath of the leg. The anterior femoral and pelvic musculature had been exposed, and I could see the Sartorius and at least two of the Quadriceps heads dangling. This was good work and I nodded appreciatively, then turned my attention to the abdominal wall.

In terms of time the abdominal muscles presented less of a problem than the thoracic ones, for there were no ribs to contend with. In addition, as long as I was careful not to puncture the viscera, I could enter the peritoneum almost recklessly. I took my scalpel and thrust it upon the xiphoid, near what laymen call the solar plexus, and started the long and penetrating incision down the linea alba, past the umbilicus, to the symphysis pubis. With one hand I lifted the margin of the wound, and with the other delicately sliced the peritoneal membrane. I reflected all the abdominal muscles, the Rectus and Transversus Abdominis, the Obliquus Internus and Externus, and detached them from their bony insertions. Grasping the peritoneum with a long-toothed forceps and peeling it back, I placed two large towel clips in the overlying muscle mass, and then, as an iceman would pick up a block of ice, lifted it above the table, passing it into the hands of the waiting technician. Another was there for the thoracic musculature, and once these were cleared from the table, I turned to the abdominal contents themselves.

Let me interject a note as to the status of our patient at that time. As deeply as I become involved in the techniques and mechanics of any surgery, I am always, with another part of my mind, aware of the human being who lies at the mercy of the knife. At this juncture in our operation I noticed, by the flaccidity in the muscles on the other half of the abdomen, that the patient was perhaps too deeply relaxed. Always there is a tension in the muscles, and this must be mollified sufficiently to allow the surgeon to operate without undue resistance, but not so much that it endangers the life of the patient. In this case I noted little, if any, resistance, and I asked Dr Guevara to reduce slightly the rate of infusion of the relaxant. This affected all the muscles, including, of course, the diaphragm and those of the larynx, and Mr Reagan took the opportunity to attempt to vocalize. Being intubated, he was in no position to do so, yet somehow managed to produce a keening sound that unnerved us all. His face, as reported by Dr Guevara, became constricted in a horrible rictus, and his eyes seemed to convulse in their sockets. Clearly, he was in excruciating pain, and my heart flew to him as to a valiant soldier.

The agony, I am certain, was not simply corporeal; surely there was a psychological aspect to it, perhaps a psychosis, as he thought upon the systematic dissection and dismemberment of his manifest self. To me, I know it would have been unbearable, and once again I was humbled by his courage and fortitude. And yet there was still so much left to do; neither empathy nor despair were distractions we could afford. Accordingly, I asked Dr Guevara to increase the infusion rate in order to still Mr Reagan's cries, and this achieved, I returned my concentration to the table.

By pre-arrangement Dr Biko now moved to the opposite side of the patient and began to duplicate there what I had just finished on mine. The sole modification was that he began on the belly wall and proceeded in a cephalad direction, so that by the time I had extirpated the contents of one half of the abdomen, the other would be exposed and ready. With alacrity I began the evisceration.

It would be tedious to chronicle step by step the various dissections, ligations, and severances; these are detailed in a separate monograph, whose reference can be found in the bibliography. Suffice to say that I identified the organs and proceeded with the resections as we had planned. Once freeing the stomach, I was able to remove the spleen and pancreas without much delay; because of their combined mass, the liver and gall bladder required more time but eventually came out quite nicely. I reflected the proximal small and large intestines downward in order to lay bare the deeper recesses of the upper abdominal cavity and to have access to the kidneys and adrenals. I treated gland and organ as a unit, removing each pair together, transecting the ureters high, near the renal pelvices. The big abdominal vessels, vena cava and aorta, were now exposed, and I had to withstand the urge to include them in my dissection. We had previously agreed that this part of the procedure would be assumed by Dr Biko, who is as skilled and renowned a vascular surgeon as I am an abdomino-thoracic one, and though they lay temptingly now within my reach, I resisted the lure and turned to accomplish the extirpation of the alimentary tract.

We did not, as many had urged, remove the cavitous segment of the digestive apparatus as a whole. After consultation with our technical staff we determined that it would be more practical — successful — if we proceeded segmentally. Thus, we divided the tract into three parts: stomach, including the esophageal segment just distal to the diaphragm; small intestine, from pylorus to ileo-cecal valve; and colon, from cecum to anus. These were dutifully resected and sent to the holding banks, where they await future purpose and need.

As I harvested the internal abdominal musculature, the Psoas, Iliacus, Quadratus Lumborum, I let my mind wander for a few moments. We were nearing the end of the operation, and I felt the luxury of certain philosophical meditations. I thought about the people of the world, the hungry, the cold, those without shelter or goods to meet the exigencies of daily life. What are our responsibilities to them, we the educated, the skilled, the possessors? It is said, and I believe, that no man stands above any other; what then can one person do for the many? Listen, I suppose. Change.

I have found in my profession, as I am certain exists in all others, that to not adapt is to become obsolete. There are many I have known, many of my colleagues, who, unwilling or unable to grapple with innovation, have gone the way of the penny. Tenacity, in some an admirable quality, is no substitute for the ability to change, for what in one age might be considered tenacious in another would most certainly be called cowardly. I thought upon our patient, whose fortunes had so altered since the years of my training, and considered further the question of justice. Could an act of great altruism, albeit forced and involuntary, balance a generation of infamy? How does the dedication of one's own body to the masses weigh upon the scales of sin and repentance?

My brow furrowed, for these questions were far more difficult to me than the operation itself, and had it not been for Ms Narciso, who spoke up in a timely voice, I might have broken the sterile field by wiping with my own hand the perspiration of my forehead.

'Shall we move to the pelvis, Doctor?' she said, breaking my reverie.

'Yes,' I countered, turning momentarily from the table to recover, while a nurse mopped the moist skin of my face.

The bladder, of course, had been decompressed by the catheter that had been passed prior to surgery, and once I pierced the floor of the peritoneum, it lay beneath my blade like a flat and flaccid tyre. I severed it quickly, taking care to include the prostate, seminal vesicles, ureters, and membranous urethra in the resection. A technician carried these to an intermediate room, where a surgeon was standing by to separate the structures before they were taken to their respective tanks. What remained was to take the penis, which was relatively simple, and testes, which required more care so as not to disrupt the delicate tunica that surrounded them. This done, I straightened my back for perhaps the first time since we began and assessed our progress.

When one becomes so engrossed in a task, so keyed and focused that huge chunks of time pass unaware, it is a jarring feeling, akin to waking from a vivid and lifelike dream, to return to reality. I have felt this frequently during surgeries, but never as I did this time. Hours had passed, personnel had changed, perhaps even the moon outside had risen, in a span that for me was marked in moments. I looked for Drs Ng and Cochise and was informed that they had left the surgical suite some time ago; I recalled this only dimly, but when I looked to their work was pleased to find that it had been performed most adequately. All limbs were gone, and the glenoid fossae, where the shoulders had been de-articulated, were sealed as we had discussed. Across from me Dr Biko was just completing the abdominal vascular work. I nodded to myself, and using an interior approach, detached the muscles of the lumbar spine, then asked for the bone saw.

We transected the spinal cord between the second and third lumbar vertebrae, thus preserving the major portion of attachments of the diaphragm. This, of course, was vital, if, as we had planned, Mr Reagan was to retain the ability to respire. It is well-known that those who leave surgery still attached to the respirator, which surely would have been the case if we had been sloppy in this last part of the operation, do poorly thereafter, often dying in the immediate post-operative period. In this case especially, such an outcome would have been heinous, for it would have deprived this brave man of the fate and rewards most deservedly his.

I am nearing the conclusion of our report, and it must be obvious that I have failed to include each and every nerve, ligament, muscle, and vessel that we removed; if it seems a critical error, I can only say that it is a purposeful one, intended to improve the readability of this document. Hopefully, I have made it more accessible to the lay that exist outside the cloister of our medical world, but those who crave more detailed information I refer to the *Archives of Ablative Technique*, vol. 113, number 6, pp. 67–104, or, indeed, to any comprehensive atlas of anatomy.

We sealed the chest wall and sub-diaphragmatic area with a synthetic polymer (XRO 137, by Dow) that is thin but surprisingly durable and impervious to bacterial invasion. We did a towel count to make certain that none were inadvertently left inside the patient, though at that point there was little of him that could escape our attention, then Dr Guevara inserted the jugular catheter that would be used for nourishment and medication. Dr Biko fashioned a neat little fistula from the right external carotid artery, which, because we had taken the kidneys, would be used for dialysis. These completed, we did a final blood gas and vital sign check, each of which was acceptable, and I stepped back from the table.

'Thank you all very much,' I said, and turned to Mr Reagan as I peeled back my gloves. He was beginning to recover from the drug-induced paralysis, and his face seemed to recoil from mine as I bent toward him. I have seen this before in surgery, where the strange apparel, the hooded and masked faces, often cause fright in a patient. It is especially common in the immediate post-operative period, when unusual bodily sensations and a frequently marked mental disorientation play such large roles. I was therefore not alarmed to see our patient's features contort as I drew near.

'It is over,' I said gently, keeping my words simple and clear. 'It went well. We will take the tube from your mouth, but don't try to talk. Your throat will be quite sore for awhile, and it will hurt.'

I placed a hand on his cheek, which felt clammy even though the skin was flushed, and Dr Guevara withdrew the tube. By that time the muscle relaxant had worn off completely, and Mr Reagan responded superbly by beginning to breathe on his own immediately. Shortly thereafter, he began to shriek.

There are some surgeons I know, and many other physicians, who believe in some arcane manner in the strengthening properties of pain. They assert that it fortifies the organism, steeling it, as it were, to the insults of disease. Earlier, I mentioned the positive association between pain and tissue survival, but this obtains solely with respect to ablative surgery. It has not been demonstrated under myriad other circumstances, and this despite literally hundreds of studies to prove it so. The only possible conclusion, the only scientific one, is that pain, apart from its value as a mechanism of warning, has none of those attributes the algophilists ascribe to it. In my mind these practitioners are reprehensible moralists and should be barred from those specialities, such as surgery, where the problem is ubiquitous.

Needless to say, as soon as Mr Reagan began to cry, I ordered a potent and long-lasting analgesic. For the first time since we began his face quieted and his eyes closed, and though I never questioned him on it, I like to think that his dreams were sweet and proud at what he, one man, had been able to offer thousands.

Save for the appendix, this is the whole of my report. Once again I apologize for omissions and refer the interested reader to the ample bibliography. We have demonstrated, I believe, the viability of extensive tissue ablation and its value in providing substrate for inductive and variant mitotics. Although it is an arduous undertaking, I believe it holds promise for selected patients in the future.

Appendix

As of the writing of this document, the following items and respective quantities have been produced by our regeneration systems:

ITEM	SOURCE	QUANTITY
Oil, refined	Testes: seminiferous tubules	3761 litres
Perfumes and scents	Same	162 grams
Meat, including patties, filets, and ground round	Muscles	13,318 kilograms
Storage jugs	Bladder	2732
Balls, inflatable (recreational use)	Same	325
Cord, multi-purposed	Ligaments	1.2 kilometres

ITEM	SOURCE	QUANTITY
Roofing material, e.g., for tents; flexible siding	Skin: full thickness	3.6 sq. kilometres
Prophylactics	Skin: stratum granulosum	18,763 cartons of 10 each
Various enzymes, medications, hormones	Pancreas Adrenal Glands Hepatic Tissue	272 grams
Flexible struts and housing supports	Bone	453 sq. metres

The vast majority of these have been distributed, principally to countries of the third world, but also to impoverished areas of our own nation. A follow-up study to update our data and provide a geographical breakdown by item will be conducted within the year.

NOTES ON THE AUTHORS

Geoff Ryman is a Canadian, born in 1951, who has lived in Britain for a number of years. He published his first short story in 1976, and his first novel, *The Warrior Who Carried Life*, in 1985. His novella, *The Unconquered Country*, which first appeared in *Interzone* magazine, will be published as a separate illustrated book in 1985/6.

Angela Carter is one of Britain's most acclaimed novelists. She was born in London in 1940, and is the author of *Heroes and Villains* (1969), *The Infernal Desire Machines of Dr Hoffman* (1972), *The Passion of New Eve* (1977), and *Nights at the Circus* (1984).

Scott Bradfield was born in San Francisco in 1955 and now lives near Los Angeles. He is a post-graduate student, but is keen to point out that he is not enrolled in a Creative Writing Course.

Malcolm Edwards was born in 1949 and works as an editor in a leading London publishing house. 'After-Images' is his first published story, which won the British Science Fiction Association's Award as the best short story of 1983.

Keith Roberts was born in 1935 and now lives in Oxfordshire. He has worked as an illustrator as well as a freelance writer. His novel *Pavane* (1968) was selected by Anthony Burgess for mention in *Ninety-Nine Novels: The Best in English Since 1939*, and he is also the author of *The Chalk Giants* (1974), *Ladies from Hell* (1979) and *Molly Zero* (1980). 'Kitemaster', which won the British Science Fiction Association's Award as the best short story of 1982, is the opening tale in a cycle which will make up Keith Roberts's next book.

Neil Ferguson, poet and bicycle journalist, was born in 1947 and now lives in London. 'The Monroe Doctrine' is his first published fiction.

Rachel Pollack is an American, born in 1945, who now lives in Amsterdam. She published her first short story in 1971 and her first novel, *Golden Vanity*, in 1980.

David Redd lives in Wales and has been writing and selling stories regularly, if not prolifically, since 1966.

John Shirley was born in 1953 and has recently returned to New York after a period of living in France. He is the author of *City Come A-Walkin'* (1980) and other novels, and he is regarded as one of the best of the newer American science-fiction writers.

J. G. Ballard was born in 1930 in Shanghai, China, and now lives in Shepperton. For more than 20 years he has been established as perhaps Britain's most original writer of science fiction, with books such as *The Drowned World* (1962), *The Unlimited Dream Company* (1979) and *Hello America* (1981). He has recently achieved new heights of fame with his semi-autobiographical novel about World War II, *Empire of the Sun* (1984).

Cherry Wilder was born in New Zealand in 1930, but now lives in Germany. She began writing science fiction in the early 1970s, and has had a number of novels published including *The Luck of Brin's Five* (1977). Her fantasy novel, *A Princess of the Chameln*, published in England in 1985, is the first novel of a trilogy and will be followed by *Yorath the Wolf* and *The Summer's King*.

Kim Newman was born in 1959, graduated from Sussex University, and now works in London as a freelance film critic. He has written books on film, including *Nightmare Movies*, and is now at work on a novel. 'Dreamers' is his first published work of fiction.

Michael Blumlein lives in San Francisco. He is a licensed physician but now devotes himself mainly to writing. 'Tissue Ablation and Variant Regeneration' is his first published story.

ACKNOWLEDGEMENTS

The following people all helped with the launch of *Interzone* magazine or have been closely involved with its editing and production since. This anthology would not have been possible without their collective efforts: Paul Annis, Scott Bradfield, Philippa Bramson, Alan Dorey, Malcolm Edwards, Abigail Frost, Graham James, Roz Kaveney, Ian Miller, Simon Ounsley, Andy Robertson and Charles Platt.

All of these stories were first published in *Interzone* magazine, except for 'O Happy Day!' by Geoff Ryman, which is published for the first time in this anthology.

Acknowledgements

Kim Newman, 'Dreamers', *Interzone* 8, 1984; copyright © Kim Newman, 1984

Michael Blumlein, 'Tissue Ablation and Variant Regeneration', *Interzone* 7, 1984; copyright © Michael Blumlein, 1984

EVERYMAN FICTION

J. G. BALLARD

'One of the most important, intelligent voices in contemporary fiction' *Susan Sontag*

'It is utterly appropriate to number Ballard among the true contemporary radicals of the imagination . . . His best work is simply a new way of looking at the world.'
New Musical Express

'The first thing to say about J. G. Ballard is not that he is among our finest writers of science fiction but that he is among our finest writers of fiction *tout court* period.' *Anthony Burgess*

The Drowned World

Ballard's classic novel, set in a tropical, flooded London of the near future, is a fast-paced narrative full of stunning images that reflect on our own society. 'This tale of strange and terrible adventure in a world of steaming jungles has an oppressive power reminiscent of Conrad.' *Kingsley Amis*

The Terminal Beach

This is one of Ballard's most brilliant collections of stories, which ranges from a disturbing picture of an abandoned atomic testing island in the Pacific to the shocking Oedipal fantasy of 'The Gioconda of the Twilight Noon'.

The Voices of Time

Ballard's extraordinary inventiveness and the unfailing grace and energy of his writing are triumphantly on display in this classic collection of stories, which includes 'The Overloaded Man', 'Chronopolis', and 'The Garden of Time', which Anthony Burgess has called 'one of the most beautiful stories of the world canon of short fiction'.

Vermilion Sands

Vermilion Sands is J. G. Ballard's fantasy landscape of the near future, where he would be happy to live himself – a latterday Palm Springs populated by forgotten movie queens, temperamental dilettantes and drugged beachcombers, with prima donna plants that sing arias, cloud sculptures, dial-a-poem computers and ravishing, jewel-eyed Jezebels.

RACHEL INGALLS
Binstead's Safari

A love story with a fantastical twist, in which an unremarkable American couple are transformed by their experiences in the lion country of East Africa. Witty, entertaining, beautifully written, '*Binstead's Safari* is a small triumph . . . It should, if there is any justice, bring Rachel Ingalls hundreds of new admirers' (Paul Bailey, *The Standard*)

Mrs Caliban and Others

In these three short novels Rachel Ingalls blends fantasy and legend with the deftly captured details of everyday life to explore the effects — sometimes bizarre, sometimes tragic — of isolation. 'I loved *Mrs Caliban*. So deft and austere in its prose, so drolly casual in its fantasy . . . but opening up into a deep female sadness that makes us stare. An impeccable parable, beautifully written from first paragraph to last.' *John Updike*

ORDER FORM

All these books may be obtained through your local bookshop, or can be ordered direct from the publisher. Please indicate the number of copies required and fill in the form below.

Name .... BLOCK

Address .... LETTERS

.... PLEASE

Please enclose remittance to the value of the cover price *plus* 40p per copy to a maximum of £2, for postage, and send your order to: BP Dept, J.M. Dent & Sons Ltd, 33 Welbeck Street, London W1M 8LX
Applicable to UK only and subject to stock availability
All prices subject to alteration without notice